After the Republic

www.AftertheRepublicBooks.com

Frank L. Williams

ISBN: **1508543232**
ISBN-13: **978-1508543237**

ACKNOWLEDGMENTS

With sincere and heartfelt gratitude for those who helped pave the way for *After the Republic*:

God, who endowed me with a creative mind and a knack for the written word.

My parents, Ike and the late Martha Williams, who expected me to be a good student from day one and who instilled in me a love for America and an appreciation for our freedoms.

The teachers at Cape Fear Baptist Church Christian School, Lincoln Primary School, Leland Middle School and North Brunswick High School.

Jenny Rebecca Keech, whose writing rekindled and inspired my own.

Rob Riffel, Scott Stone, Jeff Harvell and Rebecca Anthony, who read initial drafts of *After the Republic* and helped refine it.

The late Jackie Iler. Jackie had agreed to be the editor for *After the Republic*. Sadly, she passed away while I was still writing. This book would have been even better with her keen insight. Jackie is missed by all who knew her.

Jay Vics of JVI Mobile Marketing, who designed the *After the Republic* cover, logo and social media graphics.

Mary Fonvielle, my editor. Her insights have made this a better book, and I look forward to working with her on future projects.

Nancy Brice, my proofreader.

GET CONNECTED

Visit www.AftertheRepublicBooks.com and sign up to receive email updates on future installments of *After the Republic*. You can also connect with us on social media.

 /AftertheRepublic

 @AfterRepublic

IN A BOOK CLUB?

Visit www.AftertheRepublicBooks.com to download sample discussion questions.

PART I

Frank L. Williams

CHAPTER 1

The cold winter breeze whisked across Joshua's face as the old pickup rumbled down the narrow dirt road to the pasture. He closed his eyes and took a deep breath as the tall pines on either side gently swayed in the wind. His wife, Rebecca, would think it was too chilly to have the windows down, but he found the cold winter air refreshing. Reagan, a beagle-bulldog mix puppy, didn't seem to agree and nuzzled under Joshua's right arm. Emblazoned with black, white and tan splotches and built like a bulldog, the two-month-old pup had already taken to Joshua and Rebecca. Joshua smiled as he scratched the shivering puppy behind the ears.

Life was simpler – and Joshua's blood pressure lower – since he had decided not to run for a fourth term in the state legislature last year. It was time to give someone else a chance to serve, and he was happy to return to a quieter life on the small Chatham County farm he and Rebecca had purchased a few years earlier. Finding a buyer for the hardware store in his hometown meant one less thing to worry about. He smiled. They could *finally* take time to slow down and enjoy life together.

The energetic, attention-craving puppy seemed determined to trip Joshua, whining and pawing at his jeans as he lugged the bale of hay and bucket of ground feed to the hungry cows. "Calm down, boy!"

As the sun began setting over the tree line the 1989 Chevy Silverado rumbled back to the white plantation-style house, which was situated in an expansive yard adorned by several century-old oak and pecan trees. The billowing white clouds featured brilliant streaks of red and orange. Old Glory snapped proudly in the brisk wind.

It was peaceful here -- a totally different world than the busy, fast-paced political environment in which Joshua had lived and worked for two decades. He looked forward to spending time relaxing in those rocking chairs on the full-length front porch, which was accented by thick white columns.

A dark blue Ram pickup met them in the driveway. Joshua looked at his watch. *Is it that late already?* While the peaceful scenery on the farm had been good for Joshua's stress level, tonight was a night that had tended to *increase* his blood pressure in recent years: the president's annual State of the Union address. Joshua watched each year, even when he was not a fan of the person delivering the speech. But this year was different. Tonight, President Alan Wagner would deliver his first State of the Union address. *We've finally taken our country back!*

"We're a little early." Joshua's best friend and longtime fishing buddy, Perry Edwards, climbed down out of the truck, followed by his wife, Caroline, and their children, Charlie and Allie. Perry towered over everyone else in the group, standing nearly a foot taller than his wife and six inches taller than Joshua. Perry and Caroline were not as interested in politics as Joshua, but they did pay attention to the news and had made the trip to the farm to watch the President's speech the past couple of years.

"Glad you could make it!" Joshua shook Perry's hand. "How are ya?"

"If I was doing any better I couldn't stand it!" Perry said.

Reagan growled at Perry and Caroline but wasn't fazed by the children, who were closer to his own size. "Meet my new guard dog, Reagan," Joshua said with a laugh. "He thinks he already weighs a hundred pounds."

Reagan steered clear of Perry and Caroline as they entered the house, positioning himself across the warmly lit room from them. The living area was expansive but cozy and a small fire sparkled in the fireplace.

"I get the impression he doesn't like strangers?" Caroline pointed at Reagan.

"He hasn't met many new people." Rebecca's shoulder-length brown hair barely touched the collar of her grey sweatshirt. She wore faded jeans and white socks. "It won't be long before you two aren't strangers to him." She hugged Caroline and motioned in the direction of Charlie and Allie, who were anxiously trying to befriend Reagan. "They sure are growing up fast!"

"Too fast!" Caroline beamed. "It's hard to believe they're

eleven and eight. Pretty scary! But they're the center of my world."

"I can understand that." Rebecca looked down. "You have a beautiful family."

Joshua sensed a solemn tone in Rebecca's voice. He knew she had always wanted children, and seeing Charlie and Allie was a constant reminder that they had none. *If only we'd met a few years earlier.*

"I like that outfit." Rebecca gestured toward Caroline.

"Thank you!" Caroline smiled broadly. She was attired in a bright red skirt accented by a matching red purse, shoes and a ribbon perched atop her auburn hair.

Aren't you a bit overdressed? Joshua thought.

"So, how do you think President Wagner will do in his first State of the Union?" Perry kicked off his sneakers and claimed a spot on the dark blue love seat. Caroline sat beside him, stroking his wavy brown hair.

"He'll do fine," Joshua said. "He can't be any worse than the last guy."

"Amen," Perry agreed. "Don't even *mention* his name."

"I wasn't planning to. We've got to have realistic expectations for President Wagner. We can get America back on the right path, but it's not going to happen overnight. The country is in a hole."

"No doubt about that."

Reagan growled as another pair of headlights flashed into the driveway. The doorbell rang and Joshua introduced the newest arrival. "Perry and Caroline, this is Drew Thompson. Drew and I met while I was in the legislature. He works for the Speaker."

"Good evening." Drew sported a pair of neatly pressed khakis, white long-sleeve dress shirt and red sweater vest. *Works for the Speaker* was an understatement. Drew had served as deputy chief of staff for the Speaker of the N.C. House of Representatives for the past two years, making him one of the most powerful political operatives in North Carolina at the ripe old age of 31. Joshua knew he had led a challenging life. Both parents were killed in a car wreck when he was in eighth grade. He lived with his aunt through high school, and she passed away during his freshman year in college. Drew had been married a short time but his wife left him, complaining that he was always at work. He was not Rebecca's favorite person, but she reluctantly agreed when Joshua asked if they could invite him to holiday meals and other family events since, apart from the people he worked with, he was alone in the world.

Drew staked himself out in one of two brown leather recliners. "Joshua, how's private life treating you? You can't tell me you don't miss the political game." He pointed at a decades-old picture of a young Joshua and his late parents at a political function. "It's in your blood."

"It *is* in my blood, but that disease is curable." Joshua

5

glanced at the wedding picture on the wall. It hung opposite a picture of him and Rebecca sitting atop a bale of hay. "I'm enjoying my time here on the farm with my wife. It's good to slow down and get away from the rat race."

Joshua pursed his lips as Rebecca chuckled, perhaps louder than she realized. He offered a silent glance in her direction. *She* knew politics was still in his blood, even though the process often frustrated him. Sometimes he enjoyed it too much for his own good.

"I, for one, am *glad* he didn't run again." Rebecca ran her hand across Joshua's neatly trimmed black hair, which was dotted with a few specks of gray, and gently slapped him on the back of the head. "It's good to have him *home*."

And this truly is home, Joshua thought. It has been said that opposites attract, and in many ways that was the case with Joshua and Rebecca. He was an extrovert, she was an introvert. He enjoyed meeting people and learning what was on their minds, while she preferred a quiet, home-centered life. He enjoyed the many public events required of someone in public life, but she preferred to avoid them. He enjoyed the machinations of the political process, which often turned her off. While Rebecca didn't always appreciate the political process, she had always supported Joshua in his public service and agreed with him on the most important issues. For that, he was grateful.

"If good people like Joshua don't get involved and stay

involved, who will run things?" Drew asked. His phone rang before anyone could respond.

Joshua's mind wandered to the events of the past eight years. The national debt had skyrocketed to unprecedented levels. The government had become increasingly involved in areas he felt should be left to the free market. The country's military strength had been gutted. America had lost credibility and respect on the world stage. The nation's lack of clear foreign policy had emboldened its enemies and rattled its allies. Terrorist groups like ISIS had demonstrated renewed boldness and vigor. The previous president circumvented Congress with hundreds of executive orders, some of which were overturned by the Supreme Court. Waves of illegal immigrants had poured over the southern border in 2014. Any public mention of God, faith, or family values was increasingly frowned upon. More and more people relied on the government for their day-to-day sustenance and well-being. Private property rights were increasingly infringed upon by the government at all levels.

"What's on your mind?" Rebecca derailed his runaway train of thought.

"Sorry." Joshua looked up. "Was just thinking back on everything that's happened over the past eight years. We've got a heck of a mess to clean up. I've got faith in Wagner, but where does he start?"

"Again, that's why we need people like *you* back in the game." Drew reclaimed his seat. "One man can't do it alone." He gestured toward the television. "President Wagner has done a good job of filling his cabinet."

"Mostly," Joshua responded. "But he blew it with Homeland Security."

"Who did he appoint?" Perry asked.

"Nelson Armando from New York," Joshua answered.

Perry took a sip of sweet tea. "Never heard of him."

Drew jumped in and filled in the blanks. "Nelson Armando spent a year as Secretary of Public Safety for New York State. He has raised money and campaigned for numerous Republican candidates, including President Wagner. He also served as mayor of a town in New York."

"*Joshua*, why don't *you* like him?" Perry asked, appearing perturbed by Drew's interruption.

"He doesn't have the experience, principles or temperament for the job. His main qualification seems to be that he was a major fundraiser for the president's campaign. I expected better judgment from Wagner."

"My perspective is that the political dynamic *always* plays a role." Drew pushed his wire-frame glasses against his slightly pudgy face. "You have to consider the aspect that Wagner needed New York to win the election, and Armando helped him win it. Alan Wagner is the first

Republican presidential candidate to carry New York since Ronald Reagan in 1984."

"It didn't take Armando long to find himself neck-deep in a scandal over privacy rights and surveillance techniques after he was appointed in New York," Joshua said. "I would think that undermines any credibility he gained from his *very* brief time in that job. It also bothers me that his appointment there happened under a liberal governor – one whose views were markedly different than those Wagner espoused on the campaign trail. And he's taken some positions that are very much anti-Second Amendment, including that stupid 'turn in your guns' campaign. I'm *more* than a bit uneasy about what he *really* believes."

"Forgive my ignorance," Perry interjected. "What does the Second Amendment cover?"

"The right to keep and bear arms." Joshua cocked a brow and thought, *I can't believe you don't KNOW that!*

"Aah, okay. I don't keep up with this stuff like you guys do. I definitely support gun rights and know that's important for people running for Congress, but is it a big deal for a position like this?"

"Absolutely," Joshua answered. "It's an essential foundation of our freedom."

"I can see that," Perry said.

"Homeland Security is *not* a policy-making position."

Drew's prematurely bald forehead glistened beneath the classic traditional lighting fixture. "His beliefs on *political* issues shouldn't matter for a position that is *not* engaged in policy-making."

"I beg to differ." Joshua clenched his teeth, already irritated by Drew. "It *very* much matters what the Secretary of Homeland Security believes about freedom, our Constitution and the rights of American citizens. Besides that, homeland security is too important to be left to someone whose only real qualification is political organizing."

"Don't forget that he served as a mayor."

Joshua let out an exasperated sigh. "Of an *extremely* small town. One so small that comparing his brief tenure as mayor to serving as Secretary of Homeland Security for the United States is not even *close* to comparing apples to apples. He's *not* qualified."

Caroline sighed and rolled her eyes.

Drew shrugged. "I guess we'll just have to agree to disagree. The bottom line is that he helped Wagner win the election. I guess I'm just a bit more pragmatic than you on issues like this. We needed him to win."

Joshua waved Drew off. "Pragmatic or unprincipled? Not everyone who helps with a campaign needs to be at the leadership table *after* the campaign."

Rebecca back-handed Joshua on the thigh. "Enough back-and-forth for tonight. Let's just watch the speech!"

"Amen!" Caroline chimed in. Perry smirked.

After the dignitaries were seated, the Sergeant at Arms bellowed *Mister Speaker, the President of the United States!* President Wagner entered the House chambers, escorted by members of the House and Senate. Members of Congress gave the President a standing ovation as he slowly made his way to the dais, shaking hand after hand along the way.

As the president worked the crowd Joshua couldn't help but think out loud. "President Wagner has given renewed hope to a lot of people who had given up on America. You can tell he *truly* loves America, believes in freedom and wants us to be the greatest nation on--"

"We get it, *you like the guy.*" Perry rolled his eyes.

Joshua patted Reagan on the head. "In some ways he reminds me of my dog's namesake." The puppy wagged his tail vigorously.

Rebecca cocked an eyebrow. "Comparing a brand new president who hasn't even given his first State of the Union speech to Ronald Reagan is a pretty bold statement."

"No doubt, but one can hope. We could use another Ronald Reagan."

"I'll second that," Drew agreed. "By the way, naming your dog 'Reagan' is pretty ape."

Perry looked at Drew and then Joshua, his brow furrowed. "Ape?"

Joshua shook his head and chuckled. "Inside joke with Drew and some of his friends who work at the legislature. *Don't ask.*"

Perry rolled his eyes and let out a frustrated sigh.

President Wagner took his place on the dais. The Speaker of the House and the Vice President stood behind him, overshadowed by an American flag that stretched to the ceiling. All conversation ceased as the statuesque, silver-haired president began his address. *My fellow Americans, this will be different than most State of the Union addresses you've heard in the past. Far too often, political leaders have told you what you WANTED to hear, not what you NEEDED to hear. Far too many politicians have danced around serious issues rather than dealing with them head-on. Far too many politicians have made big promises, without telling you how they planned to pay for them. Far too many politicians have spent their time focusing on what divides us, at the expense of the ties that bind us. All too often, politicians have been so worried about the next election that they forgot about the next generation.*

Enough is enough. Tonight, we will begin a candid, adult conversation about the TRUE state of our union. We must take an honest look at where we are, reflect on how we got here, and have a serious, mature discussion about where we go from here.

Joshua smiled broadly.

The President continued: *As I traveled this great country over the past two years, one thing became even clearer than I could ever have imagined. America is filled with great people who love God, love their families, love our nation and want to work hard and make a better life for themselves and their children. And the federal government needs to get out of their way, not stand in it.*

For the better part of a century America was the undisputed leader of the free world. In World War II, our Greatest Generation helped turn back the face of tyranny by leading the fight to defeat Nazi Germany and the Empire of Japan. That war would likely have ended differently – and our world would be a much darker place today – if not for the United States of America.

Joshua glanced at his grandfather's flag from World War II, which hung in a framed case across the room. *Granddaddy would be so happy if he were alive to hear this speech,* he thought.

President Wagner continued: *We put a man on the moon. We stood down the Soviet Union and won the Cold War. Our nation has been the source of much of the world's innovation over the past 100 years. America has been a beacon – THE beacon -- of freedom and hope to those who have neither.* Joshua felt goosebumps form on his arms.

That has been our past, and it can be our future -- IF we are willing to make the tough decisions that demand to be made. Before I discuss the specific steps we must take to get America back on track, it is appropriate to reflect upon the things that made America the greatest nation on earth.

President Wagner reached into his jacket pocket and held up a small pamphlet. *Let's start with our Constitution.* The entire chamber erupted into applause, with many Members of Congress rising to their feet. Joshua glanced up at the framed print of George Washington signing the U.S. Constitution.

I challenge every person in this room, as well as every person watching at home, to read and study our Constitution. Get to know it. Understand how it applies. Learn what the framers were thinking when they crafted this great document. Don't believe the snippets you hear on television. Read it for yourself!

The Constitution of the United States outlines a framework for the greatest free government this world has ever seen. A system centered on the people, not the bureaucracy. A system in which the government derives its power from We the People, not the other way around. A system which recognizes that our rights are bestowed by God, not by the government. I fear that we have strayed from the timeless principles for which our founding fathers pledged their lives, their fortunes, and their sacred honor.

We live in a great republic. But tonight, I am reminded of Benjamin Franklin's timeless words. A lady asked him what form of government they had instituted. His centuries-old response speaks to us today: 'A republic, if you can keep it.'

I am also reminded of the words of another great American, President Ronald Reagan, who admonished us that 'Freedom is never more than one generation away from extinction. We didn't pass it on to our children in the bloodstream. It must be fought for, protected, and handed on for them to do the same, or one day we will spend our sunset years telling our children and our children's children what it was once like in the United States where men were free.'

That is the question before us today. Can we keep this great republic? Or will we one day be relegated to telling our children and grandchildren what life was like in the United States?

Again, I believe our Constitution outlines the framework for the greatest free society this world has ever seen. The Constitution protects our God-given rights -- freedom of speech, freedom of religion and freedom to assemble. It protects our private property rights. It ensures that no one person – and no one branch of government – has too much power over the people. We must return to those Constitutional principles if America is to once again be the world's greatest beacon of freedom, hope and opportunity.

America is full of God-fearing, hard-working people who

want to earn a living and take care of their families. To those of you watching at home, I believe you are more than capable of running your lives without the government watching over and micromanaging everything you do. What you need is for the federal government – and this goes for state and local governments as well – to get out of the way and let you live your lives.

Joshua clapped. "He sounds more and more like Reagan!" Perry frowned, snatched the remote control and turned up the volume.

"Let's just watch the speech!" Rebecca said.

President Wagner continued: *Unfortunately, there are some in this country, and many who have stood in this building – even some who have stood at this podium – who have pushed the federal government into more and more aspects of your lives. They promise you everything and make the next generation pay for it. It has been said that a government big enough to give you everything you want is strong enough to take everything you have. We must resist the temptation to go further down that perilous path.*

President Wagner again held up the Constitution. *If this Constitution does not specifically give the federal government the authority to do something, we shouldn't be doing it. Period. Unfortunately, for far too long our federal government has tried to be all things to all people. And every pet project, every handout, every new program costs money. The* *politicians have run up the bill with well-meaning initiative after well-meaning initiative, all of which sound good in a speech or 30-second ad and look good on paper, but none of which we can afford. That's why our national debt is now over $20 trillion. We simply cannot continue piling on more debt for future generations to pay. That's why we must--*

The screen went white and the only sound was static. Joshua cocked an eyebrow.

"What happened?" Perry rubbed his fingers across his goatee.

"I don't know." They had been watching on CSPAN. He flipped to Fox News, CNN, the major broadcast networks and even MSNBC. The result was the same each time: white screen and static.

"Probably just a problem with the satellite." Caroline pushed herself up off of the love seat. "This looks like a good time for a bathroom break."

Joshua switched to a movie channel. The scheduled program came through crystal clear. Next he flipped to a 24-hour sports network, where a sports news show was broadcasting uninterrupted. "Strange."

Joshua switched back to Fox. This time there was a picture, but it was from the studio in New York, not the Capitol.

"That's weird." Perry's brow furrowed.

"Let me see if I can find any news online." Drew fixated on his smartphone for a few moments. "Nothing. I'll try to call a few friends in D.C." He tried to make a call. "Can't get through."

Joshua left the television on Fox. The rattled anchor struggled to explain the situation. *Folks, we are not sure what is happening. We are trying to reach our Washington bureau, but have been unsuccessful thus far. We will keep--*

The screen again went blank. White picture, static for sound. All of the major news networks were again blank.

Joshua's stomach twisted like a tornado. His gut told him something was very wrong. He glanced at Rebecca, who was nervously twirling her hair between her fingers.

Joshua silently walked to his home office, returning with his tablet computer. He walked past Charlie and Allie, who were absorbed in a cartoon and oblivious to the fact that something was out of the ordinary. He went to the most reliable news source he could think of: Twitter. He felt the blood drain from his face as he looked at Rebecca, speechless.

"What?" Rebecca's jaw dropped.

Perry, Caroline and Drew stared at Joshua, waiting for a clue. Rebecca twisted her hair tightly. "Josh?"

Joshua swallowed and struggled to get the words out. "I... can't believe it."

"What is it?" Perry asked.

Joshua bit his lip. "Over Washington." His hand quaked as he held up the tablet, which brightly displayed a photo of a mushroom cloud. "From Arlington."

Rebecca's cup fell from her hand, splattering tea across the room as it crashed to the hardwood floor.

"Someone probably just downloaded that and posted it," Perry said. "Doubt if it has anything to do with the TV not working."

"I'm not so sure." Drew held up his smartphone, displaying another picture of mushroom cloud. "From Bethesda. If this is real, then it took out the president, VP and most of Congress."

Joshua swallowed hard and looked at Rebecca. "Phil..."

Drew grimaced. "Congressman Moyer would be a terrible loss."

Everyone stared at each other in stunned silence. Tears streamed down Caroline's cheeks. Joshua closed his eyes for a moment. *What is happening? Is this the start of World War III?*

"My best friend from college works on Capitol Hill." Drew frantically made a call. "Still can't get through. Fast busy signal." He frowned and sent a text.

"Who did this?" Rebecca's voice quaked as she spoke.

"Sounds like Al Qaeda," Perry said.

"Or ISIS," Joshua said. "Or a copycat."

"Or anyone else with a nuke," Drew said. "China. Russia. Pakistan. North Korea. Maybe Iran."

"What does this mean?" Caroline said between sobs. "Are we safe here? What do we do now?" Perry put his arm around her and silently wiped the tears from her face.

"We don't even know for sure if it's real," Drew said. "Twitter and Facebook are already lighting up with all kinds of wild conspiracy theories that this is hoax. Others are saying it's an inside job." He cleared his throat. "But I've got a bad feeling..."

Rebecca squeezed Joshua's hand.

"No!" Joshua stared at his tablet, gripping it tightly. A deathly chill ran down his spine.

Rebecca grabbed his knee and squeezed it. "What now?"

Joshua shook his head, a tear in his eye. "Reports of mushroom clouds over five more cities." Rebecca silently grabbed his hand.

"No way!" Perry said. "This CAN'T be happening."

Joshua scrolled though Twitter photos of mushroom clouds. "Washington. LA. New York. Atlanta. Chicago. Houston." He gulped. "I think this is real."

Perry silently rushed outside, returning with his Smith & Wesson .38 revolver. After reclaiming his spot on the love seat he double-checked the pistol to ensure it was loaded.

Caroline buried her head on his shoulder, crying. Tears streamed down Rebecca's face as she tightly gripped Joshua's hand. A dark, impenetrable tension gripped the room.

"Whoever did this clearly wants to destabilize our country by taking out our government," Drew stated with an eerie calmness. "The protocol for the State of the Union is to have at least one member of the line of succession in a different, secure location. That person is called the 'designated survivor.' There are typically a few members of Congress in a different location. Today will be remembered in the same vein as 9/11 and Pearl Harbor. I just don't know who this year's designated survivor is."

Joshua closed his eyes and took a deep breath. His head was spinning. A torrent of conflicting emotions rushed through his mind. *Who did this? Are we safe here? Is it over? We have to hunt down whoever did this. Where does our country go from here? What do I do next? I have to be strong for Rebecca.* He swallowed hard and opened his eyes. "Whatever is happening could make its way to us, here. This was well-planned. We need to make plans for what we'll do, how we'll survive when this gets too close to home. But right now we need to take care of ourselves and our families. I want to call some friends in the D.C. area and see if they are okay. Perry and Caroline, you two need to get your children home and talk to them about what's happening. Can you guys meet here tomorrow afternoon at

5:00?"

Perry shook his head. "Tomorrow will be pushing it. I need to process all of this, and I want to get some things in order around the house just in case."

"State government will be on high alert, so tomorrow is probably out of the question for me," Drew added.

Joshua pursed his lips. "How about Thursday?"

"Okay," Perry said.

"I'll do my best to be here," Drew added.

"There are a few other people I want to call. Please don't invite anyone else without checking with me. We need to know who we can trust."

Perry and Caroline nodded in agreement.

"Mama, what's wrong?" Charlie stood in the doorway between the living room and the kitchen, Allie beside him.

Caroline shot up and put her hands on her hips. "How long have you two been standing there?"

Before they could answer Perry said, "Kids, I'll explain it on the way home. We're leaving in a minute. Get ready."

"But we're in the middle of a cartoon, Dad!" Charlie said.

"Son, get ready NOW. We have to go."

Charlie huffed. "Okay."

"One more thing," Joshua said. "Let's pray before you

guys go."

The children joined the group and everyone formed a circle, joined hands and bowed their heads.

"Father, we come before you tonight as people who are uncertain and afraid," Joshua prayed. "We don't know exactly what is happening in our nation or why it is happening, but we do know that you are in control. We're not sure what comes next. We ask that you guide us as we develop our plans and we ask that you bring us back together safely. We pray for the safety and future of our nation. We pray these things in Jesus' name. Amen."

Joshua felt he should have offered a lengthier prayer given the circumstances, but was not sure what to pray.

Rebecca wiped the tears from her eyes. "You guys be careful."

"We will," Caroline responded, tears still streaming down her cheeks.

Perry, Caroline, Charlie and Allie made a beeline for their truck and Drew headed for his red, late model Corvette. The flag snapped in the wind, illuminated by an in-ground light.

Joshua waved. "Get ready for the fact that we might need to leave this area on a moment's notice."

Joshua collapsed onto the couch and Rebecca plopped down beside him. After silently staring off into space for what seemed like an eternity he looked into her puppy-dog brown eyes. Even in the midst of a gut-wrenching moment like this they still had the power to hypnotize him.

"So much for returning to a quiet, peaceful life on the farm." He stroked her cheek. "I have a feeling the next few years of our lives will be drastically different than we'd planned."

"We can't control what life throws at us. We'll make it." She wiped a tear away. "*Somehow.*"

Joshua leaned back and closed his eyes. Rebecca rested her head on his chest. "Josh, what are we going to do?"

He released a heavy sigh. "I don't know yet. But I'm working on it."

Joshua's mind raced as he anxiously searched the internet for more information on what had happened. *Who did this? How many lives have been lost? Who is in control of the U.S. government? Who is in command of our military? Who has control of our nuclear arsenal? Are the attacks over, or are there more to come? What comes next?*

CHAPTER 2

The welcome aroma of brewing coffee made its way to the bedroom. Joshua grunted as he forced himself out of the warm, comfortable bed. He dressed, covered his matted hair with a faded red N.C. State Wolfpack cap and lumbered down the hall in the direction of the coffee pot.

Rebecca greeted him with far too much energy. "Good morning!"

"'Morning," he mumbled.

"*Somebody* needs a cup of coffee."

"Even more so than usual." Joshua savored his first sip. "Long night. Took me *forever* to get to sleep. Tossed and turned half the night." He picked up the remote. "Maybe we can get some more info about what happened."

Most of the 24-hour national news networks were back up and running, broadcasting from alternate locations. The headline across the top of the screen read *America Under Attack*. The last time Joshua had seen a headline like this was September 12, 2001, but even that nightmare scenario paled in comparison to the apocalyptic devastation described by the stunned news anchor: *Eleven major U.S. cities were hit with nuclear attacks yesterday.* Joshua's jaw dropped.

"Eleven!" Rebecca exclaimed.

The clearly exhausted anchor had noticeable bags under

his eyes. *The first attack hit Washington during the State of the Union address, killing President Wagner and the Vice President and taking out most of the U.S. government. The attack on our nation's capital was followed by blasts in Los Angeles, New York, Atlanta, Chicago and Houston. Overnight, nuclear bombs also went off in Pittsburgh, Phoenix, Indianapolis, Dallas and Miami.*

Rebecca squeezed Joshua's shoulder tightly as they watched the coverage in stunned silence.

The anchor continued: *These blasts do not appear to have come from missiles, and authorities are investigating the possibility of suitcase nukes or something similar. So far, no one has claimed responsibility for the attacks. President Nelson Armando, who was administered the Oath of Office this morning--*

Joshua waved his fist at the television. "No!"

"Your favorite." Rebecca gently slapped him on the shoulder.

Joshua groaned. "Just what we need. From bad to worse. I still can't believe Wagner appointed him. He didn't have the experience to be Secretary of Homeland Security, and he sure as heck doesn't have the experience to be president."

Yet there he was: President of the United States, less than three weeks after being confirmed as Secretary of Homeland Security in a razor-thin, controversial Senate vote. His confirmation had drawn opposition from nearly all of the same conservative Senators who supported Alan Wagner in the previous year's election.

"Well, for better or worse he's who we've got now," Rebecca said.

"That's what I'm afraid of."

They got quiet as President Armando appeared on screen wearing a dark suit, white shirt and dark tie. The president spoke with a heavy New York accent reinforced by his dark complexion and slicked-back hair. *My fellow Americans, yesterday was a tragic day in the history of our great nation. We were attacked in what can only be described as a savage act of war by an unknown, cowardly enemy. Many of our major cities have been devastated and hundreds of thousands, if not millions, of Americans have been killed.*

February 21, 2017 will be remembered in infamy alongside December 7, 1941 and September 11, 2001 as days on which the United States was brutally attacked, without provocation. America was knocked down yesterday, but as we did after Pearl Harbor and 9/11, we WILL get back up. That's what Americans do.

Armando adopted a stern tone and leaned forward toward the camera. *Those who executed yesterday's attacks want to bring America to its knees. They want to destroy our freedom, our way of life. They want the United States to be a thing of the past. To those who did this, I say to you. YOU WILL FAIL. America will find you, and America will bring justice to your doorstep. You can run, but you cannot hide. You will NOT break us.* He pointed at the camera and slammed his fist on the table at which he was seated. *Make no mistake. America will NOT be broken apart, and we will not crumble. Not on my watch. I will do whatever it takes to keep this nation together. Period. Thank you, and may God bless America.* Armando disappeared through a side door without taking questions.

Joshua turned off the TV. "Well, he said all the right things. I just hope he means it. Regardless, I've got a *really* bad feeling about where we're headed. We have to get ready for the absolute worst. I'm going to head out to the barn."

Around 2:30 that afternoon Joshua and Reagan emerged from the red barn, which was topped by a black gambrel roof and accented by white trim. He had been so lost in thought that he didn't realize how late the hour was until his growling stomach alerted him.

Rebecca handed him a peanut butter and jelly sandwich as he entered the house. "Make any progress?"

"Made a few calls and did some thinking about what's going on. Still need to get up with a few people. I tried to call Thomas, but couldn't get him on the phone and his voice mail was full." After wolfing down the sandwich he looked at his watch. "I'm going to go ahead and take care of the cows."

America may have been attacked yesterday, but the cows still expected to be fed.

"I'll ride with you." Rebecca grabbed her purse and donned a tan baseball cap, pulling her ponytail through the back.

Joshua chuckled. "You're taking your *purse* to feed the cows?"

Rebecca pulled her compact Beretta .380 pistol out of the purse. "Thought we could shoot a few targets while we're out. It'll help get our minds off of what happened yesterday."

"Good idea."

Joshua reached for the power window switch in the old Silverado, but thought better of it. *The window wouldn't make it halfway down before I'd be hearing 'It's cold!'"* He smirked but wisely kept quiet.

The smell of freshly cut hay permeated the barn, offset only by corn dust as they loaded the truck. Rebecca tossed a couple of old milk jugs into the back. "Targets."

The cloudless, clear-blue sky stood in stark contrast to the interior of the dimly lit barn. The bright sun more than compensated for the chilly winter air. Reagan stood on Rebecca's lap as they drove down the short dirt road to the pasture behind the barn, where the cows greeted them at the gate. They weren't the smartest animals on the planet, but they knew this truck brought food with it. Joshua cut the strings on the hay bale and spread it out while Rebecca dumped the ground feed into the troughs.

The pond was about 100 feet long, 40 feet wide and stocked with catfish. The dirt from the pond made a nice berm, which provided the perfect backdrop for target practice and helped ensure that no stray bullets ended up anywhere they shouldn't. Joshua admired Rebecca's slender, athletic figure as she set up a milk jug about three feet up the berm.

"Josh, you go first. Three shots each."

"Becca, you just want to know what you have to shoot to beat me."

"You know I beat you *every* time."

Joshua didn't acknowledge the dig, as that would only have encouraged more of the same. He took aim with his Beretta 9mm and fired his first shot. Dust flew up from the berm above the jug, which remained unscathed. Reagan yelped, bolted for the other side of the truck and nervously peeped around the back tire.

"That was still close enough to cause damage." Joshua took aim for his second shot.

"Uh huh," she said sarcastically.

His second shot was closer, grazing the top left corner of

the jug. A few rocks scattered, but the jug remained upright. "He'd be down by now."

"Close doesn't count."

Joshua felt a drop of sweat forming on his forehead as the smell of gunpowder penetrated his lungs. He squared up and took aim. *I'll NEVER hear the end of it if I don't hit this one.* He swallowed hard and fired off his third shot, hitting the jug closer to the top than he had hoped and tipping it over.

"'Bout time you hit *something*." Rebecca moved into position.

"Okay, Miss Trash Talker, let's see what you've got. Time to put up or shut up."

Rebecca smirked and calmly fired off three quick shots that pierced the jug in a tight pattern grouped near its center.

"Any questions?" She walked toward the berm to retrieve the jug. "If not, this concludes today's lesson."

Joshua felt his cheeks flush red for a moment. "Good shooting." He loved her competitive side, but sometimes it got under his skin. *Better left unsaid,* he thought.

Just as Reagan cautiously re-emerged from behind the truck Joshua's phone rang. He looked at the caller ID. It was Thomas Page, the general contractor who had built Joshua's farmhouse and barn. Thomas was a laid-back man who rarely got excited or upset. He was also a jack-of-all-trades who seemed to know a little about almost everything. They had become good friends, and Joshua's gut told him Thomas would be someone good to keep close in the coming days. "Thomas, I'm glad you called back."

"Hey man. Heck of a two days," Thomas said. "Can you believe what's happened? Kinda scary, ain't it?"

"Scary is an understatement. That's why I called you. I'll cut to the chase. You may not remember it, but a few years ago you said that you felt like America would go through tough times one day. You said that when those times came you would most likely find a quiet, out-of-the-way corner and watch history unfold."

"Yeah, I remember. Kim and I were talking about it this morning."

"Well, history is unfolding. I know you guys like your privacy and like to be left alone, but it'll be a lot easier to make do in that quiet corner if you have the right group of people with you."

"What are you thinking?"

Joshua described the beginnings of a plan. "I've been thinking through a list of people I think we can trust, and who can contribute something in the new world we are about to face. I'm just not sure where we should go."

"I think I know just the place. We were already making

plans to go there."

"What are you up to this afternoon? If you can, come over here around 5:00 or 5:30 and we'll talk about it."

"Man, I can do that," Thomas replied. "I've got some leftover BBQ sandwiches I made for a cookout on Monday. I'll bring 'em with me."

After the call ended Joshua and Rebecca made the short drive back to the house.

"I'm going to the store to pick up some things," Rebecca said.

"Want me to go with you?" Joshua asked.

"No, you need to make your calls."

"Be careful. It could be crazy out there. Take your pistol with you."

"Josh, you know I never leave home without it."

***

Tension hung over the grocery store parking lot like a dark, angry storm cloud. Nearly every space was full. A fistfight broke out between two would-be shoppers as Rebecca drove back and forth searching for a parking spot. *This is nuts*, she thought. *People are already losing their minds.*

She spotted an empty parking place one row over. As she maneuvered toward the spot a beat-up green Pontiac station wagon with a missing hubcap abruptly cut her off and rattled into the space. Rebecca instinctively blew her horn. Her heart jumped violently as a man wearing a white t-shirt under a denim jacket shot out of the car and began yelling obscenities at her. A heavy-set woman with curlers in her hair and wearing pink tights at least two sizes too small exited the passenger side and shot Rebecca the middle finger.

Rebecca's right hand tightly gripped her pistol as she partially rolled down the window with the left. The man menacingly approached her, gesturing wildly and screaming obscenities as the sun glistened on the gold chain around his neck.

"I didn't mean to blow the horn," Rebecca said. "The space is all yours. I don't want any trouble."

He continued yelling obscenities and gesturing wildly, but turned and walked toward the store. The woman followed him, glaring at Rebecca with venom-filled eyes as she passed. Rebecca gripped her .380 tightly until they were out of sight. Relieved, her shoulders relaxed as she closed her eyes and let out a deep sigh. *I really don't want to shoot anyone today.*

Rebecca apprehensively entered the store, checking her purse three times to make sure she had her trusty firearm. She gripped the cart tightly, avoiding eye contact with other shoppers. People gathered to watch two women fight over the last steak in the meat department. Rebecca took advantage of the distraction to load her cart with soup and other canned goods. While others were competing for the last loaves of bread she snagged several jars of peanut butter, numerous bags of flour and a hefty supply of coffee, sugar, salt and pepper. *Think long term, Rebecca. What will we need to MAKE food?*

The clerk spoke up as Rebecca pulled out her debit card. "I'm sorry, but the network is down right now." Rebecca looked around nervously as she handed the clerk cash.

Outside, she quickly unloaded her cart into her dark gray Explorer.

"Looks like you've got a wad of cash in that there purse. Hand it over."

Rebecca turned and came face-to-face with the same man in the blue denim jacket. His scraggly mullet appeared to have never encountered shampoo and his white t-shirt featured several prominent brown stains. His stench was more putrid than anything her cows had ever produced.

"I don't want any trouble." Rebecca smoothly slipped her hand into her purse and squeezed the grip on her Beretta, her index finger resting on the barrel. "Just go on your way."

"GIVE ME YOUR MONEY, WOMAN!"

As Rebecca tightened her grip and started to draw her

pistol, two tall, muscular men in their early twenties appeared from behind a van two spaces away. The first man removed his sunglasses and brushed his wavy blonde hair back. "Is there a problem here?"

"None of your business, punk. Get out of here."

The second man, a clean-cut African-American, removed his red and white jacket and tossed it on the ground, revealing bulging biceps and an "N.C. State Football" t-shirt. He clenched his fist and took an imposing step toward the would-be robber. "Leave the lady alone." The troublemaker took a half-step toward him before turning and walking away, cursing.

Rebecca exhaled and slipped her hand off of her pistol and out of her purse. "Thank you so much."

"You're welcome, ma'am." He picked up his jacket, the back of which was emblazoned with a strutting wolf. "We'll stay here until you're out of the parking lot."

"Thank you so much," Rebecca repeated, her voice still shaking. "Is there anything I can do for you? Do you need money for groceries?"

"No, ma'am," the blonde football player answered. "We're just glad to help."

"Thank you again." Rebecca locked the doors, fired up the Explorer and got out of the parking lot as quickly as possible. *I'm sure glad those guys showed up or that could've been a real mess. I should've brought Josh with me.*

Joshua met her in the kitchen when she returned. "How was the store?"

Rebecca shuddered. "A madhouse. People are really freaked out. They're buying up *everything*. There were even a couple of fistfights."

Joshua shook his head. "That's what I was afraid of. And it's only going to get worse."

Should I tell him I almost got robbed? She wondered. *No, that'll just give him one more thing to worry about.*

***

Group Claims Responsibility. The anchor expounded on the unsettling details behind the scrolling headline: *A terrorist group calling itself 'AIS' is claiming responsibility for yesterday's attacks. The following is from a video the group posted online this morning.*

"Who the heck is 'AIS'?" Joshua wondered aloud. "Never heard of 'em."

The newscast cut away to the video clip, which featured a seated terrorist in a black robe and balaclava mask flanked by two men in similar attire brandishing machine guns. One of the men also had a large sword. A flag featuring bold blue, green and white horizontal stripes and red Arabic lettering underscored by a black sword hung behind them.

The seated terrorist's voice was disguised. *AIS conducted the attacks against the American infidels yesterday. This was just the beginning. The United States has bombed our countries for too long. Now it is your turn to know what it feels like to be attacked in the night, where you thought you were safe.*

Joshua leaned forward and clenched his fists. The terrorist continued: *Now you will know what it feels like to see your women and children suffer and die. We will destroy your cities. We will destroy your government. We will wipe you from the earth. We will own your land. Your country will burn like the depths of hell. The United States will be no more.*

White-hot rage surged through every inch of Joshua's being. He uttered a rare expletive.

The newscast broke away from terrorist leader and the anchor continued. *Ominous words. AIS is short for 'American Islamic State.' Sources tell us that this group gained inspiration from both Al Qaeda and ISIS. One intelligence analyst who wishes to remain anonymous describes AIS as a hybrid that has adopted the worst traits of both terror groups. Additionally, British intelligence sources tell us that AIS is methodical, organized and brutal, and that they are planning more attacks on American soil. The weapons used in yesterday's attacks appear to have been suitcase nukes. No word yet on how they got the weapons into the U.S.*

Joshua wondered if the anchor was quoting British intelligence because there were no American intelligence sources left to quote. He clenched his teeth as the newscast cut away to clips of young men burning American flags and holding up pictures of mushroom clouds in street celebrations in middle-eastern cities.

***

Reagan barked incessantly as Thomas' white Suburban turned into the driveway. Thomas rang the doorbell, and then entered before Joshua or Rebecca could make it to the door. "How are y'all doing?"

Thomas was a tall man, just over six feet, and had short, light brown hair. His tan baseball cap had seen better days and he wore faded jeans and beat-up brown work boots. Joshua envied his laid-back approach to life.

Thomas handed Rebecca several BBQ sandwiches. "Leftovers." A well-worn toothpick twisted between his teeth as he spoke.

Reagan continued growling until he realized Thomas had food with him. Rebecca poured three glasses of tea and everyone wolfed down their sandwiches.

After the meal Joshua looked at Rebecca. "This was excellent. *Nobody* cooks barbecue like Thomas."

"Thanks, man." Thomas chugged his tea. "Given how many fish I helped you put in that new pond a few months ago I'm sure it's overcrowded. My fishing poles are in the Suburban. Let's kill two birds with one stone and talk out there."

"Sounds like a plan," Joshua said. "Rebecca, we'll be back in a bit."

Outside, they grabbed their fishing poles and Thomas pulled a bait bucket and roll of papers out of his Suburban. Reagan followed them to benches near the edge of the pond as the sun faded into darkness.

After they dropped their baited hooks into the water Thomas unrolled a sheet of paper and handed Joshua a flashlight. The light illuminated a map of the Great Smoky Mountains in Western North Carolina, near the Tennessee border.

"Man, you know how I've always said I would like to move out to the mountains?" Thomas asked.

"Yes, but I was never sure if you were serious about it," Joshua answered.

"Well, last year I started getting serious about it. You remember that land I sold back in 2007, right before the market tanked?"

"I think I remember you mentioning that."

"Well, about a year and a half later, right after the market crashed, I used the money from that sale to buy about 300 acres of mostly wooded land here, near Fontana

Lake and the Little Tennessee River." Thomas used his index finger to circle an area on the map. "It was a foreclosure, so I got a good deal. Paid less than what I got for the land I sold. We've just been sitting on it waiting for the right time to do something with it. Last year I started working on plans to live on part of the land and sell or develop the rest. The plan was for this to be our retirement."

Thomas used his toothpick to point out several different areas on the map. "Kim and I are planning to keep this section for us and the kids. It's out of the way and secluded, just like we like it. And this is where we had plans to sell a few lots and maybe build some houses. It's a bit closer to the road, but still out of the way and can't be seen from the passing vehicles. It's fairly remote and the terrain is pretty rugged. Would be a good spot for y'all to get away from all the craziness."

"That sounds great, but I don't expect you to just *give* this to us."

"Man, don't worry about it. It'll all work out."

"*I'm serious.* Everyone who uses a piece of your land should compensate you somehow."

"Man, I'm sure everyone will chip in." Thomas rolled the toothpick between his teeth.

"I'm not going to assume that. Everyone we invite to come *will* have a clear understanding that they are going to somehow compensate you for the use of your land."

"You really think all of that's necessary?"

"I'm not going to let it happen any other way," Joshua insisted. "I do have a few other questions, though. First, I'm assuming there are no houses on any of this property, no infrastructure, no power, and so forth?"

"Not exactly. My cabin is pretty much ready, and I've had enough interest that I already built two cabins to use as spec houses. I've also cleared several lots, and my equipment is still there. I've run electricity to all of the spots where I was planning to sell lots. And I've got some guys up there drilling wells and putting in septic tanks today and tomorrow."

"Wow. I had no idea you had all of this going on."

"Man, you know I keep things pretty close to the vest." Thomas grinned. "So what do ya think?"

"I think it sounds good," Joshua answered.

"I do have one rule I will enforce though." Thomas leaned forward, taking the toothpick out of his mouth and gripping it tightly between his fingers.

"What is it?"

"One of those two cabins is for you and Rebecca."

"You don't need to--"

Thomas waved his hand. "It ain't negotiable, buddy.

You're going out of your way to help all of the folks you're bringing with you. If y'all are going to stay on my land, one of these cabins is yours. And don't try to change my mind. *It ain't changing.*"

"If you insist."

"Good. Done deal."

"What are you doing tomorrow night?" Joshua asked. "You need to meet some folks I've got coming over to talk about our plans."

"Thanks, man, but I can't make it tomorrow. Me and Kim are headed to the mountains in the morning to take a load of stuff. If you think they're good people I'm sure they are."

"I still think you need to meet them. How about Friday?"

"Friday is good. What time?"

"5:00?"

"All right, man." As Thomas nodded his float disappeared beneath the surface of the water. He frowned as he removed the catfish from his hook and threw it back. "Let's let him get a little bigger."

"Another question," Joshua added. "If we all show up at one time there will only be room for so many people in the cabins. Some of the folks we'll bring along have campers and RVs. Will those work?"

"Man, we can make 'em work."

Thomas was a talker who was known for making a short story long. The pitch-black sky was dotted with innumerable stars, and the Big Dipper was clearly visible between several wispy clouds. Joshua felt the temperature dropping as their conversation veered off into a wide range of less-serious topics. Several hours later Thomas' phone rang. "I bet that's Kim wondering where I'm at."

Thomas hung up the phone and they pulled their lines out of the water. Joshua nudged Reagan, asleep on the ground near the end of the bench, and they returned to the house.

***

The next afternoon Joshua sat down on the couch, leaned back and closed his eyes, hoping for a few restful moments after a long day of preparation. The gravity of the situation weighed on him like an anchor around his neck. He was jarred out of his brief moment of peace when Reagan started barking and ran to the window. Joshua let out a frustrated sigh as he spotted Drew's Corvette coming down the driveway. *So much for a few minutes of peace and quiet,* he thought.

"Drew's here." Joshua looked at his watch. "Quarter till five. Always on time, if not early."

"Sometimes he seems a bit *too* eager," Rebecca said.

Drew had barely gotten out of his car when his phone rang. "Sorry, but I need to take this." He walked away from the house, immediately diving into a deep conversation.

"Always busy, too," Rebecca said quietly, but loud enough that Joshua could hear. "Or at least trying to *look* busy."

"Give him a chance, Becca. He's a good kid, but he's young."

Rebecca shook her head. "A bit too ambitious for my taste."

"You didn't know me then, but I wasn't so different when I was his age." Joshua had been 37 when he married Rebecca and they had recently celebrated their eighth anniversary.

"Well it's a good thing you grew up *before* I met you or both of our lives might be different today. Just keep an eye on him."

Joshua heaved a heavy sigh. Reagan started barking again as the Edwards' Ram pickup made its way down the driveway.

"Good to see you guys." Rebecca invited them in. "You didn't bring Charlie and Allie?"

"No," Caroline answered. "My parents are watching them tonight so that we can focus on what we need to discuss. They're going out for pizza in downtown Raleigh."

An old, beige Jeep Grand Cherokee turned into the driveway as they were talking. Jim Davidson, a country guy who had served on the pastoral staff at a church in Raleigh, had arrived. Jim had introduced Joshua to Rebecca in 2007. Sunday, December 16, 2007, to be exact. They both attended a Christmas program at the church where he worked, and Jim had a hunch they should meet. His hunch was on point, and he had officiated their wedding on April 25, 2009.

"How are y'all doing?" Jim's thick Georgia accent echoed as he got out of the jeep and walked toward the house. He was a slender man, just under six feet tall with thinning brown hair. Reagan ran to greet Jim as though he'd known him for years.

"Thanks for coming." Joshua pointed at Reagan. "You're the first stranger he hasn't growled at. I hope he's not getting soft on me."

"He's just a smart dog." Jim scratched the pup behind the ears. Reagan nuzzled his snout against Jim's jeans.

Joshua chuckled. "Crazy dog." He motioned for Jim to follow him. "I'm looking forward to hearing your thoughts, but first, let's fire up the grill. We can't plan the future of the free world on an empty stomach."

Joshua waved for Drew to join them. Drew hurriedly ended his phone call and quickly followed them inside. After Joshua introduced Jim to Drew everyone migrated to the back deck. Perry helped Joshua man the grill while Reagan sat nearby, fixated on the food. Rebecca and

Caroline huddled in a corner, shielding themselves from the brisk wind. Joshua felt his stomach growl as the aroma of sizzling burgers and hot dogs enveloped the deck.

Jim and Drew set up camp in two folding chairs on the corner of the deck and dived headfirst into a conversation, tuning out everything around them.

"That's interesting," Joshua muttered quietly.

"What?" Perry asked.

Joshua nodded in the direction of Drew and Jim. "Those two just met tonight and they seem to have hit it off. I thought they'd be like oil and water."

"Hopefully your friend Drew will learn something from Jim."

"What do you mean?"

"Nothing specific. Just have a funny feeling about Drew. Can't put my finger on it."

Joshua also secretly hoped they would connect. Even though Jim was only a couple of years older than Joshua he had been a mentor to him and many other men at the church. *Maybe Jim can be mentor for Drew like he was for me.*

After a few minutes the burgers and hot dogs were ready, along with a veggie burger for Caroline. Rebecca always went out of her way to accommodate their friend's quite finicky dietary preferences.

Jim blessed the food. As Joshua enjoyed his hamburger, he pondered what he would say to the group. His instincts told him that the worst was yet to come, that the attacks on America were not over. His gut said the future attacks would hit close to home. He and Rebecca and their friends needed a plan if they were going to survive. He was working on his plan, but it was still coming together. *We need the right people involved, and we need to be prepared to leave if this conflict comes to our back yard.* Joshua shuddered. *What if my plan fails?* He shook off the worry. *I just have to have faith.*

After the meal Joshua got down to business. "Thank you guys for coming. Some of you know Thomas Page. He came by for a while yesterday, but couldn't make it tonight. Let's get to the point -- we all know why we're here. America changed Tuesday. The *world* changed Tuesday. We need to have a plan for the worst-case scenario."

"Worse than what's already happened?" Perry asked.

Joshua pursed his lips. "Unfortunately and frighteningly, yes. My gut tells me this thing isn't over. We need to be ready."

"What are you proposing?" Jim inquired.

"I haven't worked out the details yet, but if there are more attacks that cause the situation to deteriorate further we have a better chance of getting through it if we work as a group and have a plan. We need to know where we will go and who we will take with us. And we need to set some ground rules."

"What do you mean 'go'?" Rebecca asked. "You've mentioned the possibility of leaving a couple of times. Why couldn't we stay here? Our farm is pretty out-of-the-way."

"Not far enough. We're too close to Raleigh, and we're too close to major highways like US 1 and 64, not to mention the Shearon Harris Nuclear Plant. If it hits the fan we need to be as far 'off-the-grid' as possible, away from population centers."

"You mentioned ground rules," Rebecca followed up. "What kind of ground rules, Josh?"

"For starters, no freeloaders," he answered. "Everyone has to pull their weight, unless they are simply unable to contribute."

"I agree that everyone needs to pull their weight in some way," Jim said. "With that said, we need to realize that not everyone will contribute in the *same* way. And we need to have compassion for those who cannot help themselves."

"Agreed," Joshua said, "But we have to differentiate between people who cannot take care of themselves and those who just *won't* do anything."

"Can't argue with that."

"Again, my instincts tell me that these attacks aren't over," Joshua continued. "This 'AIS' group selected an ominous name, 'American Islamic State,' which tells me that they plan on putting boots on the ground here in the United States. I just think this thing is going to hit close to home."

"And what do you think about the acting president?" Perry baited him.

Joshua took the bait. "Not a lot. I don't think he's anywhere near qualified or ready to take on the job that's now in his lap, and I fear he will handle it very poorly."

"He's not *that* bad," said Drew, who had been unusually quiet thus far. "Let's give him a chance. And he's not 'acting' – he is POTUS."

"POTUS?" Perry asked.

Drew pushed his glasses tightly against his face. "It's an acronym for 'President of the United States'."

"Oh, okay." Perry rolled his eyes. "Political insider jargon, I guess."

"Drew, I hope you're right about Armando not being that bad, but I'm not holding my breath," Joshua said before changing the subject. "Seconds, anyone?" He started making another hamburger. "We'll get back to business in a few."

Without warning the deck shook so violently that Joshua nearly lost his balance. A deathly chill overcame him as a bright flash illuminated the dark sky like the middle of a clear summer day. A deep, echoing boom consumed his ears. Reagan let out a yelp, vaulted off the steps and disappeared into the darkness underneath the deck.

"What the...?" Perry exclaimed.

Joshua dropped his plate onto the deck and stared in horror at a mushroom cloud reaching for the sky over the distant horizon. *Here. In North Carolina.* His heart pounded violently.

"Oh my God!" Caroline cried out.

Rebecca moved over and tightly gripped Joshua's arm with both hands, a tear streaming down her cheek. Everyone was speechless. Silent for what seemed like an eternity, staring as the glowing ball of deadly heat and toxic radiation expanded toward the heavens. *What do we do now?* Joshua thought. *We're far enough away that there is no immediate threat to us here, but--*

Perry broke the silence. "What direction is that?"

Joshua's heart sank as Perry asked the question. He looked at Rebecca in stunned silence. "Ummm...."

"What direction?"

"Umm, the deck faces south... umm... so that is east – maybe slightly north of east."

The blood drained from Perry's face as he looked at Caroline and then Joshua. "Raleigh?"

Joshua's chest tightened. "I... probably so."

Perry turned ghost white. "Charlie and Allie..."

Caroline screamed and fell to her knees on the deck. "My babies... and my parents... NO!" She leaned back against the guardrail, shaking violently and sobbing uncontrollably. Perry sat beside her and put his arms around her, tears streaming down his face. A lump formed in Joshua's throat as he turned away from the mushroom cloud and stared off into the darkness. He closed his eyes and took a deep breath.

Joshua opened his eyes and looked at Jim, silently asking for advice. None was forthcoming. Drew still stood motionless, staring at the mushroom cloud off in the distance. Trembling, Reagan made his way back onto the porch and planted himself next to Joshua.

Perry rose to his feet, his eyes watery and his jaw clenched. "I have to go to Raleigh." He took his keys out of his pocket. "I have to find my children."

"Perry!" Joshua implored. "You can't go into a nuclear blast zone. You'll wind up dead yourself!"

"You're not the one whose two children are there." Perry walked down the steps. "I *have* to go." He turned and pointed at Joshua. "And *don't* try to stop me!"

"Then I'm going with you," Caroline said in a choked voice, standing up.

"Perry... Caroline--" Joshua's voice quaked as he took a step to follow them. Jim reached out and silently blocked his path, shaking his head. Joshua swallowed hard as he heeded Jim's unspoken advice and stopped pursuing his heartbroken friends.

Perry turned and looked down at the much-shorter Caroline, putting his hands on her shoulders. "Honey, you need to stay here where it's safe. *I'll handle this.*"

Caroline's face flushed red and she poked Perry in the chest. "No! They're *my* children too! And my parents were with them. *I'm going!*"

Jim whispered under his breath as Perry and Caroline argued. "Joshua, you'd go if those were your children. And I know you well enough to know that no one would stop you without a fight." Joshua knew Jim was right. He teared up as he nodded.

Rebecca stepped off the deck and grabbed Joshua's hand, tears streaming down her cheeks. Perry and Caroline, who had apparently come to an agreement, silently walked to their truck. Always the gentleman, Perry opened Caroline's door before walking around to the driver's side.

Joshua gulped and called out. "I'll pray for you guys. If you can, be here Saturday morning at 8:00 with everything you want to take with you."

Rebecca and Jim looked at Joshua quizzically. Perry

continued walking as asked, "Where are we going?"

"I'm not sure yet, but I'm working on it. I'll hammer that out between now and then. *You just be careful and get back here.* And call me if you are able and let me know about Charlie and Allie."

Joshua's eyes filled with tears as Perry gave a thumbs-up and slammed his truck door. The Ram kicked up gravel as it sped down the driveway toward the road. Joshua's pounding heart felt as heavy as lead. He sat on the steps and planted his face in his palms. *How can this be happening?* Rebecca sat beside him and put her arm around him, speechless. Reagan wedged himself between them, still trembling. Jim sat silently facing Joshua and Rebecca.

After a few long minutes Joshua lifted his head up to reveal red, watery eyes. He sighed heavily as he grabbed Rebecca's hand and squeezed it tightly. *What do we do? Where do we even start?* He looked at Jim, then Rebecca, then back at Jim.

"I... I cannot imagine what Perry and Caroline are going through," Joshua said, his voice trembling. "Jim, you're right that if my children were in Raleigh tonight I would go, but I hate to see Perry and Caroline put themselves at risk. We've already lost a lot today, and I don't want to lose my best friend too."

Jim nodded and spoke in an even, reassuring voice. "I

understand, but he has to make that decision for himself. And I think you'll see them here Saturday morning."

"How can you be so calm?" Joshua asked.

"Appearances can be deceiving. But I know that God is in control, even when things seem out of control."

"Speaking of Saturday, what's your plan, Josh?" Rebecca asked.

"Let's go inside and talk about it." As Joshua rose from the steps he realized Drew was still standing motionless, fixated on the mushroom cloud glowing on the eastern horizon. He had not spoken a word since the blast. "Drew?"

Drew jumped as though suddenly snapped out of a trance. He silently looked at Joshua and Rebecca, white as a ghost.

"Are you okay?" Jim asked.

"Umm, yeah," Drew stammered. He looked in the direction of the mushroom cloud for another moment, and then staggered toward the door in a manner reminiscent of a drunkard.

"My apartment is... *was*... in downtown Raleigh." Drew pointed toward the mushroom cloud. "If I had been home, that would've killed me. I can't imagine what your friend Perry and his wife must be feeling now. *That should have been me, not their children.*"

"Drew, you can't let yourself feel guilty because you were

here instead of there," Joshua said. "You couldn't predict that."

"I… um…" Drew paused for a moment, appearing to search for the right words. "My boss. The House and Senate leadership. *I was supposed to be with them.* The governor and his cabinet. All dead--."

"But we don't know for sure that the blast was in downtown Raleigh," Rebecca said.

"Where else would it be?" Drew shot back. "That's where I'd put it."

"Are you saying you believe our state's leadership was taken out by what we just saw?"

Drew shook his head and looked down at the floor. "That's *exactly* what I'm saying. I *told* them to meet off-site, away from Raleigh, but they wouldn't listen. I told them I was sick and couldn't come. I just had a feeling I shouldn't be there." Drew paused and then started toward the bathroom. "I think I *am* going to be sick." The closed bathroom door didn't completely muffle the sound of him violently vomiting.

"I'm going to check on my wife and kids," Jim said with a sense of urgency. "We'll plan to see y'all Saturday." Jim hugged both Joshua and Rebecca and headed for his jeep. "We'll talk tomorrow. *If* the phone networks are working."

Joshua plopped down on the couch. Rebecca sat beside

him and rested her head on his shoulder. Reagan sat at his feet, still trembling. Joshua put one arm around Rebecca and ran his fingers through her straight brown hair. He used his free hand to turn on the television, but there was no satellite signal. His tablet was still working. *I'm amazed this still works,* he thought. Tears came to his eyes as a news website confirmed that downtown Raleigh was the location of the nuclear blast they had just witnessed.

The anchor explained that the second wave of attacks had not been confined to Raleigh. Bombs had breached several levees in New Orleans, flooding low-lying residential areas without warning. San Jose had been hit with an electromagnetic pulse weapon, wreaking havoc on electronic devices in Silicon Valley. A dirty bomb had gone off in Cincinnati, several car bombs had detonated near crowded areas in Austin, a suicide bomber had blown himself up in a mall in Boston and there had been an explosion near the naval yard in Norfolk.

Joshua shook his head. "This is spiraling out of control faster than I ever imagined."

Rebecca looked up and sniffled. "Yes it is. So what's the plan for Saturday?"

"Saturday..." Joshua rehashed the plan that he and Thomas had discussed the night before.

"He's just going to *give* the land to us and whoever goes with us?" she asked.

"Not exactly, and I wouldn't ask him to do that. It's *his* land, and we shouldn't expect something for nothing. Anyone who wants to go will have an agreement with him to provide something for his family in exchange for the use of his land. If they don't follow through, they're out."

"Sounds like a good rule, but who'll enforce it?"

"You remember me talking about my friend, Bob Kendall?"

"The guy who was in the Army for so long and worked at the legislature?"

"That's the one. He's going with us. And he and Thomas are meeting here tomorrow afternoon."

"That'll be interesting," Rebecca said skeptically. "Thomas is so laid back and Bob sounds like a 'shoot first, ask questions later' kind of guy."

"It'll be definitely interesting to see how they mesh." Joshua chuckled. "But we need them both."

Drew finally emerged from the bathroom, pale and looking like he could get sick again at any moment. He trudged into the living room and silently collapsed onto a vacant recliner. After a few moments Joshua broke the silence. "Drew, you mentioned that your apartment was in downtown Raleigh. Where are you staying tonight?"

"Umm, I hadn't thought about it yet. Don't know."

Joshua glanced at Rebecca, who silently nodded her

approval to the unspoken question. "You're welcome to stay here. We have a spare bedroom."

"Thank you so much. Still processing what happened today. Can't believe it hit *Raleigh*."

Rebecca showed Drew the guest room while Joshua finished reading news coverage of the second wave of attacks. After a few minutes she returned and joined him on the couch. "Josh, are you sure about this? Packing up and moving to the mountains and abandoning our farm?"

Joshua felt a pang of guilt. "I don't like it either, but in my gut I know it's the right move. I love it here, but all hell is breaking loose in this country and we're too close to too many people here. We have to get out of the line of fire while we can."

"Okay, Josh," she said unconvincingly. "But I don't like it."

Joshua bit his lip. "Me either, but I need you to trust my judgment on this."

"I do, but I still don't like it."

"Thank you, Becca. That means a lot. Especially now."

CHAPTER 3

Perry gripped the steering wheel tightly with both hands. He drove in silence down the winding, pitch-black road toward the mushroom cloud billowing over Raleigh. Caroline sat in the passenger seat, bawling like a baby. He fought back a tear as he reached over and squeezed her hand. She squeezed back for a moment, then withdrew her hand and turned away, silently staring out the window.

Flashing blue lights overcame the darkness as they rounded a curve and approached a roadblock. An officer approached Perry's truck. "Sir, you're going to have to turn around. We can't allow any vehicles beyond this point."

"I understand, but our children are there. *Please* let us go look for them. I realize we'll be on our own if we go in, but we have to find them."

Caroline looked up at the officer through tear-filled eyes, her lower lip quivering. "Please..."

The officer pursed his lips. "Hold on a moment, I'll be right back." He walked toward a vehicle surrounded by several men in suits and uniforms. Perry cocked an eyebrow as he noticed the U.S. Department of Homeland Security logo on the vehicle. *They sure didn't waste any time getting here.*

While Perry was waiting two of the officers approached the car in line ahead of him. He leaned out the window to hear what was said. He clenched his teeth as one of the officers barked out a command. "Give us your gun."

The driver objected loudly enough for Perry to hear. "But I have a concealed carry permit, and concealed weapons are allowed in this area."

"President Armando has imposed martial law and we need your gun."

"I am not giving it to you."

Perry's heart leapt as one of the officers drew his Glock .40 on the man, who put his hands in the air and surrendered his pistol. He glanced at Caroline, who was fixated on the officers. "Honey, we have to cooperate with them or this could get ugly fast." She sniffled and nodded.

The officer returned to Perry's window, accompanied by a man in a dark suit and a uniformed Homeland Security police officer. The man in the suit spoke sternly. "You need to turn around, now. We cannot allow you to enter this area."

"I understand, sir," Perry calmly responded. "We're just trying to find our children. They were supposed to be in Raleigh."

"Did you hear me? You need to turn around, *NOW*."

"Yes, sir." Perry said. "We will do so."

"And we need your cell phones."

Perry's brow furrowed. "Our cell phones?"

"You heard me. Hand 'em over."

"Why do you need our phones?"

"You ask too many questions. Hand them over *now*."

Perry bit his lip as he looked at Caroline and handed their phones to the agent. Caroline began sobbing loudly.

"Do you have any weapons in the vehicle?"

"No, sir." Perry swallowed hard.

"Turn around and get out of here."

"Yes, sir." Perry did a quick three-point turn and drove away from the roadblock. He exhaled a sigh of relief as the blue lights disappeared from his rear view mirror. "We'll try again tomorrow, but there was no getting past those guys."

Caroline wiped a tear from her cheek. "Why did you tell him we don't have any weapons?"

Perry squeezed her hand. "The pistol is hidden, and I feel safer having it with us. I took a chance they wouldn't do a thorough search."

***

A thick, haunting fog hung over the farm the next morning. Joshua was on the front porch with his cup of coffee perched precariously on the rail and his Bible in his lap when Rebecca finally made her way outside. She leaned over and kissed him. "Good morning. You're up early."

"Hey," he responded in a monotone voice. "A lot on my

mind. So much to ponder."

"Me too. And I'm worried about Perry and Caroline." Rebecca shivered as the brisk wind knifed through the yard. "It's cold out here. I'm going inside."

"I'll be in shortly." Nearly an hour later he made his way into the house and turned on the television. "Let's see if this works. I'm almost afraid to watch if it does."

Joshua cocked an eyebrow when the TV flared to life. The news anchor rehashed the prior day's events. *In addition, car bombs exploded in crowded areas in Detroit and Austin and a small fishing boat loaded with explosives damaged a docked U.S. Navy vessel in Norfolk. There are reports of looting and violence in some areas. Many federal government services have ceased operations due to the loss of personnel and infrastructure, and the same is likely to happen in states like North Carolina where the state capital was hit yesterday.*

British intelligence sources are privately telling us that they are still picking up a high volume of terrorist chatter and that they believe AIS is planning more attacks on U.S. soil. Analysts are warning citizens to be on the alert for potential copycat terrorists. Additionally, we are receiving reports that cargo ships, many of them transporting food and other essential items, are refusing to dock at American ports due to heightened security concerns.

Meanwhile, President Armando has reassigned officers

with the Department of Homeland Security's Federal Protective Service, commonly referred to as FPS or 'Homeland Security Police', to help maintain order in areas victimized by looting and violence in the wake of this week's attacks. Sources close to his administration tell us that he may enlist the military to assist as well. These Homeland Security officers were stationed throughout the country prior to this week's attacks. President Armando has declared martial law in many areas. This move has several governors and local officials crying foul, with some voicing concerns that the federal government should assist local governments, not take the lead. One local official even went so far as to say that he worried federal police and the military would not leave once they are entrenched. The Armando administration rejected these concerns as 'irrational fringe conspiracy theories driven by fear-mongering political extremists with selfish agendas'.

The anchor paused for a moment, turned and looked to the side as if communicating with someone off-screen, then continued. *We have breaking news that a bomb has damaged a major commercial rail line used to transport food and other critical items up and down the east coast. There are reports of accidents, traffic jams and multiple instances of road rage on major highways, especially near cities. Communication lines are down in many areas, but the nation's wireless infrastructure seems to be holding its own. Authorities are encouraging people to stay in their homes unless travel is absolutely necessary.*

Joshua shook his head as he muted the television. "This is getting worse and worse. It's a good thing we're leaving tomorrow, but we've got a lot to do today. We need to pack *everything* we want to take with us so that we can do it all in one trip. I'll work on big items from the barn, and you start packing the things we need from the house."

He walked toward the door. "A few more things... can you try to call Perry and Caroline and see if you can get up with them? And keep the tabs on the news? And check on Drew?"

"Will do," she answered. "Were you expecting anyone this morning?"

"Not until this afternoon."

Rebecca pointed out the window. "Well, we've got company. It's only 8:00."

Joshua looked out and saw a dark green GMC Yukon pulling a small, enclosed utility trailer making its way down the driveway.

"I'm not sure who that is." Joshua tucked his 9mm into his back pocket before stepping onto the porch. Rebecca watched from the doorway behind him and Reagan stood at his feet, barking incessantly.

Joshua squinted, trying to discern who was driving this strange vehicle. He exhaled a sigh of relief when a familiar face emerged from the driver's side. The new arrival was a tall, clean-cut, stocky man in his late 50s. He had short, gray hair and sported neatly pressed khaki cargo pants, dark brown boots and a long-sleeve black shirt featuring a U.S. Army logo.

"It's Bob Kendall." Joshua looked back at Rebecca. "I wasn't expecting him until later this afternoon."

An even taller man unfamiliar to Joshua emerged from the passenger side of the vehicle. He was slender and muscular, appeared to be around 30 years old and had blonde hair in a neatly trimmed crew cut. He looked the part of an active duty Army Infantryman or Marine who wouldn't shy away from a bare-knuckles fight.

"Good morning, Joshua," Bob said. "I hope we didn't startle you, but we thought you could use some help with your preparations." Bob pointed in the direction of his guest. "This is Kane Martin. Martin served under my command in Operation Enduring Freedom after 9/11." Joshua thought it odd that Bob addressed Kane by his last name.

Kane stepped toward Joshua, stood at attention as if greeting a high-ranking officer and extended his hand. "Nice to meet you, sir!"

Joshua was caught off guard by the level of military formality in Kane's greeting. "Umm, nice to meet you too." He gestured in Rebecca's direction. "This is my wife, Rebecca."

Kane extended his hand. "Nice to meet you, ma'am!"

"Becca, you've heard me talk about Bob," Joshua said. "He worked at the legislature as a sergeant at arms for a few years before retiring in 2012. Before that he was in the Army for 30 years and reached the rank of Command Sergeant Major. Oh, and he tells the best stories of anyone I know."

Bob let out a rare laugh. "No time for stories now. Let's get started. Joshua, what is the plan and what do you need help with?"

Reagan followed them at a distance, warily eyeing Bob and Kane as they walked to the barn.

"Well, Bob, given your military background I was hoping you could help me figure that out. Let me start by telling you where we're going. A friend of mine has land in the mountains, west of Asheville. He is going to let us set up and stay there."

"Who is this friend?" Bob asked.

"Thomas Page."

Bob lit up a cigar. "What is his background? Do you trust him?"

"I've known Thomas for years. Yes, I trust him. As a matter of fact, he built this house and barn for us."

"How secure is the property in question?"

"I don't really know. I haven't seen it yet. It's near the

Fontana Dam. Pretty remote area."

"I know the area. That is away from population centers and major highways. Good."

"I'm going there under the assumption that we will be there indefinitely," Joshua explained. "We need to take *everything* we need to be able to make do. What do you think should be on the list?"

"First, you need protection," Bob puffed on his cigar. "Second, provisions for food. Third, shelter."

Joshua's brow furrowed. "What *specific* items do you think we need to take on Saturday?"

Bob rattled off what sounded like a checklist in a survivalist handbook: "Guns. Ammunition – as much as you can get. Other weapons if you have them, such as bows or crossbows. Knives. Matches and other ways to start a fire. Cooking utensils. A portable grill, if you have it. Blankets and sleeping bags. Flashlights and all the batteries you can get your hands on. Rope. Twine. Canteens or jugs to store water. Warm clothes and boots. Sleeping bags. Fishing gear, given that we'll be near a lake. Tools, including saws and axes to cut wood. Machetes. Binoculars or a telescope. Work gloves. Any and all non-perishable food items. Anything that can be traded and bartered for other things we may need."

Joshua furiously scribbled every item Bob mentioned onto a piece of scrap paper he found in the barn. "Anything else?"

"Every bit of cash you can get your hands on, although it may not be worth anything soon. Let's take a look around your barn and see if we need to take anything else you have."

The sound of frantic cackling filled the barn as they approached a small, caged area near the back. Bob pointed at the chickens. "They go, and we'll need wire to build a coop."

"I'm assuming we should we take the cows, too?" Joshua asked.

"Yes. Correct. And we'll need fencing for them."

Joshua scribbled on his list as Bob went into to the next room. Kane silently followed them while Reagan explored the barn.

"What are these?" Bob pointed at small, dust-covered paper pouches stacked on shelving along the wall.

"Seeds," Joshua answered. "Sweet corn. Cucumbers. Tomatoes. Watermelon. Green beans. Peas--"

"They all go," Bob said. "And if you have it, we'll need a way to preserve food, even if we do not have electricity."

"You mean like canning supplies?"

"Affirmative. How do you plan to transport all of this?"

"That's a good question," Joshua answered. "We'll be

stuffing our personal items into Rebecca's SUV and pulling our trailer behind it. We could take my old farm truck if I had someone to drive it, but I'm not leaving Rebecca alone in the SUV."

Bob turned to Kane. "Martin, you're driving Mr. Winston's farm truck and pulling his cattle trailer. Get started loading the truck."

"Yes, sir!" Kane immediately began loading the truck, not muttering a word as he worked.

"Let's talk logistics," Bob said. "We need to get from here to there undetected. And once we get there, we need to stay off the grid. The fewer people who know where we are, the better. Speaking of people, who is going with us?"

"Six families and one individual in addition to you, Kane, Rebecca and me."

"How do you know these people?"

"Some through work, some through politics, others through church. And some indirectly through others who are going."

"Who are they?"

"Thomas, who owns the property, and his wife and kids."

"What does he do?"

"A little bit of everything. He grew up on a farm and has been involved in everything from construction to real estate to land development."

"Who else?"

"Jim Davidson. He was a pastor at a church I once attended and works for a non-profit ministry. He's an outdoorsman who hunts and fishes."

"Who else?"

"Drew Thompson. Drew worked at the legislature for the Speaker of the House."

Bob cocked an eyebrow. "What does he bring to the table?"

Joshua cringed. "I'm not going to leave him out to dry. Hopefully, my best friend Perry and his wife will be joining us."

"Hopefully?"

Joshua fought back a tear. "They were here Thursday night when the bomb went off in Raleigh. Unfortunately, their two children were supposed to be in downtown Raleigh. Perry and Caroline left to go look for their kids, and we have not seen or heard from them since."

"Hmmm. Who else?"

"Let's see. We have a Marine veteran who makes his living as a firearms instructor--"

"Excellent!" Bob grinned broadly.

"Assuming Perry and Caroline make it we have someone

who works in finance, a computer software engineer, a nurse, a teacher, a business consultant, someone who works in IT and a former deputy sheriff."

"How well do you know these people?"

"Some better than others, but I believe everyone on the list is trustworthy and will do their part. There will be some kids in the group as well."

Bob audibly groaned at Joshua's mention of children. "Everyone in the group needs to have clear instructions tomorrow. We don't need to draw attention to ourselves. We must get from here to the mountains as quietly as possible. And when we get there, we need to remain as off the grid as possible. That means *discipline*. And with that said, we need to be prepared to defend ourselves if necessary."

"I agree," Joshua said. "Can you take the lead on organizing travel logistics for tomorrow?"

"Affirmative," Bob said. "Make sure everyone who shows up tomorrow has a full tank of gas and that their cell phones are fully charged."

"Will do. I'll email or text everyone when I get into the house."

"Negative! No email or text! They are too easy to monitor. We don't know who we can trust, therefore we must remain below radar as much as possible. Call them, from a landline if you have one. Additionally, instruct everyone to turn off their GPS devices and the GPS functions on their phones. They do need to bring their phones and have them fully charged, *but should use them for emergency purposes only from this point forward.*"

"Will do, but half of these people will be lost without their GPS."

"Well, it's time they grow up and learn how to use a stinking map." Bob blew a puff of cigar smoke in the air. "If they can't get there without a GPS that may be a sign that we don't need 'em holding us back."

A lot of people are going to be in for a dose of culture shock when they meet Bob tomorrow, Joshua thought. "By the way, don't forget that Thomas will be here at 5:00. I hope you can stick around and meet him."

"Affirmative."

"Also, what time will you be here tomorrow morning?"

"With your permission, we will sleep here tonight. Martin and I have everything we need and will pitch our tents out here by the barn."

"Why am I not surprised?" Joshua chuckled. "That's fine. I'm going in to check on Rebecca, run this list by her, see what else we need to pack and then start making calls. Do you need anything from me?"

"Negative. Martin and I will handle packing your large items. We will let you know if we need additional information."

"Yes, sir!" Kane agreed.

Inside, it was immediately evident that Rebecca had been hard at work. The living area floor was covered in boxes, several of which contained canned goods. Others were filled to the brim with clothes, dishes and utensils.

"Wow, you've been busy!"

Rebecca wiped her brow as she looked up from her seat among the sea of boxes. "I've gotten a lot done. If we *have* to make this move, I want it to feel like home when we get wherever we're going. Trying to pack everything we'll need. What have you guys been up to? They seem like interesting characters."

"They're definitely interesting." Joshua chuckled. "We'll need them. Bob helped me make a list of things everyone should bring, and now I have to call everyone and share the list. Now he and his friend Kane are getting some of our large items ready to go." Joshua looked over the boxes. "Let's make sure we take some pictures and personal items with us. That will help it feel a little like home."

"Already working on it," Rebecca said as Joshua picked up an empty box and started toward his office. "What are you going to put in that?"

"A few books I don't want to leave behind."

"Books?" she quizzed him. "Won't those just take up

space that could be used for things we *need* to take with us?"

"I think we'll *need* some of these," Joshua responded without further explanation. Before he made it down the hall he stopped, closed his eyes and took a deep, heavy breath. "Umm, were you able to get up with Perry and Caroline?"

"No." Rebecca solemnly answered.

Joshua shook his head. His stomach tightened into knots as he walked to his office. He began putting books he felt were worth taking into the box: *The Bible. The Art of War. The Boy Scout Handbook.* Pocket-sized copies of the U.S. Constitution. Books on leadership. Biographies of George Washington, Winston Churchill and Ronald Reagan. *Robert's Rules of Order.* A survivalist handbook he had purchased a few years earlier out of morbid curiosity, and which now seemed eerily relevant. Joshua retrieved his Rotary "Past President" pin and a coin which bore the Rotary motto, "Service Above Self," which he had always sought to uphold while in public life.

After packing the books Joshua took a seat in his office chair, pulled out his smartphone and silently stared at it for a moment. A lump formed in his throat as he dialed Perry's number but got a fast busy signal. "Network is down," he muttered to himself. The call went through on his landline. *Please pick up.* It went straight to voice mail.

Joshua left a long-winded message: "Hey, Perry. Rebecca and I are worried about you guys. Please let us know how you're doing and what you've found out about Charlie and Allie. We're getting organized and are still planning to meet here tomorrow morning at 8:00 to travel to a secure location. I hope you two can be here and go with us. We need you, and we miss you guys already. If you can make it, please come prepared to leave here for good. Bring any weapons and ammunition you have, matches, cooking utensils, sleeping bags, clothes, non-perishable food, tools – anything you can think of that we might need. As far as getting ready, bring as much cash as you can, and anything that we could use to barter for other things we need. Oh, and have a full tank of gas." Joshua paused for a moment, then choked up. "Perry, I *really* do hope we see you guys tomorrow."

He hung up the phone and sat silently for a moment before realizing Rebecca was standing in the doorway.

"I take it Perry didn't answer?" she asked.

"Nope." He cleared his throat and fought back a tear before turning to face her. "Becca, we've lost our sense of security, we're losing our farm, and I'm worried that I've lost my best friend."

Rebecca walked over and hugged him for what seemed like an eternity. "You've still got me." She leaned over and kissed him. "You need to make the rest of your calls, and I need to finish packing." He nodded and dialed the next number.

***

The sun was already dropping toward the western horizon when Thomas turned into the driveway from the main road. Joshua and Reagan walked out to the barn to greet him. Bob emerged through the barn doors just as Thomas parked his Suburban.

"Thomas, good to see you," Joshua said. "This is Bob Kendall. Bob will be coordinating the logistics of our trip."

"Hey man, nice to meet you." Thomas extended his hand.

Bob shook Thomas' hand. "Likewise." In typical no-nonsense Bob Kendall fashion, he dispensed with the pleasantries and got down to business. "Do you have a map of the property with you?"

"Yeah, let me get it out of the truck."

Thomas retrieved the rolled-up maps and handed them to Bob, who immediately unrolled them and spread them out on the hood of the Suburban.

"Where is the property boundary?" Bob asked.

Thomas outlined the borders of his land.

Bob continued, "Mr. Winston said you were keeping a portion for your house. Where is it?"

Thomas used his toothpick to point out the area where his cabin was located.

"What are the routes in and out?"

"We have one road in at this point, right here."

"We will need a backup emergency exit. Where will livestock be kept?"

Thomas shrugged. "Hadn't thought about that."

Bob grimaced. "We need a plan, as that will be part of our food source. What are your power sources?"

"We are connected through the TVA, and I know some folks who work up at the dam."

"Good. Do you have a security plan?"

Thomas shook his head. "Hadn't thought about that either."

"We will take care of that. What are the routes from the property to the lake?"

Thomas showed him.

"How will you decide who lives where on the property?"

"This is my area." Thomas again pointed to the portion of the tract where his home was located, then to another square. "Joshua and Rebecca will have this cabin. I have another cabin that's open. Haven't really thought about it beyond that."

Joshua interjected, "Everyone is being instructed that

they *will* provide Thomas with some form of compensation for the use of his land. I'll leave it to him to negotiate the specifics of that with each person or family."

"Understood." Bob pointed at a wooded area on the map. "With your permission, Martin and I will set up camp here and our camp will serve as a security watch. I assume handling security for the property will suffice as compensation for the use of your land."

"Martin?" Thomas twisted the toothpick between his lips. "Who's that?"

"Martin!" Bob called out. Kane came jogging out of the barn. "Mr. Page, meet Kane Martin."

"Nice to meet you, sir!" Kane extended his hand.

"You too, man."

Kane stood silently until Bob said, "Dismissed!" He did a quick about-face and returned to the barn. Thomas looked at Joshua with an expression of combined bewilderment and amusement.

Joshua smirked. "C'mon, let's take a look in the barn."

Inside the barn, Joshua's Silverado was packed to the gills. Kane had loaded the truck with shovels, hoes and rakes, a pickaxe, two machetes, bags of corn, axes and wood splitters, a variety of hand saws, a bush axe, a box of nails, post-hole diggers, chicken wire, heavier wire for the cattle fence and a large toolbox containing hammers and other basic tools. He had also constructed a portable cage large enough to transport the chickens.

"You've been hard at work," Joshua observed.

"Yes, sir!"

"Martin is a workhorse," Bob said. "One of the hardest working men I've ever commanded. Follows orders precisely."

Thomas flashed another perplexed grin in Joshua's direction. Joshua chuckled quietly to himself. *Oil and water. I hope they can get along.*

Suddenly Reagan ran to the barn door, growling and barking at the headlights turning into the driveway.

"Expecting anyone else tonight?" Bob asked.

"Nope."

"Do you recognize the vehicle?"

Joshua walked to the barn door and studied the silver king-cab F-150 with a camper shell and large box trailer making its way toward the house. "No."

"Martin!" Bob bellowed. "Unknown vehicle. Observe."

Kane grabbed his .308 rifle and disappeared out of the back of the barn.

"Bob!" Joshua clenched his teeth. "He's not going to do anything rash, is he?"

"Martin will not initiate," Bob calmly replied.

Joshua pursed his lips.

Bob stepped outside and shined a spotlight at the truck. "Identify yourself!"

The lights on the truck went dark, the engine shut off and the door opened. "I'm Drew Thompson. Who are *you*?"

Bob looked at Joshua.

"Drew's with us," Joshua said. "He's okay."

"Martin!" Bob called out. "Stand down!"

Out of the corner of his eye Joshua saw a quick movement as Kane lowered his .308 and retreated from his vantage point near the corner of the barn, disappearing into the darkness like a ghost. Bob did an about-face and reentered the barn.

"Those two cats are wound a little tight, ain't they?" Thomas nodded toward the barn.

Joshua chuckled but did not answer. "Drew, I take it you got a new vehicle?"

Drew was sporting what appeared to be pair of brand new khakis, a light blue dress shirt and green sweater vest, polished brown dress shoes and leather jacket. He was also carrying a dark blue backpack on one shoulder.

"Yes I did. I needed something that would move more cargo than my little car."

"Looks like you also found a change of clothes. I thought

your apartment was destroyed?"

"It was. I still own my parents' old house in Dunn and had some items in storage there. I went there to get a few things and convinced a friend who owns a used car dealership to trade me this for the 'Vette."

Joshua nodded. "Drew, this is Thomas Page. Thomas owns the land where we'll be going."

Drew and Thomas exchanged pleasantries as the three of them walked into barn.

"Drew, there are two more people I'd like you to meet," Joshua said. "This is Bob Kendall. Bob is a retired Army Command Sergeant Major who worked at the legislature a few years ago. He left just before you got there. And this is Kane Martin."

"Nice to meet you." Drew extended his hand to Bob.

Joshua gritted his teeth when Bob did not return the handshake, instead thumping Drew's chest. "That sure is a real *purty* sweater vest you've got there, boy," he said with a sneer reinforced by a derisive laugh from Kane. "You're too soft for where we're going. Do you have any idea what you're going into?"

"Probably not," Drew admitted without hesitation.

"Didn't think so." Bob blew cigar smoke in Drew's face and turned to walk away. "Joshua, I hope this one won't drag us down. *No weak links!*"

Joshua cringed. "Come on, Bob, give the kid a break."

Joshua grimaced as Bob grunted and walked to the back of the barn, where Kane had resumed working.

"Drew, don't worry about him," Joshua said. "He's just a bit old-school and rough around the edges."

"Duly noted," Drew responded dryly. "Mr. Page, may I have a word with you in private?"

"Sure thing, man," Thomas said. "Let's go outside."

Joshua watched curiously as they disappeared through the barn doors. *What could Drew want to speak privately with Thomas about? They JUST met.* He walked to the back of the barn.

"Bob, please go easy on Drew. He's a good kid."

"I saw enough of these political operative types at the legislature to know what they're all about. He's just a hack. It only takes one look to tell that boy is *soft*. He'll hold us back."

"Don't forget you met me at the legislature."

"That's different. You were elected by the people, and I could tell from day one that you were there to serve, not advance yourself."

Joshua shook his head. "Give him a chance. I'm going to go help Rebecca. I'll see you guys in the morning."

***

The next morning Joshua turned on the television in their farmhouse one last time. Unsurprisingly, the news anchor was talking about the aftermath of the week's attacks.

All across the country, people are in a state of panic. A line of people wrapped around a grocery store flashed across the screen, followed by empty shelves inside the store. *People are buying up everything in stores.*

Next, the newscast showed a clip of looters carrying away stolen items in a downtown area. *There are countless reports of looting, carjacking and armed robberies. The situation is worse in areas closer to the attacks, where state and local governments and law enforcement agencies have been decimated. Major roads are clogged with people trying to flee the fallout from the blasts. Those medical facilities that are open are overwhelmed with patients, many of whom relied on the now nonexistent federal healthcare plan to pay their doctor bills.*

Next came a clip of military vehicles in the streets. *President Armando has imposed martial law in the attack zones and other areas where there is unrest. Citizens in those areas are being ordered to remain indoors, surrender any weapons they have and, in some cases, house troops and Homeland Security police. Local officials in many areas have protested, but with most of Congress and the Supreme Court gone there appears to be no one to stand in the President's way.*

"Wow." Joshua's nostrils flared. "Unbelievable. Looks like my worst fears about Armando are being realized. It's a good thing we're getting out of here."

"Sounds like it," Rebecca said. "But do you really think we would have to worry about it *here*?"

"Sadly, yes."

Rebecca looked down at the floor and shook her head. "I know you're probably right, but it's just all so hard to believe."

A few minutes later Joshua savored what would likely be the last cup of coffee he would ever drink on the porch at their beloved farmhouse. He closed his eyes and thought of the day he and Rebecca found this tract of land. They had worked together, along with Thomas, to design the house and barn and determine where everything would be placed. This was truly their dream house. No, it was more than that. It was HOME -- where he had planned to spend the rest of his life with Rebecca. *This doesn't seem real*, he thought. *We're actually leaving. Is this the right move?* He looked at his watch. *Everyone will be here within the hour. I can't believe this is actually happening.*

Rebecca joined him and a jittery Reagan tightly wedged himself between them. "This is all hard to believe. I still don't like it, but I trust your judgment," she said. "I've got a few more things to get ready."

Joshua went to the barn to do a quick check for any

last-minute items that needed packing. When he walked through the high, arching doors into the dimly lit interior he noticed the old Massey Ferguson tractor. It had belonged to his father. Joshua felt a lump form in his throat. They were leaving the antique red tractor behind. Joshua perked up as Bob greeted him. "Joshua, we are ready to proceed."

"Thanks for all you've done, Bob. One question. I'd like to stay connected to the outside world so we know what's going on. Do you think we should take our satellite dish and see if we can get it working?"

"Affirmative. Martin, remove the satellite dish from the residence and prepare it for transport. We will ascertain its functionality when we arrive at the new location."

"Yes, sir!" Kane removed a ladder that was tied to the cattle trailer. Joshua and Bob loaded the television while Kane removed the satellite dish.

As Joshua walked back toward the house he again dialed his phone, praying that his best friend would answer. His heart sank when the call went straight to voicemail. "Perry, this is Joshua. Just trying to get in touch with you. We're leaving in a bit and are worried about you. Hope we see you this morning. *Please* let us know how you're doing. *We miss you guys.*"

Joshua walked back into the barren house, where a teary-eyed Rebecca sat on the empty floor. He sat down beside her and grabbed her hand. "Well, this is it." He put his arms around her and hugged her tightly as she buried her head in his chest. Joshua closed his eyes as the reality of the moment swirled around him. They were leaving their beloved farm behind. Joshua was parting ways with an entire library of books, many of which had belonged to his mother. The high-back leather chair featuring the North Carolina State Seal that he retained from his days in the legislature would also remain, along with most of his business suits and a mountain of plaques and certificates from his years of civic and political involvement. Rebecca was devastated to leave her wedding dress behind, along with her grandmother's antique China and sewing machine. So many important memories were attached to these items. Precious items which were being swept out of their lives by the tides of history.

CHAPTER 4

The flag whipped gently in the breeze, its colors shimmering in the radiant morning sunlight. A few wispy clouds graced the sky. Joshua and Rebecca looked out over a driveway teeming with vehicles and people. The crowd included several children and three dogs. The group looked like an ancient convoy of nomads who took all of their belongings when they traveled, apart from the fact that this group had automobiles rather than camels. Reagan was unnerved by the crowd of strangers, particularly the three much larger dogs, and hid behind Joshua.

"Any sign of Perry and Caroline?" Rebecca asked.

"None." Joshua heaved a morbid sigh.

She squeezed his hand. "I'll try them one more time. You go talk to everyone and make sure they're ready."

"Thanks. And can you go ahead and put Reagan in the Explorer? He seems a little spooked."

She nodded. Joshua worked the crowd and spoke to those who had arrived, then found Bob. "Are you ready to give everyone their marching orders?"

"Affirmative," Bob answered. "I will execute on your signal."

Rebecca frowned as she rejoined Joshua. "No luck."

A feeling of hopelessness enveloped Joshua. "I guess there's nothing we can do but hope and pray." He looked down and shook his head, a tear in his eye. "Regardless, it's time to get this show on the road."

Joshua climbed onto the Silverado's tailgate and addressed the crowd. "Good morning everyone. It's 8:00 and we've got a long trip ahead of us, so let's get organized. I'd like to begin by introducing a couple of people. First, this is Thomas Page. Thomas owns the land where we are going." Thomas waved and smiled. Joshua continued, "As I've communicated to each of you, you should compensate Thomas in some way for the use of his land. Whatever arrangement you work out is between you and him, but I will *not* stand idly by and let anyone freeload off of him. Thomas, do you want to say anything?"

Thomas took the toothpick out of his mouth and rolled it between his fingers. "How are y'all doing? Glad we're able to help you folks. I only gave Joshua one rule. One of the cabins goes to him and Rebecca. We owe 'em that since he's taking the lead on this. Look forward to getting to know y'all better."

"Thomas does have another cabin that is up for grabs, so talk with him if you are interested in that."

"Actually, that one is taken," Thomas said. "Drew and I have an arrangement."

Joshua looked at Thomas and Drew, puzzled. "Okay." He cleared his throat. "Next, I'd like to introduce Bob Kendall. Bob and I met when I was in the legislature. He worked there as a sergeant at arms for a couple of years. Before that he was in the Army for 30 years and reached the rank of Command Sergeant Major, which proves he knows a little something about leadership and getting things done. Bob has agreed to handle logistics for our trip to ensure that we get there safely and will oversee security once we arrive. Please listen to him carefully and follow his instructions. He knows what he's doing."

Bob effortlessly jumped onto the tailgate as Joshua climbed down. "Good morning, patriots! Today you will embark on a journey through unknown conditions to a strange place that will be your home for the foreseeable future. There are reports of violence and unrest in urban areas, including larger cities here in North Carolina. We do not know if there will be a hostile presence on our routes, so we must assume that there *will* be and prepare accordingly. We will avoid major highway routes and major cities. You must always be on the lookout for potential threats and must be prepared to defend yourselves with force if necessary."

"We will travel in groups of two or three vehicles," he continued. "Every convoy should have at least one weapon held by someone who knows how to use it. Deactivate the GPS functions on your phones and in your cars before we leave. You will be provided with maps outlining your route. If you do not know how to navigate without your GPS, now is the time to man up and learn. Every vehicle will be given an encrypted radio to communicate with others in the group. Our objective is to travel in a way that avoids drawing unwanted attention. Is this clear?" He blew a puff of cigar smoke as he looked over the crowd. "Do you have any questions?"

Jim raised his hand.

"What is your question?"

"What should we do if we encounter law enforcement at a checkpoint or otherwise?"

"First, you will alert other groups using the radios provided. Second, tell them you are delivering items to a family member in Athens, Tennessee. That is all they need to know. At this time Kane Martin will distribute the maps and radios. Martin!"

Kane walked silently from group to group, handing each driver a map and radio. As Kane worked Bob bellowed, "Any further questions?"

Jim again raised his hand. "You mentioned defending ourselves. If something happens, to what lengths should we go?"

Bob puffed on his cigar. "Again, sir, you must be prepared to use deadly force if necessary."

Jim didn't appear satisfied. "How will we know if it's necessary?"

Bob answered in his drill instructor-like manner. "You

will know. But do not hesitate. Hesitation could cost you your life and the lives of those you love."

Jim did not press the issue.

"If there are no further questions we will now assign your vehicles to groups," Bob continued. He systematically divided the vehicles into groups of two. "You are to watch over the other vehicle in your group at all times during the trip. You must have each other's back. Each group will leave precisely four minutes after the group ahead of them. Travel exactly five miles above the speed limit to avoid attracting attention. Martin or I will communicate your departure times over the radios. Timing is critical. Discipline will keep you alive. Do you have questions?" Bob looked at his watch. "Seeing none, take your place in your vehicles. Departures will commence in precisely ten minutes."

As Bob jumped down from the truck Jim climbed onto the tailgate. "Folks, I'd like to pray for us before we leave. Please remove your hats and bow your heads."

After the prayer Jim pulled Joshua aside as they walked toward their vehicles. He nodded in the direction of Bob and Kane. "Those two guys scare me. They're *way* too intense. I think they'll to get us in trouble."

"Bob is all business, but he knows when to stop," Joshua assured him. "We'll be okay."

Jim's brow furrowed. "I hope you're right."

Joshua caught up with Thomas before he reached his vehicle. "Thomas, did I hear you say that Drew had made an arrangement with you for the second cabin?"

"Yeah man, you sure did. We made a deal last night."

Joshua cocked his head to the right, perplexed. "Is he compensating you? I'm not going to let anyone take your land without giving you something in return."

"Don't sweat it, man. He did me right. In fact, he owns that cabin and piece of land free and clear."

"*Really?* What did he give you for it?"

"Yeah man, really. But I'll leave it up to him tell you the details."

Joshua shook his head in bewilderment as he walked away. *How in the world?*

The parade of vehicles assembled in the order dictated by Bob. As Joshua settled into the drivers' seat Reagan made his way to the floorboard between the bucket seats. "Don't worry, boy." He scratched the whimpering puppy on the head. "We'll be settled into our new place in no time."

Bob approached the drivers' side window as Rebecca got comfortable in the passenger seat. "Joshua, it's go time. Are you ready?"

Joshua's eyes narrowed as he fired up the engine. "Let's do this."

Bob nodded and called out marching orders over his

handheld radio. "First group departing in one minute."

As the Explorer began creeping forward Joshua reached over and grabbed Rebecca's hand, attempting to force a smile as he looked into her tear-filled eyes. As he did the wind picked up and out of the corner of his eye he noticed the American flag snapping in the breeze. He slammed on the brakes and jumped out. "One more thing! I want to take the flag with us."

Bob grabbed his radio. "Martin! Front and center." Kane and Bob lowered the flag and folded it with military precision.

Another vehicle turned into the driveway as Bob was storing the flag in his SUV. He started toward the new arrival, hand on his holstered sidearm. "Martin, strange vehicle approaching. Get into position."

Joshua bounded out of the Explorer and waved Bob off. "This is no strange vehicle!"

Rebecca vaulted out of the SUV and sprinted to greet Perry and Caroline. Caroline ran to embrace her.

"Oh my God, I was worried you guys were dead!" Rebecca said. Sobbing uncontrollably, Caroline buried her face on Rebecca's shoulder.

Joshua hugged Perry. "I'm glad you guys are okay and that you got here before we left." He called for Thomas to join them. Bob had already done so, without invitation.

"Perry, meet Thomas Page and Bob Kendall. Thomas is providing the land where we're going, and Bob is handling security. Guys, this is my best friend Perry. I told you that he had gone to look for his children, who were supposed to be in Raleigh when..." Joshua's stomach twisted violently. "I... um... what did you find out about Charlie and Allie?"

Perry shook his head and answered in a shaky voice. "When we got to Raleigh they wouldn't let us into the blast zone. We went back to our house in Wake Forest and made dozens – hundreds – of calls. The restaurant where they had planned to eat was destroyed, and no one has heard from them or Caroline's parents." He closed his eyes and took a deep breath. "At this point we have to assume they were--" Perry began bawling like a newborn baby.

Joshua embraced his heartbroken friend. "I am so sorry." Caroline continued sobbing on Rebecca's shoulder but did not speak.

After what seemed like an eternity of awkward silence Perry wiped the tears from his eyes. "You mentioned security. That's good. We're going to need it."

"What do you mean?" Bob perked up.

"People are starting to lose it," he said. "One of my neighbors in Wake Forest got stopped and robbed at gunpoint on a usually calm, upscale neighborhood street while driving home from the grocery store. The robbers didn't want money. They took her *food.* We've heard other similar stories. And when we were trying to get into Raleigh we were stopped at a roadblock. There were some local law enforcement personnel there, but there were also some federal Homeland Security police."

"And?"

"Well, the fact that they were there didn't surprise me given that there had been a nuclear attack. But they took our cell phones and asked if we had any weapons. I saw them confiscate a pistol from a car in front of us at the roadblock, *even though the driver had a concealed carry permit.* They grilled us and said President Armando had declared martial law. They treated us like *we* were the enemy."

"Why would they want your cell phones?" Joshua pursed his lips.

Perry shook his head. "I have no idea, but that was disturbing. Joshua, maybe you were right about this Armando guy. And in regard to our discussion about why the Second Amendment matters, I think I get it."

Joshua looked at Rebecca. "*Now* he knows why."

Bob's brow furrowed. "Joshua, when you were making calls providing people with instructions to meet here, did you leave specifics on voice mail messages?"

Joshua nodded.

"Did you leave Mr. Edwards a message on the phone

that was seized?"

Joshua frowned and again nodded.

"Mr. Edwards, do you know if you were followed here this morning?"

Perry shrugged. "I have no idea. Didn't think about that."

Bob immediately went into high alert. "Martin! Front and center!" Kane joined the group. "Martin, climb to the highest possible vantage point and look for strange vehicles or other threats."

"Yes, sir!"

Kane retrieved his binoculars and rifle, bolted to a tree behind the house and shimmied up it.

Joshua said, "Bob, we'll add Perry to the first travel group. Please give him a map and radio and explain the logistics."

Kane scanned the horizon for potential threats from his vantage point high atop the tree. Joshua squinted as he zeroed in on Kane's location. "If I didn't know he was there I wouldn't be able to spot him."

"That's the idea, son," Bob said.

After a few moments Kane turned and issued several hand signals. Bob issued a signal in return, then turned to Joshua. "Two men in a strange vehicle are parked on the road near your driveway. No other bogeys in sight." Kane rejoined the group. "Martin and I will investigate and neutralize if necessary."

"Bob, we don't want any trouble if we can help it," Joshua said. "Don't rush to judgment."

"If they are already here watching us they *cannot* be allowed to know where we are going," Bob said. "Martin, stand guard and I will draw them out. Joshua, I will drive to the road. You remain stationary unless I signal otherwise." Bob picked up his radio. "On guard. Potential threatening vehicle on road. Action imminent."

Joshua swallowed hard. *What have we gotten into?*

Bob gave Perry a rapid-fire overview of the travel plans, instructed him to disable his GPS and provided him with a map and radio. Everyone returned to their vehicles and Perry joined the line immediately behind Joshua. As Bob began driving toward the road Kane hid himself behind Joshua's vehicle. Joshua rolled down his windows to ensure that he could hear any conversation outside the vehicle.

Rebecca pointed toward the end of the driveway. "Oh, no!"

Joshua felt the hair stand up on the back of his neck as a black SUV pulled into the driveway, blocked the exit and two men in black uniforms got out. One brandished what appeared to be an AR-15 and both had holstered pistols. Bob immediately stepped out of his vehicle to confront the unwelcome visitors.

"You folks look like you're in a hurry," one of the agents called out. "Where are you going?"

"Sir, we are going to a friend's farm down east," Bob answered calmly. "We don't want any trouble, and we don't plan to cause any. We just want to go on our way."

The agent took a step forward and puffed out his chest. "Then why do you need that gun on your side?"

Bob remained calm. "Sir, we have heard reports of violence and simply want to protect ourselves."

Joshua squeezed Rebecca's hand as they anxiously watched and listened from their SUV. "So far Bob is keeping his cool. I was afraid he'd blow a gasket as soon as they showed up."

Rebecca wasn't convinced. "So far. But you may need to step in if it gets heated." Joshua swallowed hard.

The lead agent adopted a more threatening posture. "We need to know where you are going, *now!*"

"As I said, we are going to a friend's farm down east."

Joshua's heart pounded like an earthquake as the increasingly agitated agent raised his voice. "We need more details than that. *Where are you going?*"

"Sir, those are all of the details you need." Bob's face flushed red. "Now please step aside and allow us to peacefully go about our business. We do not want any trouble."

"Peacefully?" the agent snarled. "Trouble? That sounds like a veiled threat!"

"Josh, you'd better try to calm this down," Rebecca said.

Joshua nodded, chewing on his bottom lip. As he stepped out of his vehicle the second agent immediately trained his AR-15 on him. "Put your hands on your head!"

Joshua complied. "Sir, as my friend said we don't want any trouble. We just want to go on our way."

"This looks like the kind of group that would *cause* trouble," the lead agent declared. "Like some kind of organized resistance."

"Resistance to *what*?" Bob fired back. "We are American citizens who just want to live our lives in freedom. We have done nothing to warrant this kind of gestapo-like inquisition."

"A voice mail retrieved from a Mr. Perry Edwards' cell phone, left by someone identifying himself as 'Joshua,' indicated that this group was meeting here today," the agent said. "The message included code words like 'organizing,' 'getting ready' and 'secure location' and encouraged Mr. Edwards to bring survival supplies, weapons and ammunition, which resulted in this gathering being flagged as a potential extremist militia organization looking to capitalize on the current crisis. Now, sir, I am telling you for the last time, *put your gun down!*"

Bob stood his ground. "Sir, I am a Veteran of the United States Army, and I took the same oath you took. We have done nothing wrong, and the Constitution you and I *both* swore to uphold protects our rights to assemble and to keep and bear arms. Now please step aside and let us go on our way peacefully."

The agent was having none of it. "President Armando has directed us to help keep the peace, and we will do whatever it takes to uphold his order."

"How does threatening American citizens who are just trying to live their lives keep the peace?" Bob demanded, his face flushing red. "You are a disgrace to the American government and an abomination to the Constitution, you maggot!"

"We are just following our orders."

"Is your loyalty to Nelson Armando or to the Constitution you swore an oath to uphold?"

Joshua's stomach twisted as the agent avoided the question. "Everyone needs to exit their vehicles slowly and bring any weapons you have forward and lay them on the ground, *NOW!*" He pointed at Bob. "That begins with you, old man."

Bob didn't budge. "Stay in your vehicles! Do NOT exit your vehicles!"

"I said get out of your vehicles, NOW! Or your friend here dies." The lead agent pointed at Joshua, who was still in the second agent's sights.

"No!" Rebecca's door shot open and she was out of the Explorer in an instant. The lead agent quickly drew his Glock .40 and pointed it at her. Two shots rang out. The world stood still. The only sound Joshua heard was his heart thumping like a bass drum. *Oh my God!* he thought. *They've shot her!*

The cold specter of death overcame Joshua as a pair of knees hit the ground, followed by a body. Joshua's heart raced as he heard the sound of someone desperately gasping for air. Regaining his senses, he realized it was not Rebecca. It was the agent whose rifle had been trained on Joshua. The lead agent also fell, landing on his back in a pool of blood. The twin emotions of horror and relief fought for control of Joshua's consciousness.

Kane emerged from behind the Explorer, his still-smoking .308 trained on the fallen agent who had pointed his gun at Rebecca. Bob's Springfield 1911 .45 was trained on the lead agent. He had drawn and fired so quickly that no one had noticed until the man went down. Kane checked the second agent's pulse, looked at Bob and shook his head, indicating there was none.

Joshua silently stared at the fallen agents for a moment before running to Rebecca and embracing her. "Are you okay?" Shaking, she nodded but did not speak.

Bob retrieved his still-burning cigar from his Yukon. He stood over the lead agent, who still was gasping for air. "You should have let us go peacefully." Bob puffed on his cigar, spit in the man's face and coldly fired the kill shot between his eyes.

"We did what we had to do," Bob said to Joshua as he holstered his pistol, which featured a silver barrel and wooden grip.

"I... know," Joshua stammered, still shaken.

"Remain here," Bob said. "We will clean this up. This will delay our departure. Martin, check the road for additional threats."

Joshua helped Rebecca into the Explorer. She was still trembling as he hugged her. "It'll be okay."

Rebecca looked at Joshua through teary eyes. "I'm trained in self-defense. Always thought I'd know how to handle myself. But I've never actually seen anyone shot before..."

"Me either." He kissed her and stroked her cheek. "You stay here. I'm going to keep an eye on Bob and Kane." She nodded and wiped away a tear.

A stocky man with sandy blonde hair left his vehicle in the fifth travel group, dubbed Zeta Group, and approached Bob. "Do you need any help, sir?"

Bob didn't beat around the bush with pleasantries. "What are your name and background, son?"

"Jack McGee. I was in the Marines and have worked as a firearms instructor for the past few years."

Bob appeared sold at "Marine" and immediately gave Jack marching orders. "Yes, McGee. Help me search these bodies and retrieve anything valuable, then cover the evidence of what happened here."

"Will do, sir."

Bob and Jack removed the agents' identification badges, radios and weapons.

Kane returned from the road. "No sign of additional threats, sir."

"Good work," Bob said. "Martin, this is Jack McGee. Marine. He'll be a big help. McGee, meet Kane Martin."

"Nice to meet you, sir!" Kane said, once again standing at attention as if greeting a high-ranking officer.

"Martin and I will dispose of their vehicle," Bob said. "McGee, stand guard here."

"Will do, sir."

Kane retrieved a gas can from the Silverado and drove off in the agents' vehicle, followed by Bob. Jack stood guard near the Explorer with his AR-15.

Joshua approached Perry's Ram pickup, followed by

Thomas, Drew and Jim. "Perry, it looks like you were right," he said. "This is getting bad quickly."

"Man, I wasn't sure what to think of that Bob guy at first, but it looks like it might be handy to have him around," Thomas said.

Jim nodded and Drew offered his opinion: "Maybe, but he still seems like a jerk to me."

Perry pointed. "Look!" A plume of thick, black smoke drifted toward the sky, coming from the direction in which Bob and Kane had taken the agents' vehicle. An explosion was heard off in the distance as Bob's Yukon returned to the driveway.

"The vehicle has been disposed of," Bob assured Joshua. "Martin, check the agents' radios for GPS or other tracking devices."

As Kane disassembled the agents' electronics Bob picked up his radio. "We will leave in five minutes and will adhere to our plan to travel in five small groups. The groups will leave four minutes apart. If you need to exit the vehicle for any reason prior to leaving do so now and then return to your vehicle. Be on high alert throughout the trip. No unnecessary stops. Stay in communication. Over and out."

Kane looked up from the radios. "No tracking devices, sir."

"Are you certain?" Bob inquired.

"Yes, sir. I will reassemble the devices now."

"Good work, Martin."

Kane finished reassembling the devices just as everyone was re-entering their vehicles. Bob walked to Joshua's vehicle window, followed by Kane and Jack, and motioned for everyone to be silent. He pulled out the lead agent's identification badge and radio. "Agent Bedford reporting. We have secured the group's weapons. They claim to be traveling to a farm in Jones County to escape the violence and unrest. They are on their way, traveling east. While they bear watching I do NOT deem them a threat at this time."

The response came in a strong New York accent. "Very good, Agent Bedford. Keep an eye on them."

"Will do. Are there any other agents in our area if we need backup?"

"None in your area at this time. Do you need assistance?"

"No, sir. We will be in touch if help is required. Agent Bedford out."

Bob waited a moment for a response; none was forthcoming. He puffed on his cigar. "Martin, put these radios in my vehicle and prepare for immediate departure."

"Yes, sir!"

"Joshua, let's roll," Bob said. Joshua nodded and Bob

returned to his vehicle. Bob's voice crackled over the radios: *Alpha Group, prepare to depart on my lead.*

Sadness fell over Joshua as he and Rebecca left their beloved farm, the place where they had hoped and planned to enjoy the rest of their lives. Bob's vehicle turned right onto the road in front of the house. Joshua followed, as did Perry. Rebecca watched through the window as their farm faded from sight. She turned and looked at Joshua, tears streaming down her face. "I just can't believe it. I don't think we'll ever see this place again." Joshua squeezed her hand tightly, trying to think of some way to console her, but the words did not come.

Suddenly Bob's voice came over the radio. *Sigma Group, prepare to depart in 30 seconds.* Exactly thirty seconds later his voice again came over the system. *Sigma Group, depart now.* Like clockwork, he instructed each group when it was time to leave.

As the final group left the farm another voice came over the radio. *Jack McGee here. Zeta Group departing now.*

Bob responded with a question. *Is there any indication that you or any of us are being followed?*

None at this time, sir, but I will keep an eye out.

Bob commended his new helper. *Good work, McGee.*

The journey to a new home had begun.

CHAPTER 5

The convoy navigated down a series of winding back roads, avoiding main highways and population centers. The narrow, two-lane roads weaved between fields and farmhouses accented by century-old trees, past country stores and through a series of quaint small towns. In many cases a mile or more passed between homesteads. *How did I wind up here, leading my friends across the state to an unfamiliar place?* Joshua took a deep breath. *Maybe this wasn't such a good idea, but there's no turning back now.*

Some time later Bob broke a fairly long period of radio silence. *Approaching overpass to cross Highway 220 and Interstate 73. Major highway. All groups check in after crossing and report any issues immediately.*

One by one the groups reported crossing the highway safely. They continued moving down back road after back road.

Rebecca pointed at a towering column of thick, black smoke that came into view to the south. "What is that?"

Joshua's brow furrowed. "Don't know. Looks like it's coming from Charlotte. Haven't heard about any attacks there, though."

Rebecca shook her head. "Not a good sign."

After some time, Bob's voice again rang out over the airwaves. *Interstate 85 ahead. All groups check in after crossing.* A few moments later he issued a warning. *Be aware, military presence on 85. Proceed with caution.*

Joshua gripped the steering wheel tightly with both hands. As they crossed the overpass he saw a large convoy of military and other vehicles below headed toward Charlotte, many bearing the U.S. Department of Homeland Security logo. *Awfully strong Homeland Security presence,* he thought. *I guess that's understandable given what has happened.* Once again, all groups checked in with no issues.

Next the route stretched north, paralleling Interstate 77. They crossed I-77 near Mooresville and skirted around Lake Norman before again traveling south to avoid Interstate 40.

"Smooth sailing so far," Joshua said.

Rebecca cocked an eyebrow. "Almost *too* smooth."

They continued winding down country road after country road. After some time a voice came over the radio: *This is John Moore in Zeta Group. My van is running low on gas and I don't want to push it too far. We need to stop at the next gas station.*

Bob responded, *There is a station five miles ahead on the right. All groups stop there. Maintain the appearance of being unconnected to those in other groups. All groups fill up, take care of any other necessities and leave with your group. Check in once you have safely departed.*

When they reached the gas station Joshua and Rebecca both made a beeline for the bathrooms. He got in line to pre-pay for gas while she picked up a couple of soft drinks. When she joined him in the checkout line he was fixated on the newscast blaring from the small television on the wall.

Federal officials continue their aggressive crackdown to combat the unrest in the wake of this week's attacks. Here in North Carolina authorities are searching for two federal agents who went missing this morning in Chatham County, just outside of Raleigh.

"Dude, you gonna pay?" the scraggly looking clerk called out to Joshua, who had been so focused on the newscast that he didn't realize he was next in line.

"Sorry. Got sucked into the news. Crazy stuff going on."

"It dang sure is," the clerk said. "Them dern feds are going crazy this week. Ain't hardly even America no more."

Joshua handed the clerk the drinks and snacks Rebecca had picked out.

"That it?" The clerk started ringing the items up.

Joshua nodded and Rebecca chimed in. "What about gas?"

"Oh, yeah, I need to pre-pay for gas," Joshua said.

"We take cards at the pump."

"I know, but I'm paying cash today," Joshua answered.

"Worried about the feds tracking you or something?" the clerk asked with a tone that implied he was not joking.

"Something like that." Joshua forced a chuckle as he handed his cash to the clerk.

Joshua and Rebecca returned to their SUV and Alpha Group left the station.

***

The sun was dipping toward the horizon and the parking lot at the gas station was remarkably empty other than the members of Zeta Group. Jack's son, Billy, was pumping gas and John Moore was filling up his minivan. Inside the otherwise empty store Jack was carrying on a conversation with the clerk, who was still ranting about the federal government. Jack's wife, Andrea, and John's wife, Ruth, picked out snacks and drinks. The clerk was getting increasingly agitated as he ranted. After the three of them paid they walked toward the door.

Jack froze as he heard John's voice ring out across the parking lot. "Sir, we don't want any trouble." He clenched his fists when he spotted three men holding Billy and John at gunpoint near an older, full-sized brown van.

"Neither do we," the man who appeared to be the leader of the group answered. He was tall and skinny and his greasy hair awkwardly protruded from beneath his dingy yellow baseball cap. He waved his revolver wildly. "We just want this truck and trailer."

John started to speak but a tall, stocky carjacker with a shaved head and goatee punched him and sent his wire-frame glasses sliding across the parking lot. "Get back in your van right now, old man, or we'll shoot you and the boy."

Jack silently motioned for Andrea and Ruth to stop. "I left my pistol in the truck," he whispered. "You two stay out of sight."

John quickly made eye contact with Jack before putting both hands in the air. "Okay, I'll do what you ask. Just don't hurt us." He cautiously got into his van and locked the doors.

***

Joshua perked up as his radio flared to life. *This is John Moore in Zeta Group. We've got a problem. Two guys with guns. They've got Billy and Jack.*

Rebecca looked at Joshua. "Oh, no! What do we do?"

Before Joshua could respond Bob's Yukon skidded to a near-stop and did an abrupt 180-degree turn on the road ahead of them. His voice boomed over the radio: *Joshua and Perry, continue on your own. I will handle this.*

Joshua swallowed hard as he watched Bob speed away in his rear-view mirror. "Oh boy. Here we go."

***

Jack tried to negotiate with the men. "Guys, we don't

want any problems. If you just go on your way and let us go on our way that'll be the end of it."

"Shut up!" The carjacker in the yellow hat puffed on the cigarette dangling between his equally yellow teeth. "Seeing that I'm the one with the gun I don't see where you're in a position to make demands. We're taking your truck and trailer. The only question is whether you survive this or not." The short, partially bald man in a red flannel shirt who was holding Billy whispered something to the leader, who grinned and upped the anté. "And just because you've been a pain we're taking your boy. We need some labor on the farm."

Jack's eyes narrowed as a shot of adrenalin spiked through him. "I don't think so!"

The clerk emerged from the store with his shotgun trained on the lead gunman. "Get off my property or I'll put you down!"

The short carjacker spun and fired his revolver in the clerk's direction, missing him but shattering a store window. The clerk shouted an expletive, retreated into the store, ran past Andrea and Ruth and hid behind a display rack.

The gunshot woke up Jack's chocolate lab, Sarge, who had been sleeping in the back seat of his crew-cab Sierra. Sarge's incessant, agitated barking echoed throughout the surrounding area.

Jack stood his ground. "You'll take my son over my dead body!" He took a step toward the gunmen.

"Sounds like a good arrangement to me." In one quick motion the carjacker with the yellow hat fired a shot that hit Jack in the mid-section, sending him to the ground.

***

Andrea heard three gunshots outside the store. Sarge's barking faded into a yelp, then went silent. She peeked around the display, clenching her teeth she when saw Sarge lying in a lifeless heap. A chill shot down her spine when she spotted the men trying to force Billy into their van. She bolted through the door, fixated on her only son. "No!"

The lead carjacker spun and fired a shot. Andrea felt the air move as the bullet whizzed over her head. She zeroed in on Billy as sparks and glass splinters flew from the illuminated sign above the door. "Let him go!" The carjacker fired a second shot. Andrea felt searing pain tear through her right bicep. She fell to the pavement, then struggled to stand. "Let my son go!" The carjacker again pointed his pistol at Andrea and took a menacing step toward her.

A shot rang out, and one of the windows on the carjackers' van exploded into a million tiny pieces of glass. Then another, which pierced one of the van's tires. The shots were followed by a booming voice. "Put your weapons down or I will end you. You cannot see me, but as you can tell I can see *you*. My next shot will take your life." Andrea watched as the confused carjackers laid their weapons on the pavement. Several tense moments of eerie silence passed before the deep, authoritative voice called out again. "Now get on the ground, face-down, and put your hands behind your heads." The carjackers complied with the unseen gunman's demands. After another few moments of silence the voice rang out once more, saying "Good. Now remain in that position. If you move, it will be the last movement you ever make. *Do you understand me?*"

Andrea exhaled when she spotted Bob walking out of the shadows with his 1911 trained on the three men.

"Are we glad to see you!" Andrea forced herself to her feet, then called for Ruth to join them. Her body twisted into knots as Billy emerged from behind the gunmen's van and ran to his father, who was lying motionless. "Jack!" She ran to Jack's side. *I was so focused on Billy that I didn't even realize Jack had been shot. How could I?* Andrea knelt down beside her motionless husband, stroked his thinning, dirty blonde hair and put her hand on his face. "Jack?"

There was no response. She began shaking and tears ran down her face. *"Jack?"*

Andrea jumped, startled when Jack opened his blue eyes. Her tears became tears of relief and joy.

***

As Jack regained consciousness he felt a hand on his

cheek. A soft hand. He opened his eyes and was greeted by the welcome sight of Andrea. Her piercing green eyes focused on him like a laser. "Surprised to see me?" he asked, then pulled her down and kissed her, running his fingers through her curly, light brown hair.

"Oh my God, I thought you were dead!"

"No such luck." The sharp pain pierced Jack's ribcage like a dagger. He groaned as he fought through it and forced himself to sit up. "I'm okay, but that's going to hurt tomorrow!" He gritted his teeth, slowly stood up and unbuttoned his shirt, revealing a bullet-proof vest. "Actually it hurts *now*. I sure am glad I decided to wear this." He removed the slug embedded in the vest. "That's what I get for leaving my gun in the truck." Jack pointed at the blood on Andrea's right bicep. "Are you okay?"

Andrea looked down at her arm. "I was so focused on Billy and you that I barely noticed it."

"It just grazed her," Bob said. "She'll be fine." Bob thumped Jack's vest. "I'm glad you had that on, McGee. Next time, have your weapon with you and maybe you won't need the vest."

"Absolutely." Jack grimaced as the pain intensified with each step, as though he was being stabbed again and again. He felt like the knife was being twisted for good measure as he knelt beside his lifeless dog's body and put his face beside Sarge's, fighting back tears. "Sarge, I'm so sorry." He cupped the dog's head in his hand.

After a few last moments with his beloved pet Jack forced himself back to his feet. Rage consumed him as he looked at Sarge's carcass. Fueled by his fury, Jack gritted his teeth as pain radiated from his ribcage, pulsating throughout his body like lava in his bloodstream. His anger grew as he walked to the face-down bandit with the yellow hat and summoned the energy to kick him in the ribcage. "That's for shooting me." The man balled up in pain.

Next Jack made his way to the shortest bandit, again fighting through his own pain to kick the man in the ribcage. "That's for even thinking about kidnapping my son." He repeated the process with the carjacker with the shaved head. "And that's for killing my dog. You're lucky I don't put a bullet in your bald head."

Bob blindfolded the gunmen, tied their ankles and wrists and taped their mouths shut. As he taped the last man's mouth the clerk emerged from the store, shotgun in hand, walking with a swagger as though he had played a key role in the victory. He gave a thumbs-up. "Looks like we've got this here under control!"

Bob wheeled to face him and answered with a derisive tone. "You didn't wet your pants, did you, boy?" He laughed condescendingly. "We're leaving. I assume you will handle this from here." Bob did an about-face and walked toward his vehicle without giving the clerk a chance to respond.

"Move out!"

***

Bob's long-awaited update came over the radio. *Zeta Group is secure and has returned to the route. All groups check in.*

"Thank God," Rebecca said. "That had me worried."

"Me too." Joshua let out a sigh of relief. "I just hope Bob didn't kill anyone."

"At least there wouldn't be any witnesses." Rebecca chuckled.

One by one the groups checked in over the radio as they continued their westward trek on hidden back roads that rarely saw out-of-town traffic. They crossed Highway 321 between Hickory and Lincolnton. After continuing west for a few miles the group turned south, and then west again. The full moon helped illuminate the otherwise pitch-black two-lane roads.

Rebecca pointed at the road sign as they came to an intersection. "This is definitely the scenic route. Dirty Ankle Road. Interesting name."

The group continued uninterrupted for some time before another voice broke radio silence. *This is Perry Edwards. My truck is trying to overheat. We are stopping at the next gas station.*

Affirmative, Bob replied. *Everyone refuel and acquire any other essentials while we are stopped.*

Less than a mile later Joshua pulled into a large gas station adjoined by two garage bays, followed by Perry. Joshua and Rebecca both double-checked to make sure their pistols were loaded and ready for use, then concealed them before exiting the Explorer. Perry popped the hood on his pickup and spotted a leaking hose. He purchased several jugs of anti-freeze and went to work fixing the leak.

As Bob exited his vehicle Joshua approached him. "It's been a long day, and taking these back roads has made this a long trip. It's 9:00 now. Should we stop somewhere for the night?"

"Negative. We are in unknown territory. Stopping for long periods is dangerous. Drive on."

Joshua frowned. "If you say so. I'm just worried about people driving at night, in the mountains, when they don't know where they are going and are this tired."

"Tell them to stock up on caffeine, man up and push through it."

Joshua shook his head, concerned but also convinced that he was not going to persuade Bob. About 30 minutes later Perry fired up his Ram. "I'm done. Let's roll."

Bob marched to his vehicle and barked out instructions over the radio. *Groups should depart four minutes apart. Same protocol as before.* The group resumed its trek, crossing Interstate 26 just north of Hendersonville and turning south toward Brevard.

Joshua picked up his radio. "Bob, why are we going so far south? Isn't this a bit out of the way?"

To avoid population centers and Interstate 40, Bob answered, with no further explanation.

After some time Thomas' voice came over the radio. *Hey man, this is Thomas. We took a wrong turn a few miles back. The road we're on will get us to where we're going, so we're just gonna stay on this route and meet up with y'all in a bit.*

Negative, Bob responded. *We will cease travel and wait for you.*

Nah, man, we're good.

That is not wise, but I cannot force you to do the smart thing.

Some time later Joshua started seeing signs for Lake Fontana. "We're *finally* getting close."

Shortly thereafter Thomas' voice again rang out. *Hey, we're on 74 between Bryson City and where you guys will come in off of 28. Got a flat on the van. Should have it changed in a bit. See y'all shortly.*

We will wait at the rest area, Bob answered. *Please notify us when you have resumed travel.*

Fifteen minutes passed at the rest area with no communication from Thomas. And then thirty.

"Something's not right." Joshua pursed his lip as he picked up his radio. "Thomas, are you there?"

Nothing.

"Thomas?"

Radio silence.

"Let's give them a few more minutes." Joshua's heart pounded.

"A few," Bob said.

After another fifteen minutes Joshua tried again. "Thomas, are you there? *Thomas?*"

Still nothing.

"We've got to go check on him." Joshua said.

"I will go," Bob answered. "You come with me."

"Should we take anyone else?"

"Affirmative." Bob looked at Perry. "Mr. Edwards, do you have a weapon?"

"I have a .38 revolver and a 30-30 hunting rifle."

"Get them both and come with us."

They piled into Bob's vehicle and headed east on Highway 74 – the opposite direction from their destination. As they rounded the first curve Bob asked, "Mr. Edwards, have you been trained with those weapons?"

"No formal training, but I hunt and play a lot of

paintball."

Bob chuckled. "Paintball, huh? Well, son, today you might get to take off the training wheels."

They continued winding around sharp mountain curves for several miles before Bob abruptly pulled over and killed the lights.

"What is it?" Joshua's stomach twisted.

Bob pointed to the other side of a narrow valley where the road curled back around and traveled on a downhill slope. "Down there." Joshua peered off into the darkness but saw nothing.

"Mr. Page's vehicles are down there." Bob walked to his utility trailer and pulled out what looked like a pair of souped-up safety goggles.

"What is that?" Perry inquired.

Bob strapped the goggles on. "Night vision."

Joshua shook his head. "Why am I not surprised?"

Joshua's heart raced as Bob silently surveyed the situation for what seemed like an eternity. "What do you see?"

"Thomas and his family appear to be unharmed at this point, but they are blindfolded, bound and gagged. Two men are going through their belongings. While I cannot see any weapons from here we must assume they are armed and dangerous. The two men are driving an older pickup truck. No sign of another accomplice."

"So what's the plan?"

"Surprise them. Joshua, you drive and have your pistol ready. Perry, have both of your weapons ready. I will ride in the back with the top hatch open. They will likely try to stop you. If they do, go along with it. If they do not try to stop you, stop before you get to them and ask if anything is wrong. Again, make sure you stop *before* you get to them in order to avoid compromising my position. Play along with them and occupy them with conversation until you hear me slap the back of the SUV twice. Then you should protect your ears."

"Are you going to kill them?" Perry asked.

"Not unless it becomes necessary, but if they force my hand I will not hesitate."

Joshua swallowed hard. He and Perry assumed their positions in the cab while Bob retrieved a utility belt from his trailer. He hung a .22 rifle around his shoulder and climbed into the back of the Yukon.

"Here we go." Joshua gulped. His heart raced wildly as he put the vehicle in gear. So far, this was the opposite of the peaceful life he had planned after leaving the legislature. Joshua laid his 9mm in the console and began slowly moving forward. Perry laid his rifle beside his seat and gripped his revolver. They remained silent, slowly and methodically approaching Thomas' vehicles.

Joshua's heart leapt as a man stepped in front of the SUV, raised a pistol and shined a light in his face. "Stop your vehicle!"

Joshua complied, putting the vehicle in park. He felt the vehicle jump ever so slightly. "Bob's out," Perry whispered.

"You guys having car trouble?" Joshua called out. "Need any help?"

The man responded with a demand. "Get out of your truck and put your hands in the air. *Now!*"

Joshua's heart pounded violently. "Why do you want us to do that?"

"Because we will shoot you if you don't." Joshua bit his lip as the man's accomplice joined him in the road. "We don't want to hurt you, but we are stocking up for the new world order."

Suddenly Joshua heard two taps on the back of the SUV. He and Perry quickly covered their ears.

The bandit took a menacing step forward, weapon raised. "I said--" Joshua felt a blast concussion as a bright flash overtook the darkness. As the two bandits recoiled and fell backward they came face-to-face with the terror that was Bob Kendall, who shot through the smoke cloud like a rocket. Bob hit the leader in the head with the butt of his rifle, knocking him out cold. The second man tried to get up, but Bob spun and kicked him in the chest, knocking him back to the ground, and then spun again and knocked him out.

"Flash grenade." Joshua shook his head. "This guy has everything."

"Where did you find him?" Perry asked.

Bob bound both men with duct tape and covered their mouths and eyes. "You two go release Mr. Page and his family and change their tire. I'll scout the area."

Bob pulled the two unconscious bandits off to the side of the road and surveyed the area with his night vision goggles, but did not go into the woods. He removed several items from their truck, then started the engine and sent it careening off the mountainside. It erupted into flames as it hit a rock below.

"Man, I really appreciate this." Thomas nursed his wrists, which had been rubbed raw by the ropes. "I thought we were done for."

Bob responded with a stern rebuke. "I *told* you not to go off on your own. There is strength in numbers. I'm just glad we found you when we did."

When the two bandits began stirring Bob knelt down beside the leader. "You listen to me carefully, you pathetic piece of human garbage. We were just minding our own business and you had to go and cause problems. Against my better judgment I am going to leave you alive. But if I ever see you again, I *will* kill you. Do you understand?"

There was no acknowledgement that the bandits were listening to him. Bob leaned closer and yelled into the man's ear. *"DO YOU UNDERSTAND?"* The robber jumped and then nodded. Bob got up, spit on him, then lit up a cigar as he began returning items to his utility trailer.

"Thomas, your tire is fixed," Perry said. "Now let's get the heck out of here."

Thomas nodded. "Amen to that."

"We'll lead the way," Bob said. "Get in."

As Bob's Yukon began retracing its route to the rest area he picked up his radio. "Sigma Group secure and in tow. Returning to your location. Please acknowledge."

Kane's deep voice boomed over the radio. *All secure at rendezvous point. Awaiting your arrival.*

***

A slender young woman in black attire slipped out from behind a large rock in the edge of the woods and made her way to the two bandits. She gently removed the tape from their eyes, mouths, wrists and ankles.

"That was close," she said. "I thought for sure they were going to kill you guys."

"Too close," the leader said. "Those last guys obviously knew the people we were robbing. I don't know how they found us, but that old man is lucky he caught us by surprise."

"Maybe we'll run into them again," the second man said.

***

Bob picked up his radio. "Change of travel protocol. When we leave the rendezvous point we will travel as one large group until reaching our objective. All vehicles fall in line behind me and monitor those in front of and behind you. McGee, are you there?"

McGee here.

"McGee, bring up the rear and report any problems."

Will do, sir.

After Joshua and Perry returned to their vehicles the convoy made its way to Route 28.

"We're almost there," Joshua said.

"Finally!" Rebecca let out a deep sigh. "This has been one heck of a trip. I just hope we don't have any more issues between here and there."

"Amen." Joshua rubbed his weary eyes. "I'm exhausted, and I'm sure everyone else is as well."

After 25 uneventful miles Thomas' voice came over the radio. *Hey guys, we're almost there. Just drive on into my property on the dirt path. I'll lock the gate behind us and meet you outside the first cabin you come to once you're inside.*

Bob immediately responded. *Roger that. McGee, stay with Mr. Page while he locks the gate.*

Minutes later Joshua saw Bob's brake lights illuminate. He slowed and turned past an unlocked, open gate onto a tiny dirt path that disappeared upward onto the mountain. The parade of vehicles made its way up the winding dirt path, which was bordered on both sides by thick woods and underbrush. The darkness of the night was undisturbed apart from the headlights on the vehicles. The group made its way to a clearing beside a wood cabin.

Thomas arrived a few minutes later. "Man, we finally made it."

"What's the plan from here?" Joshua asked.

Thomas pointed at the closest cabin. "Well, that's yours." He pointed at a second cabin further up the path. "And that's Drew's. For those of y'all in campers, just stay right here tonight. We'll sort it out in the morning. Do you guys need help putting your beds in your cabins?"

"Yes, but not tonight," Joshua said. "We'll crash on the floor and do that tomorrow."

Thomas nodded. "That works, man. I'll come down and meet you guys at about 10:00 tomorrow morning and we can figure things out. We do need to get your cows out of the trailers."

Thomas, Joshua and Perry set up a temporary fence

using aluminum corral panels Kane had packed on the Silverado. Once the cows had water and some hay Thomas provided, the group dispersed to their appointed locations. Thomas drove up the mountain to his secluded cabin. Bob and Kane took backpacks, sleeping bags and weapons and retreated into the woods.

Joshua flipped the light switch as he and Rebecca entered the cabin. The bulbs flared to life, bringing a warm feeling to the otherwise vacant living area.

"This feels empty." Joshua scratched a trembling Reagan on the head.

"That's because it is," Rebecca answered. "But it has potential. We can make this feel like home. Starting tomorrow. I'm going to sleep."

"I *love* the way you think," Joshua embraced her. "I'm glad you have a positive attitude about this. Let's get some rest."

They unrolled two sleeping bags. Reagan curled up nearby and Joshua kept his pistol within reach. His mind wandered as he drifted off to sleep. *What will the future bring? How long will it take the conflict to find its way to us?*

PART II

CHAPTER 6

Joshua was awakened by a cold nose on his arm. Reagan nudged him a couple of times. "Okay, boy." Joshua rubbed his still-heavy eyes as he slowly sat up.

What a difference a week has made, he thought. Just a few days earlier, Joshua had watched President Wagner's first State of the Union address with renewed hope for America. This was a man who truly believed in America, who understood what made it great. Now, he was gone, along with most of Congress. A series of deadly attacks had crippled the nation, and now those attacks had made their way to North Carolina. A wholly unqualified man with questionable principles, Nelson Armando, was now the President. Joshua's best friend, Perry, had lost his two beautiful children in the attack on Raleigh. Now, just a few short days later, Joshua had led the love of his life, Rebecca, and a group of friends across the state to a new home. Without the leadership and tenacity of Bob Kendall and Kane Martin, they might not have made it here. To this strange new place in which he now found himself. *How did all of this happen?*

Rebecca rolled over and forced her eyes open. "Good morning," she mumbled.

"'Morning." Joshua yawned. "How did you sleep?"

"Not bad, considering we slept on a floor. I was completely wiped out."

"Same here. I could use a cup of high-test coffee."

"We'll have to dig the coffee pot out of the Explorer." Rebecca stretched and then yawned.

Reagan didn't waste any time, making a beeline off of the front porch. While the dog did his business Joshua surveyed the vehicles parked around their cabin. Rebecca joined him on the porch. "Well, we got all of these people here," he said. "What the heck do we do now?"

"We'll figure it out." She trudged down the steps and retrieved the coffee pot, a note pad and Joshua's tablet.

"Well, this won't do us much good." Joshua held up the tablet and frowned. "No signal."

"It'll do us some good to disconnect from everything. Those things can be a ball and chain anyway."

Joshua shook his head. "Maybe, but we still need to know what's going on in the world."

"Let's get some coffee and look around our new place," Rebecca said. "I'd like to at least have a few things settled in by tonight. It would be nice for this to at least *resemble* home."

While the coffee was brewing they explored the cabin. In many ways it was similar to the farmhouse they had left: there was a large master bedroom, a master bathroom, two smaller bedrooms – one of which would become Joshua's study – a small bathroom and a large living area. The kitchen was undersized but functional and had room for a table. The walls featured wood paneling and had a rustic look about them, and the living area featured a large brick fireplace with a wood stove.

"Thomas did a good job," Rebecca observed. "I like it."

Joshua nodded and looked at his watch. "It's 8:00. I've got two hours to get ready. They're going to be looking to me for guidance, and I need to start off on the right foot."

Rebecca kissed him on the cheek. "You go get ready. I'll start moving the small things in and figuring out where I want the bigger items."

Joshua sat back down on the steps. Reagan rejoined him as he began scribbling furiously on his note pad, mapping out an agenda and his opening remarks. An hour and a half later he looked up and realized people were beginning to stir.

***

It was 10:00, and everyone had gathered around Joshua's front porch when Thomas' Suburban made its way down the mountain. "Let's get started," Joshua said. "Rebecca has agreed to take notes. Jim, will you open us in prayer?"

After Jim offered the invocation Joshua continued. "First, we'll have Thomas give you an overview of the property. Before he does that, don't forget that everyone will need to make an arrangement with him for the use of his land. Thomas, come on up."

"'Morning, y'all," Thomas took off his well-worn baseball cap and scratched his head. "I'm glad to have y'all here. Heck, I'm just glad we all *made* it here. That was quite a trip." Thomas' son, Tommy, passed out maps.

"The building in the middle with a 'J' on it is Joshua's cabin, where we're standing now." Thomas twisted his toothpick in his mouth. "The building marked with a 'D', just up the path, is Drew's. Thanks to Drew, there will be a community shelter across the path from his cabin."

Joshua glanced in Drew's direction, perplexed. *That's interesting,* he thought.

"This is the road where we came in," Thomas continued. "I'll get each of y'all a key to the gate. This little path leads to the lake, and this one leads up to my cabin." Thomas paused and cleared his throat. "My family and I tend to keep to ourselves. That doesn't mean we won't hang out with you guys some. Just respect our privacy and let us keep this area for ourselves."

"Absolutely," Joshua interjected.

Thomas continued. "The red spots are where my guys have drilled wells, dug septic tanks and added power connections. Come see me after the meeting and we'll decide who gets which spot." Thomas pointed at a space on the map adjacent to the areas earmarked for cabins. "You guys can fence this in and use it for the cows. This stream will give 'em water unless it's overly dry, then you'll have to bring it from the lake. There's a path just past Drew's cabin that leads up to the Appalachian Trail. That's about it. Any questions?"

Drew raised his hand. "I was glad to see the power working in mine and Joshua's cabins, and I'm assuming it's connected at the other home sites. Obviously the power company expects to get paid. How will we handle that?"

"Man, that's a good question," Thomas answered. "Right now it's all on one account, so you guys can just make arrangements with me and I'll take care of it. I've got some contacts with the power company and with some guys who work down at the dam."

"Thomas, I hate to see you bear the responsibility for paying all of our bills," Joshua interjected. "Don't you think it would be better to put these on separate accounts?"

Bob jumped in. "Negative. That could attract unwanted attention and unnecessarily expose us."

"Good point as always, Bob," Joshua responded. "Everyone make arrangements with Thomas to cover their power bills."

"That works for me, man," Thomas said. "Any more questions?"

Drew again raised his hand. "Similar question.

Obviously, whatever county we are in will expect property taxes to be paid on this. How do you want to handle that?"

Bob again piped up. "To avoid drawing attention to our presence we should make arrangements with Mr. Page and pay him for the taxes. No deeds should be altered with the county tax office at this time."

"Thomas, is that okay with you?" Joshua inquired.

Thomas shrugged. "All right with me."

"We must all be prepared for the fact that we could eventually lose electrical power," Bob added. "We must be prepared to make do without it for extended periods of time, perhaps permanently."

Caroline audibly groaned.

Joshua tried to move the meeting along. "Any more questions for Thomas before we move on to the next item?"

Once more, Drew raised his hand. "I do. I'm not getting a cell phone signal here. Are the rest of you guys able to get one? If not, how do we stay connected to the outside world?"

"Man, I don't get much of a signal up here either," Thomas said. "But I think it's kind of nice. Pretty much everyone I need to talk to is right here. If I do need to make calls I tend to do it when I'm in town."

Bob offered a warning. "Contact with the outside world could compromise our position. You are advised to remain off the grid as much as possible." Bob looked in Drew's direction. "And you, boy, you need to break your addiction to all of those gadgets. They are a crutch and make you a liability for the rest of us."

"Whatever," Drew muttered under his breath. "Jerk."

Joshua scratched the back of his neck. "Guys, that's enough. We don't need to be bickering among ourselves on our first day here." Drew and Bob both nodded begrudgingly, but Bob kept his glare on Drew. Drew avoided eye contact with Bob.

"I agree with Bob that communication with the outside world – particularly electronic communication – could endanger us," Joshua added. "But I also agree with Drew that I would like to know what is going on elsewhere in America. Thomas, we brought our satellite dish and TV with us. Do you think we can get it working?"

"Be careful," Bob interjected. "While I advised you to bring the dish, upon further consideration if you use the satellite box you had at your farm it could contain identifying information. In light of the incident at the farm, they will be looking for you."

"Y'all, I think we can work around that," Thomas said. "I've got satellite hooked up at my cabin and a guy that works at the satellite company owes me a favor. I'll see what I can do about getting you a new box."

"Thanks," Joshua said. "If we can get the satellite

working, without compromising our position, that will enable us to monitor the outside world. Does anyone have any more questions for Thomas?"

There were no additional questions. Thomas said, "One more thing, some of my workers will be here this afternoon and can help y'all unload and get set up. They've been up here working the past two weeks, and they're good folks."

Bob frowned. "Their presence concerns me. How do we know they will not compromise us?"

Thomas took the toothpick out of his mouth and twisted it in his fingers. "Let's just say they don't want to draw attention to themselves either. They just want to get paid and be left alone."

"How can you be sure?"

"Man, you don't have to worry about them. They know I've been trying to sell lots and cabins. It'll seem normal to them. And they don't want to be bothered either."

"Hmm. We'll see."

Joshua moved on. "Next, we need to discuss the rules under which we will operate. I'll go over these and then find a way to get you all printed copies. We'll officially vote on them next week after you've had time to read them."

"You mean we don't have to pass it to find out what's in it?" Drew chuckled.

"I guess not." Joshua grinned and then reviewed the

proposed rules:

- *We will operate under the authority of the United States Constitution and the Constitution of the State of North Carolina.*
- *If we arrive at a point at which the United States government is no longer functioning, we will continue to operate according to the tenets of the U.S. Constitution unless we voluntarily join forces with another sovereign national entity.*
- *We will not cede our autonomy to the United Nations or any other international entity.*
- *We will elect a governing council comprised of five adults who reside within the camp.*
- *We will operate under a free-enterprise barter system.*
- *Everyone is expected to contribute to developing a sustainable food supply.*
- *No one should expect anything for free.*
- *The camp will hold council elections each February. Every adult over the age of 18 who resides in the camp shall have one vote. Voting shall be by secret ballot and the top five vote getters will be elected. If there is a tie for fifth place there will be a second election between the candidates who are tied.*
- *The governing council shall elect one of its members as chair at a meeting immediately following the council elections. A majority of the council votes cast shall be required for the election of the chair.*

- *The council will discuss issues which impact the security and general welfare of the camp.*
- *The council will not pass any rules restricting free trade or free enterprise within the camp.*
- *The council will not pass any rules restricting the private property rights of those within the camp.*
- *Everyone is free to come and go as they please.*
- *If the camp comes under attack every able-bodied male is expected to assist in the defense of the camp.*
- *Every adult shall be expected to own and maintain a functioning weapon and know how to use it.*
- *No one will invite an outsider into the camp without permission of the council.*
- *The council shall not make any formal alliance with any outside entity without a vote of the full village, either in the annual meeting or a special called meeting.*
- *There shall be no standing taxes required of residents by the village. However, the council may, by a 4/5 vote, require one-time assistance for specific projects.*
- *The council may be called upon to settle disputes between camp residents. If the dispute involves a council member a special meeting of all residents will be called at which a three-person panel will be elected to hear the dispute.*
- *All decisions of the council may be appealed to a full camp meeting.*

- *If three or more residents sign a request for an appeal of a council decision, the council must call a special camp meeting to hear the appeal within ten days.*
- *Once established, these rules may be amended by a two-thirds vote of those present at a called meeting of the camp, provided that a detailed notice of the proposed changes is given to all residents at least ten days prior to the vote.*

"These rules are based on a few important, fundamental principles," Joshua continued. "Those include personal freedom coupled with personal responsibility, free enterprise, private property rights, due process and limited government. No one person will be the 'dictator' of this camp. The power to make decisions lies with you and the people you elect to the council. I believe these rules will help ensure that everyone here is treated fairly and that we are all on the same page. Additionally, I would like to thank Drew for helping put these together. Does anyone have questions based on what you've just heard?"

"I don't have any questions, but just wanted to say that this is impressive," Jim said. "It's almost like we're developing our own Constitution."

"In a manner of speaking that's the idea, but I hope the real one will remain in effect for the foreseeable future." There were no further questions. "We will get you copies of these and make them official next week. Without objection, we will consider these rules of operation to be in effect until they are formally adopted next week."

"Mr. Winston, when do you plan to hold elections for the council?" Bob asked. "The past few days have shown us that events can happen very quickly. We need leadership in place."

"I was planning to open the floor for nominations after we conclude our other business today," Joshua answered. Bob nodded in approval.

"Next, I'd like to bring up Bob Kendall," Joshua continued. "As you all know, over the past twenty-four hours Bob has gotten us out of hot water more than once."

A round of applause sprang up from the crowd. Joshua cocked an eyebrow as he noticed Drew doing a half-hearted obligatory golf clap. "I believe we can all agree that Bob *earned* that applause over the past day. Now he is going to discuss security protocols which, after the troubles we encountered just trying to get here, are *very* much needed. Bob, come on up."

Bob stepped onto the porch and addressed the crowd. "As the events of yesterday demonstrated, danger is all around. In the wake of this week's incidents, people outside of this camp will become increasingly desperate. They will be desperate for food. They will be desperate for some sense of normalcy. *They will be desperate for the very thing we will build here.* Desperation leads to lawlessness. And if they find out that we are here and discover what we will have here, they will be a threat to us. While you are free to come and go as you please, I advise you to be cautious. Do not travel alone. If you travel outside the camp, let someone here know where you are going, who is with you, and when you expect to return. *Always* have a weapon with you. McGee learned that lesson at the gas station yesterday, didn't you, son?"

"Yes sir, I did."

Bob nodded. "Good. Further, if you encounter anyone outside of this camp, do not under any circumstances tell them where we are. Give them misinformation if you must, but do not lead them here. Always be vigilant in making sure no one is following you. Mind your surroundings at all times. Additionally, it is noteworthy that, other than the incident at the farm, the two altercations in which we were involved happened after dark. People will do whatever they deem necessary to survive, and they will use the cover of night to do it. If possible, all travel outside the camp should be done during daylight hours."

"Next, I know many of you are accustomed to using these so-called 'social media' sites. If you find a way to access social media, it is imperative that you disable any functions which would divulge our location. Do not post photos. I recommend that you cease all usage of social media, period." Bob puffed on his cigar and pointed in Drew's direction. "That means you, boy." Drew did not acknowledge the jab. Joshua cringed.

"Instruct your children on the importance of refraining from social media use or otherwise divulging our location," Bob continued. "Additionally, we may want to investigate acquiring different vehicles than those we used to travel here. Further, wear dark clothes that do not stand out, even when you are in the camp. We do not want to draw attention from anyone whether on the road, on the trail, on the lake or in the air. With Mr. Page's permission, Martin, McGee and I will construct a security perimeter around the camp to obscure our location and make it difficult for intruders to enter undetected. We will inform you of the appropriate places to enter and exit."

"Every able-bodied male should be prepared to defend this camp if necessary," Bob concluded. "Martin, McGee and I will hold trainings for the men who wish to assist with our defense. I advise every real man to participate. The trainings will continue daily until those who participate are prepared and will then be held with less frequency to ensure that you remain sharp. Do you have any questions? If not, that is all."

"We'll move on to the next item, elections," Joshua said.

Jim interjected, "Joshua, before you get to elections, may I have a moment?"

"Sure, come on up."

Jim stepped onto the porch. "As some of you know I was a pastor for a number of years. I'd like to have a worship service every Sunday. No one will be forced to come, but I'd love to see all of y'all there."

"Good idea," Joshua said. "Where do you propose to hold it?"

Drew offered a suggestion. "As Thomas mentioned earlier, there will be a community shelter up the path near my cabin. You are welcome to have it there."

How in the world did he strike a deal for a cabin AND a shelter? Joshua's brow furrowed. *I hope he's not pulling one over on Thomas.*

"Thanks, Drew," Jim responded. "I'll take you up on that. We'll meet at 11:00 every Sunday, beginning one week from today."

"Thank you, Jim," Joshua continued. "I agree that worship will be an important part of our community here. As Jim said, no one will be forced to come, but I encourage everyone to participate. And Drew, thank you for agreeing to provide a place."

Ruth Moore raised her hand. "Jim, what kind of service will it be?"

Jim smiled. "Excellent question, Ruth. Well, I was a pastor at a Southern Baptist church, but I've always believed that denominations are unnecessary divisions based on man-made biases. I'll discuss what I feel led to discuss based on Scripture, without regard to denominational divisions. We will focus on the foundational items that should unite us as Christians."

"What are those?" Ruth's shoulder-length blonde hair ruffled in the morning breeze.

Jim smiled. "I'm glad you asked, and I'll be glad to explain what I believe. First, the Bible says in Romans 3:30, *there is one God.* Additionally, the Bible says in Romans 3:23 that *all have sinned and fall short of the glory of God.* Romans 6:23 adds that *the wages of sin is death.* Put another way, each and every one of us has sinned against God and there is *nothing* we can do on our own to repay that debt. That's the bad news, but there is good news. As written in Romans 5:8, *God demonstrates His own love toward us in that while we were still sinners, Christ died for us.* Put another way, Jesus Christ paid a debt that we were unable to pay ourselves. So what does that mean in our lives? Romans 5:8 not only states that the wages of sin is death, but also that *the gift of God is eternal life in Christ Jesus our Lord.* However, it is not enough for a gift to be offered to us; we must accept that gift. The Bible states in Romans 10:9-10 that *if you confess with your mouth the Lord Jesus and believe in your heart that God has raised Him from the dead, you will be saved. For with the heart one believes unto righteousness, and with the mouth confession is made unto salvation.* If you have questions about how you can accept this gift I would love to talk with you after the meeting."

"Hmm." Ruth's bright blue eyes narrowed, but she did not speak.

Joshua continued. "Thank you, Jim. If you have questions about what he just described, please talk to him *today*. Now we will move on to elections. As I stated earlier there will be five council positions. The floor is now open for nominations."

Perry raised his hand. "I nominate Joshua Winston."

Drew jumped in. "I move that we elect Joshua to the council before accepting any further nominations."

Before Joshua could object the entire crowd yelled "aye." Joshua felt his face flush red with embarrassment. "Thank you." The group applauded. "That's one spot filled and we have four remaining. I nominate Perry Edwards."

Perry started to object. "Joshua, I don't..." He was interrupted by a sharp elbow to his side from Caroline, who offered an equally sharp glare. "I accept. And I nominate Bob Kendall."

Drew frowned but did not publicly object.

Jim raised his hand. "Given that Thomas Page is providing us with this land, I think he should serve on the council. I nominate Thomas."

"Man, I don't have to be on the council. But I will if y'all want me to."

Jim stood firm. "I feel strongly about it. This is *your*

land, and you should be on the council."

"So far, we have nominations for Perry Edwards, Bob Kendall, and Thomas Page," Joshua said. "That's three nominations for four open seats. Are there further nominations?"

For a few moments no one spoke. Many in the crowd looked down to avoid making eye contact. Perry broke the awkward silence. "Joshua, what happens if we only have four council members?"

"We could call a special meeting at any time to fill the vacancy if someone was willing to step up. However, with only four people we would have the potential for tie votes, which could be problematic."

Thomas spoke up. "Man, I'd like to nominate Drew Thompson. He seems to have a lot of experience with government-type stuff."

Drew eagerly accepted the nomination. "Thank you. I would be honored to serve." Bob let out a loud groan.

"We have nominations for Perry Edwards, Bob Kendall, Thomas Page and Drew Thompson," Joshua said. "That's four nominations for four remaining spots. Are there further nominations?"

Jim offered a motion to close nominations and elect the four nominees. The motion passed unanimously.

"We have our council," Joshua said. "Perry Edwards,

Bob Kendall, Thomas Page, Drew Thompson and myself. Council members, do you have a nomination for chair?" Joshua was unanimously selected as the council's new chair.

"Thank you," Joshua said. "As most of you know, I had been looking forward to *not* being in any kind of political office at any level. However, this is different. These are uncertain times, and I will do my best to uphold the trust you have placed in me. We do have a few more items to cover. We need to discuss our food situation. We asked everyone to bring as much non-perishable food as you could get your hands on. Rebecca and I have about three weeks' worth of canned goods. Perry and Caroline, how much do you have?"

"Probably a couple of weeks," Caroline answered.

"Bob, how about you?"

"Martin and I each have one week of rations and are prepared to begin implementing survival techniques, effective today."

"Okay," Joshua continued. "Drew?"

Drew's answer turned a few heads. "About six months' worth."

"Hmm." Bob cocked an eye.

"Very good. Jim, how about you guys?"

Jim's answer included an invitation for lunch. "We have

about two weeks of canned goods, and we also brought along a bunch of hamburgers on ice that need to be cooked today."

"Excellent. Lunch is on Jim. Jack, how about you guys?"

"Maybe a week."

"Thanks. Chuck and Sheri Jones, how about you?"

"Probably about ten days," Sheri answered.

"John and Ruth Moore?"

"About two weeks," John answered.

"Thomas, how about you guys?"

"Man, we're good. Don't worry about us."

"As you can see our food supply could run out in fairly short order. This is the one critical area where we will have to work together, and *everyone* will need to contribute. A month will pass before we know it. If we don't plan, we'll have major problems. If we're going to survive, we must become as close to self-sufficient as possible, as soon as possible. Your non-perishable food supply is not communal, it is *yours*. The longer you can make it last, the better. Those of us who have experience hunting and fishing need to put that experience to work starting *today*. The sooner we can begin generating new food sources, the longer our non-perishable supplies will last."

Caroline raised her hand.

"Yes, Caroline?"

"Where are you guys planning to clean the animals you kill? Hopefully not too close to where we're living..."

Most of the women in the group nodded in agreement. Joshua noticed a quick smirk from Rebecca. "Good point. We'll set up a cleaning station somewhere a bit removed from your living areas."

"Thank you." Caroline sighed in relief. Bob let out a low chuckle.

Caroline again raised her hand. "Joshua, one more question. As you know I'm a vegetarian. So far you've talked about hunting and fishing. What vegetarian options do you have?"

"Well, I can't promise that we *will* have vegetarian options. We'll all have to get out of our comfort zone to survive." Caroline frowned and groaned. Joshua continued, "However, that brings me to my next point. If you have experience farming or gardening, we will need you to put those skills to use. Rebecca and I are amateurs at best."

"I grew up on a farm," Thomas chimed in. "We grew corn, soybeans and had a huge garden."

"Good," Joshua said. "We will need to consider two parts of our agriculture operation, animals and crops. Rebecca and I have a few cows, and we need to keep them alive. Thomas is bringing a bull, so we can hopefully expect the herd to grow and provide a secondary meat source."

"Secondary?" Perry asked

"Secondary to whatever our hunting and fishing efforts yield. Thomas is also getting a couple of dairy cows. We should have those tomorrow. Rebecca and I have chickens, which will provide both eggs and meat. The biggest challenge will be protecting them from predators."

Chuck Jones raised his hand. A hulking African-American, he had played linebacker in college, worked as a deputy sheriff and later started a security consulting firm. "Our dogs, Ace and Sampson, are Great Pyrenees. Their breed is often used to protect livestock from predators. They've always just been pets to us, but we'd be glad to put them in the area you fence in for the cows and chickens and see if they help."

"Thanks, Chuck," Joshua said. "We'll take you up on that. Additionally, at the appropriate time we will need to begin planting and growing vegetables and, if possible, some fruits. If any of you have experience canning or otherwise preserving food, please see Rebecca after this meeting. We'll also need to protect our crops from deer and other animals that will try to eat them."

"Any deer or anything else that tries to eat our plants should become our next meal," Jack said.

Joshua chuckled. "I cannot understate the importance of getting started shoring up our food supply *today*. If we don't, we'll be in dire straits in very short order. Anyone who doesn't have experience with hunting, fishing or farming and is willing to learn, let me know."

"Over the next two days, we should try to get everything we need from outside the camp," Joshua continued. "Bob will work with Thomas to coordinate trips to stores, farmers' markets and other sites in the area. We'll take different vehicles and people each time. That will allow us to ensure that every vehicle in the camp has a full tank of gas, and will also help avoid drawing unnecessary attention."

"How will that help avoid drawing attention to us?" Perry asked.

Joshua explained. "Well, all of us except Thomas are brand-new to this area. If a brand-new person to a small area like this suddenly starts showing up at the same store over and over, locals will notice. We don't want to be noticed. For safety purposes either Bob, Kane or Jack will go along on every trip outside of the camp for now. We don't know what's going on out there and should take every possible precaution. We'll begin trips to area stores and markets tomorrow morning, so please let Rebecca know of anything you think we need. She'll be keeping the master list. Are there any more questions?"

Sheri raised her hand.

"Yes, Mrs. Jones?"

Sheri put her arms around two of her children. "Chuck and I have our three children with us. There obviously isn't a school in the camp. We don't know if there are schools nearby, and even if there are, based on what I'm hearing we shouldn't enroll our children there as that would draw attention to us. We want them to continue their education somehow."

Andrea raised her hand. "I'm a teacher, and Jack and I want Billy to continue his education. I don't have any supplies here but I'd be willing to help with that as best I can."

"We have a few books," Rebecca chimed in.

"Man, I've got all kinds of books up in my cabin," Thomas added. "Y'all are welcome to use any of 'em."

"Thanks, Andrea," Joshua said. "I appreciate you taking the lead and will do what I can to help. Are there other questions or comments?" This time, none were forthcoming. "We've got a lot to do. We are adjourned."

After the meeting Joshua and Perry caught up with Thomas. "Thomas, thanks again for everything. I don't know what we would have done if you had not been so gracious as to allow us to come here."

"Don't sweat it. Glad to do it. I'm sure y'all will help me out, too."

Drew, sporting a pair of khakis and a blue dress shirt

with red suspenders, walked up as Thomas finished his sentence. He spoke in his usual nasally voice. "Thomas, thank you for nominating me for council. I was starting to worry that I wasn't going to be nominated. I am honored to serve." Drew blew his nose into a handkerchief, resulting in a honking noise that sounded remarkably like a duck call.

"No problem, man."

"Did I just hear what I *think* I heard?" Perry asked Joshua after Drew and Thomas left them. "Did Drew really say he was *worried* that he wouldn't be nominated?"

"I think so." Joshua shook his head.

Everyone got busy unpacking and setting up the camp. Thomas greeted his workers and immediately took three of them up the path to Drew's cabin. Bob and Kane erected a metal pole in front of Joshua's house and raised the American flag. Joshua and Rebecca invited John and Ruth to stay with them until they made other arrangements, and Joshua was pleased to learn that Jim and his family would be staying with Drew.

After the unloading was complete the delicious aroma of grilling hamburgers permeated the camp. Jim said grace and everyone gathered around Joshua's front porch. Some sat on the steps, others on folding chairs they had brought with them, and others on the ground. Joshua and Rebecca sat with Jim's family and the others sat grouped with their own families. Reagan and the other dogs paid close attention to the hamburgers and were even treated to a few scraps. An eerie quiet infiltrated only by the low murmur of people quietly talking with their families overcame the camp.

"Jim, you've always had good insight into people. How do you think everyone is doing?" Joshua asked.

"Hard to tell." Jim wiped his mouth on his sleeve. "I think everyone is still a bit on edge, but glad we made it here in one piece. Generally nervous about what the future holds."

Joshua nodded as he took another bite of his burger.

After lunch Drew and two of Thomas' contractors headed back up the path to his cabin. Jack, Perry, Chuck, Thomas and Jim teamed up to erect a fence for the cows, a job made easier by some extra posts Thomas provided, while Bob and Kane took their rifles and disappeared into the woods. Reagan watched the fence construction project from a distance.

***

Bob pushed his way through the thick underbrush. Kane silently followed him as they made their way to the secluded area where they had camped under the stars the night before. Upon arrival Bob did a quick scan to make sure no one else was in earshot, then got down on one knee and motioned for Kane to join him. Kane dropped to one knee and removed his hat.

"Martin, something fishy is up with that Drew Thompson character," said Bob. "Go see if you can get eyes on what he is unloading."

"Yes, sir!" Kane donned his hat, retrieved a dark green backpack and began traversing the thick underbrush near their campsite. After some time the back of Drew's cabin came into view. Kane dropped to the ground and crawled toward the edge of the woods. He camouflaged himself with a ghillie suit and studied the scene with a small telescope.

Drew's moving trailer was backed up to the side door, so close that Thomas' workers could step directly from the trailer into the cabin. Kane watched as the workers carried black bags from the truck through the living area into a hall. *Command Sergeant Major Kendall will want to know what's in those bags and where they're storing them,* he thought.

Kane crawled to a different vantage point that offered a view through another window. The workers were still moving bags and placing them in a closet. Kane gritted his teeth, irritated that he could not tell what was it the bags. *Command Sergeant Major will want more information.* After the process repeated several times he retreated from his position and quietly slipped away into the woods.

***

The fencing crew had enclosed a small area and moved the cows from their temporary fence. "We'll have to expand this over time," Perry said. "But it's a start."

Chuck brought Ace and Sampson to the newly fenced in area. The cows were spooked by the new arrivals, but the dogs seemed right at home. Reagan seemed unsure about these giant, shaggy white behemoths.

Joshua and Perry built a chicken coop adjacent to the cattle fence, used some leftover wood to build nests and released the chickens into the coop. Joshua did a head count: five red hens, four speckled gray ones and three white ones, plus two roosters: one red, the other a speckled gray dominecker. The chicken coop included a shelter, roosts, nests and a wire roof to keep predators out.

"We'll keep them locked up for a few days and then start letting them roam some during the day," Joshua said.

***

Kane silently made his way through the woods from Drew's cabin to their campsite in the woods, where Bob was waiting. *Command Sergeant Major is going to be disappointed that I could not discern what was in the bags,* he thought. He felt a bead of sweat form on his forehead.

Bob got straight to the point as Kane reached their campsite. "What did you find out, Martin?"

"Sir, the workers were unloading a large quantity of black bags from the travel trailer into the cabin. They were storing them in a closet in the home."

"What was in them?"

Kane looked down at his feet. "I was unable to get eyes on what was in the bags. I apologize, sir."

Bob put his hand on Kane's shoulder. "It's okay, Martin. Another opportunity will present itself. Regardless, we need to keep our eyes on that boy."

***

Joshua's heart warmed when he entered the cabin. The tan couch, love seat and two leather recliners from their farmhouse were in place in the living area. His parents' family Bible was displayed in one corner. The print of George Washington at the signing of the U.S. Constitution hung over the couch, as it had at their farmhouse.

"So, what do you think?" Rebecca asked.

"Wow! This actually looks like home!"

He walked down the hall to the first bedroom. It was empty, except for a mattress on the floor; this was where John and Ruth would be sleeping. In the second bedroom his desk and office chair were in place and books were stacked on the floor. Joshua felt a lump form in his throat when he saw the framed, folded American flag that had belonged to his grandfather during World War II hanging above the desk.

Their bed was assembled in the master bedroom and the sheets and comforter were in place. Joshua and Rebecca's wedding picture hung on one wall and a casual picture of him and Rebecca on their beloved farm hung on another.

Even the washing machine, dryer, refrigerator and kitchen table were in place.

Joshua fought back a tear as he gave Rebecca a bear hug. "I can't believe it!"

"Well, if we're going to be here, we should make the best of it.," Rebecca said. "Thomas' workers were a godsend. And I'm still amazed we were able to stuff everything into that trailer."

Joshua's excitement faded as he looked out the window. He heaved a despondent sigh as he spotted Perry's camper trailer just across the clearing. Jack's camper trailer was barely visible down a trail on the opposite side of the clearing and Chuck's RV was parked up the hill near a scraggly old tree.

"I almost feel guilty." He looked down at the floor. "We're living in this nice cabin, and it's almost like nothing has changed." He pointed out the window. "These guys are staying in campers and RVs."

"*Don't!*" Rebecca admonished him. "They wouldn't even *be* here if it weren't for you." Joshua hesitated, then shrugged and nodded.

Joshua jumped as the sound of a gunshot rang out. "What the?" Then another shot. Reagan yelped and darted toward the back of the cabin. Joshua grabbed his rifle and headed out the door and Rebecca followed, her .380 in her back pocket. Perry and Chuck were already in the clearing, guns in hand, and Jack was running down the hill with his 30:06 hunting rifle.

"Where did that shot came from?" Joshua asked in a voice barely louder than a whisper.

Perry pointed left. "That way, I think. Toward the lake." Chuck nodded in agreement.

"Any sign of Bob or Kane?" Joshua's heart raced.

Everyone shook their heads. Joshua took a deep breath, raised his .22 and began slowly walking in the direction of the shot. The others fanned out and followed his lead.

"It's us!" Bob emerged from the thick woods.

Joshua exhaled and lowered his rifle. "Who fired the shots?"

"Martin."

"What happened?"

Before Bob could answer Kane worked his way up the hill into the clearing, a large deer draped over his shoulders. "Our first kill, sir!"

"Good job, Martin," Bob said.

Jack laughed. "You guys scared the heck out of us!"

"I think we're all still on edge in general," Joshua added.

"Bob, can you guys pick a spot a bit out of the way and clean the deer? One far enough away that it won't bother the ladies?"

Bob chuckled. "Yes, and away from that Thompson boy?"

Joshua cringed. "Thank you. And good job, Kane." He headed back to the cabin, where Rebecca had been watching from the porch. She was seated in one of two rocking chairs from their farmhouse.

Joshua's brow furrowed and he pointed at the rockers. "How did these get here?"

Rebecca smiled. "Thomas had room in his van and he snuck them onto the porch a few minutes ago. Thought I'd surprise you."

"I love you." Joshua leaned down and kissed his wife. "You sure know how to make a guy feel at home."

An hour later Bob and Kane returned with the venison from Kane's kill. Rebecca prepped some of the meat for the grill and stored the rest in their refrigerator.

Joshua looked at his watch. "I'm going down to the lake to set up a trotline."

"I will assist," Bob said. Joshua retrieved his tackle box from his utility trailer. Bob returned with a bucket containing some unusable portions of the deer and they headed down the trail to the edge of Lake Fontana. They walked along the shoreline about 100 feet away from the trail until they found a small clearing.

"This is the place," Bob said. They constructed a trotline with five hooks, using deer parts as bait. Joshua dropped a piece of the leftover entrails, which Reagan promptly snatched and bolted into the woods.

"Nasty dog!"

Bob laughed. "I've eaten worse."

Joshua shook his head. "Somehow, I believe it. You've probably eaten things that would make Reagan puke."

Joshua floated the trotline out into the water. "We'll come back tomorrow and see if we've caught any fish."

They arrived in camp just as the sun was setting. Jim and Jack were hard at work grilling the venison. Perry and Chuck cleared leaves and straw, created a fire pit and built a fire. As Joshua walked onto the porch he overheard part of a conversation between Rebecca and Caroline.

"You're *really* going to eat deer meat?" Caroline asked. "What will there be for *me* to eat?"

"I've eaten it plenty of times. Look, I know you're a vegetarian, but at some point you may *have* to give it a chance. It's not *that* bad, and we're not going to have a lot of options here."

Caroline frowned. "Yuck!"

"We're *all* going to have to do some things that are

different than what we're used to," Rebecca said. "It's really a matter of *survival*, Caroline."

Did I make a mistake bringing these people here? Joshua thought. *If they can't adapt this could turn into a total disaster.*

CHAPTER 7

Joshua shot out of his bed, jarred out of a deep early morning sleep. Unfamiliar with his surroundings, it took him a moment to realize he was in the master bedroom of his new cabin. Rebecca was asleep beside him. "What was that?" he asked.

"What was what?" Rebecca rolled over and rubbed her still-heavy eyes.

"That sound. I heard something."

Rebecca sat up, her eyebrows furrowed. Joshua grabbed his pistol as he walked to the bedroom door and opened it. "Who's there?"

A man's voice came from behind the closed door to the front bedroom. "It's John and Ruth."

Joshua lowered his weapon. "I forgot they were staying with us." He exhaled a deep sigh of relief. "Guess I'm a bit jumpy."

"Don't shoot our new houseguests." Rebecca chuckled. "That's not much in the way of southern hospitality."

Joshua took his Bible and coffee onto the front porch. It was still dark out and there were no sounds of civilization, only the winter breeze whisking through the treetops. He closed his eyes and deeply inhaled the cool mountain air. Off in the distance he heard what sounded like a wolf howling. A squirrel rustled in the nearby undergrowth. This was the perfect time of day.

Half an hour later Rebecca and Reagan joined him on the porch as sunlight slowly invaded the pre-dawn sky. "It feels like we're light years away from the life we were living just a week ago." Joshua sipped the still-warm coffee.

"It is a different world, but so far it's peaceful here," Rebecca said. "Based on what we saw before we made it here, I am guessing it's *not* so peaceful out there."

Joshua pursed his lips. "I'm just worried that we'll have to face what's happening out there sooner than later."

Bob and Kane emerged from the woods and raised the Stars and Stripes. The flag began snapping in the mountain breeze. "Martin, conduct perimeter security sweep."

"Yes, sir!" Kane disappeared into the woods.

Joshua polished off his coffee. "Bob, let's go see if we caught a fish last night."

They made their way down the trail to the lake. The incline was steep, and the winding trail was so narrow that they walked single file. Trees that seemed as tall as the mountains crowded them on either side. As they made the quarter-mile trek, the incline gradually leveled out and the expansive lake came into view. The trotline they had set up the night before was washed up against the shore, tangled up in some limbs.

"What a mess." Joshua frowned. "And no fish."

"You untangle that. I'll look for a better spot." Bob walked further up the shoreline.

As Joshua struggled to untangle the matted fishing line he stepped in a hole, lost his footing and fell. A sharp pain pierced his right hand and shot up his arm like lightning. He let out a deep, feral yell. Frightened, Reagan ran the other way at first, then did an about-face and ran to Joshua.

Bob came running through the woods with his Springfield 1911 drawn. "What is it?"

Joshua held up a bloody right index finger that had been completely penetrated by a fish hook. The barb protruded from the exit wound and searing pain radiated up his arm.

Bob holstered his pistol. "That looks bad. I'd better get you back to camp *now*. We can fix this trotline later."

Bob helped Joshua up. His entire arm throbbed in pain with every heartbeat. Increasingly short of breath, the relatively brief trip up the mountain to the camp seemed like an eternity.

"Are you OK?" Bob asked.

"I'm just not used to these hills," Joshua panted.

The first person they saw upon entering the camp was Jim. "What in the world happened?"

Joshua held up his blood-covered finger.

"Ouch." Jim winced. "I'll go get Keri."

Out of breath, Joshua sat on a log near the edge of the clearing, his head spinning. Reagan planted himself at his feet. Rebecca ran out of the cabin to meet her wounded husband. Jim and his wife, Keri, arrived moments later and Bob returned soon after.

Keri opened a small bag of medical supplies and examined Joshua's hand. "That's nasty." She frowned. "The first step is to get the hook out, but we can't just pull it back through because the barb will stick. We'll have to cut it off." Joshua cringed as Bob held up a pair of wire cutters.

"Joshua, we're going to have to push the hook a bit further through so that Bob has enough room to cut it," Keri said. "This is going to hurt." Joshua nodded. Rebecca held his left hand and put her arm around him as Keri slowly pushed the hook further through to expose the barb. Sharp tentacles of pain streaked from his finger as the hook tore through the nerve endings. Joshua let out a muffled shriek, his finger throbbing violently.

"Hold still," Bob slowly positioned the wire cutters around the end of the hook protruding from his finger. Joshua gritted his teeth as Bob gradually squeezed. The next few moments seemed like hours. Joshua's arm jerked as the barb was severed, sending a fresh round of stabbing pain up his arm. He let out another screech and doubled over.

"I'm sorry," Bob apologized in a rare moment of compassion. "It was harder to cut than I anticipated."

Keri slowly pulled the hook back through Joshua's finger, gently removing it. "We need to make sure that doesn't get infected. Let's go to your cabin and get it cleaned up."

Joshua stood up for a moment and then sat back down. The clearing seemed to be spinning around him. "Give me a minute."

Bob offered another warning. "We need to take care of this internally. We do not need to go to a doctor outside of this camp unless absolutely necessary."

After a few moments Joshua forced himself up and trudged up the slope to the cabin, Rebecca at his side. Reagan took off and sprinted to the porch. Keri and Jim followed with Perry and Caroline, who had joined them.

Rebecca washed the wound and Keri treated it. Joshua let out a groan as the alcohol penetrated the puncture wound. The throbbing pain was replaced by a burning fire that radiated throughout his body.

"You need to keep this clean, and we need to check it and change the bandage twice a day," Keri instructed as she applied the bandage. "And you need to rest it for a day or two as well."

"I'll try," Joshua said unconvincingly. "It's a good thing

we brought a nurse along."

Rebecca corrected him. "He *will* do what he needs to do to let it heal."

Three strong knocks were heard on the door, and a deep voice boomed out. "It's Bob."

Rebecca invited Bob in. Upon entering he removed his hat and held it at his side. "Joshua, I just wanted to check on you and see if there is anything you need me to do while you are healing." Perry also volunteered to help pick up any slack.

"Thanks, guys," Joshua said. "Bob, we need to find a way to get that trotline set up. We need to start catching fish in short order. That's all I can think of right now. I'm going to lie down for a bit." *Please leave before I throw up. I just need to be left alone.*

"I will study more effective means of fishing, and Martin and I will organize the men who wish to hunt," Bob said. "Get some rest."

Joshua and Rebecca disappeared down the hall and everyone else left the cabin.

***

Joshua was in the recliner with his bandaged hand elevated and Reagan curled up on his stretched-out legs when Perry arrived later that morning. Rebecca took advantage of Perry's presence to go out and check on the chickens.

"How's the hand, buddy?" Perry asked.

Joshua held up the bandaged finger. "Still stings a little. The biggest challenge is remembering not to use it. I feel pretty useless today."

"You'll be fine. Bob, Jim and I got three trotlines set up, so hopefully we'll start bringing in some fish."

Rebecca returned, a frown on her face.

"What's wrong?" Joshua asked.

"Twelve hens, and not one single egg. *None.*"

Joshua shook his head in concern. "Seriously? Not good."

"Not at all. If they don't start producing soon we'll go through our non-perishable food supply much faster than we'd like."

Concern flooded Joshua's mind. *She's right. We really need to start generating a sustainable food supply. If not we'll have big trouble.* He sighed, then picked up the remote and changed the subject. "Thomas got our TV working!"

He switched to a channel showing the local forecast. *Bitterly cold weather will drop down into the south this week. We are expecting sub-freezing temperatures, heavy snow and possible freezing rain in the Appalachian Mountains and into the Carolinas and Georgia.*

Joshua shook his head. "Not the kind of forecast I like to hear. We should let everyone know."

"Doesn't sound promising," Perry said. "Anything on the news that we should know about?"

Joshua changed the channel to a 24-hour news station. *British intelligence sources tell us that the AIS terrorist organization smuggled their suitcase nukes across our southern border, some as early as 2014 – the year our nation saw a flood of immigrant minors crossing the border. Additionally, intelligence sources tell us that the level of terrorist chatter remains high and that Americans should be alert for the possibility of more attacks on our soil.*

Meanwhile, President Armando continues to face criticism for what some are describing as his "heavy-handed" use of military troops and Homeland Security police to quell unrest throughout the nation. The Governors of Texas, Tennessee, South Carolina and Georgia have all activated the National Guard in response. Joshua clenched his teeth as the station broke away to a clip of the governor of Texas speaking. *If American citizens are being terrorized by our own military and these so-called "Homeland Security police," are we really any better than those who attacked us? I will not stand idly by and allow the people of Texas to be terrorized by this administration's thugs, and our sovereign state is prepared to use the National Guard to defend our citizens.*

"We're on the brink," Joshua said. "And they mentioned

Tennessee, South Carolina and Georgia. We are close to all three states here. Maybe *too* close."

***

That afternoon, three loud knocks echoed into the cabin from the front door. Rebecca opened it to find Perry and Caroline.

"Hey Rebecca. Perry and I are going to take a hike up the Appalachian Trail to the overlook before dinner," Caroline said. "It's probably a mile and a half. Do you want to go? Joshua, you're obviously welcome as well. I think it'll help get our mind off of things."

"That sounds good, and I could use the exercise," Rebecca said. "Josh, do you feel up to it?"

Joshua shook his head. "No, I'm going to stay here and rest. Doctor's orders! But you go ahead."

Rebecca put her Beretta in her back pocket and headed out the door. Reagan bolted after her. "Looks like you've got a security escort!" Joshua laughed. After Rebecca left he turned off the television, stretched out on the couch and closed his eyes, thankful for some much-needed quiet time.

***

The sun's warmth more than made up for the cool temperature as Rebecca made her way up the trail. The hike energized her. In many places the trail was narrow and rocky, and some of the inclines seemed to reach to heaven.

After fifteen minutes Perry and Caroline both stopped and leaned against the rocks, panting.

"I need to catch my breath," Perry said between labored breaths. "This is a little different than the trails I'm used to in Raleigh."

Caroline nodded and leaned against the rock wall, her hands on her knees. Rebecca stretched while Reagan nosed around, sniffing everything in sight. After a few minutes they resumed their trek up the mountain, stopping several more times along the way.

After an hour they arrived at a spot which offered a clear, unobstructed view. Wispy clouds intermingled with the rolling mountaintops, some of which featured patches of snow. In the valley below, Lake Fontana zig-zagged between the mountains and seemed to stretch to eternity. Rebecca and Caroline took a seat on a rock and admired the view, while a jittery Reagan avoided venturing too close to the edge.

"This view makes the hike up here worth it," Caroline said.

"Just think, after doing this for a year we'll all be in good enough shape to make this climb with no problem," Rebecca said. "I wish Josh were up here with us."

After some time Perry said, "Well, we'd better head back. We don't want to miss dinner."

Reagan led the way as the group headed down the trail. As they rounded a corner in a thickly wooded area the puppy froze in his tracks and began growling. Perry raised his hand and motioned for everyone to stop. Rebecca's stomach churned as she spotted two black bear cubs on the trail ahead of them.

"Cubs," Perry whispered. "If they are here then Mama can't be far away."

They slowly backed away. Rebecca's heart leapt when a large bear bounded out of the woods in front of them. The animal's barbaric roar sent a horrific chill down her spine. In lightning-quick fashion, the bear unleashed the full force of her maternal instincts with a vicious slap that began on Perry's shoulder, slashed diagonally across his midsection and sent him careening off the trail. Rebecca heard several violent thuds as he crashed into trees along the way. Reagan let out a terrified yelp, ran between the bear's legs and disappeared down the trail.

As the bear took a menacing step forward Caroline sent forth a shrill scream that echoed throughout the mountaintops. Rebecca drew her Beretta and stepped between Caroline and the advancing beast. "Caroline, run!"

Caroline turned to flee, which only incited the already enraged bear. Rebecca's jaw dropped as the monstrosity of an animal stood on its back legs, towering over her. As the bear issued another echoing roar she fired a shot, connecting with its shoulder. The wound only angered the bear. Rebecca pivoted and ran a few steps, then spun and fired another shot. This one hit the bear's stomach, but did not stop its charge. As Rebecca turned to flee from the approaching monster she felt her foot tangle with a root. Her pistol flew from her hand as she stumbled and fell forward. She watched helplessly as her trusty Beretta skidded down the trail, out of reach. She could sense the bloodthirsty animal bearing down on her.

"Rebecca!" Caroline screamed as the angry bear approached its prey.

***

Joshua was suddenly wide awake, his much-needed nap rudely interrupted. *What was that sound?* He used his uninjured left hand to push himself out of the recliner. Bob and Jim rushed into the clearing as Joshua stepped onto the porch.

"Did you hear something?" Joshua asked.

"Yes," Bob said. "Two shots from up on the mountain."

A cold chill bolted down Joshua's spine. "Rebecca is up there." Joshua pointed up the trail. "Hiking with Perry and Caroline." As he finished his sentence Reagan zoomed down the trail and planted himself at his side, trembling. Joshua's stomach twisted. "That can't be good."

Another shot rang out. Then another. And another.

"That's a larger caliber weapon," Bob said. "I will investigate."

Joshua stepped off of the porch, gently gripping the railing with his bandaged hand.

Bob turned and pointed at Joshua. "*You* stay here. We need you healthy. I'll handle this!" He bolted up the trail.

***

Rebecca sat on the ground, shaking. The dead bear's bleeding carcass was scarcely a foot in front of her. The two cubs lay dead on the trail behind their mother.

Caroline ran to her. "Oh my God, Rebecca, are you okay?"

Rebecca nodded, unable to speak. Nearly hyperventilating, she struggled to catch her breath.

Jack stepped onto the trail from the mountainside, replacing the spent rounds from his 30:06. "Are you okay, Mrs. Winston?" Rebecca nodded, still unable to speak.

Frantic, Caroline ran to the spot where the bear had sent her husband careening down the steep slope. "Perry?" No response. "Perry?" she yelled out. Still no response. "*Perry?*"

Jack walked to the edge of the ravine and scanned it. "I can't see him from here."

Bob rounded the curve, running at a breakneck clip with his 1911 drawn. "What happened?" He showed no signs of being out of breath after his sprint up the mountain.

"They stumbled onto a bear with two cubs," Jack answered. "The mother bear knocked Perry down this hill. Thankfully, I was close enough to take them out before they hurt anyone else."

Bob holstered his weapon. "What were you doing up here, McGee?"

"Hunting these bears. Spotted their tracks yesterday."

"Good work, McGee."

Jack smiled. "And the predator becomes the prey."

"And dinner," Bob said with a chuckle. "Mrs. Winston, are you okay?"

Rebecca nodded. "I... I will be."

"Where is Mr. Edwards?"

"We haven't found him yet." Jack pointed. "He went down here."

Caroline began sobbing.

"McGee, you go down the incline and look for him." Bob opened a small telescope. "I'll survey the area from up here." Jack climbed down the hill while Bob scanned the mountainside below them.

Bob chuckled as Jim staggered around the curve, panting. "What took you so long?"

Jim put his hands on his knees, gasping for breath. "What happened?"

"Sir, did I hear gunshots?" Bob and Jim turned to see Kane walking down the trail. "I was hunting further up the mountain."

"Found him!" Jack's voice rang out from the ravine below. "He's unconscious but breathing. Help me get him out."

Kane laid his rifle on the ground and made his way down the hill. Bob and Jim cut sticks and vines and constructed a makeshift stretcher. Perry regained consciousness as they reached him.

"You're lucky to be alive," Jack said. "That bear laid you out. Try to be still and we'll get you out of here."

The four men slowly carried Perry up the steep embankment. Jim stumbled when his foot slipped on a rock, nearly sending Perry careening back down the incline. Caroline's sobbing intensified when she saw the bloody gash that stretched diagonally from Perry's shoulder across his midsection, almost to his waist. Jack and Jim carried Perry down the trail, flanked by Rebecca and Caroline. Bob and Kane stayed behind to prepare the dead bears for transport to the cleaning station.

***

A number of people had gathered around Joshua's

cabin, where he was pacing nervously on the porch when Jim and Jack came into sight carrying Perry's stretcher. He heaved a deep sigh of relief when he saw Rebecca. She ran to meet him in the clearing and collapsed in his arms, unleashing a torrent of pent-up tears.

"What happened?" he asked.

Jack explained what had taken place. "Perry was knocked out, and as you can see he has a pretty bad wound."

Keri disappeared up the path, returning a few minutes later with her medical supplies to treat and bandage Perry's wounds. Joshua put his unbandaged arm around his trembling wife and walked her back to their cabin, where John and Ruth were trying to comfort a still-nervous Reagan.

***

That night the smell of grilling venison began emanating throughout the camp. When Joshua arrived at Drew's cabin he was surprised to find a fully constructed A-frame shelter and a second shelter attached to the cabin, under which Drew had parked his truck and trailer.

"That's interesting." Joshua nodded in the direction of the makeshift garage.

"Sure is," Rebecca said. "How is Drew able to do all of this?"

"Good question," Joshua answered. "He made decent money at the legislature, but I can't figure out how he could afford to buy that cabin from Thomas free and clear, not to mention this."

"Just keep an eye on him." Rebecca cocked an eyebrow. "He still seems shady to me. I just don't trust him."

Joshua worked his way through the line to Jim. "Nice shelter. And that's a nice structure Drew has over his vehicle."

"Sure is."

"How is Drew able to afford all of this? And how is he compensating Thomas?"

"That's his business," Jim answered. "I'm not going to stick my nose into it. I respect his privacy."

"As should I." Joshua looked down. "Is Drew here?"

"No, he took off with Thomas. Not sure where they went."

A few minutes later Thomas' Suburban made its way up the winding dirt path to the camp followed by a small, unassuming motorcycle.

Bob walked to Joshua, his hand on his holstered weapon. "Who is that on the motorcycle?"

"I'm not sure. Jim said Drew went somewhere with Thomas. Could be him."

Thomas stepped out of his truck. "Hey, folks. How are y'all?" The motorcycle pulled up beside him and the rider shut off the engine and removed his helmet. It was Drew.

"Hey guys," Joshua greeted them. "Drew, when did you get a motorcycle?"

"Today. Thomas helped me find it. I thought it would draw a little less attention than a big, brand-new pickup truck." He pointed at two black canoes protruding from the open hatch on Thomas' Suburban. "Thomas also said you guys needed some canoes for fishing, so I got these for you."

Joshua returned to his seat, shaking his head. *I can't figure him out.*

***

The next day Joshua had just finished lunch when he heard a knock on the cabin door.

"Hey, buddy." Thomas opened the door. "I'm gonna ride down to the store and pick up a few things. Want to ride with me to learn a little more about the area?"

"Sounds good. We need to take either Bob, Kane or Jack with us for security purposes."

"If you insist. Let's invite Jack. He seems a little more laid back than those other two cats. Tommy's going, too."

They departed the camp thirty minutes later. Thomas pointed out a few key spots as they toured the area and then headed south to Robbinsville. "Most of the stores I use are down here. It's a bit of a hike, but there ain't much close to us up here."

Joshua and Jack navigated the narrow aisles in the grocery store, which was smaller than a typical pharmacy in a larger city. The store was relatively empty given the current crisis.

"I'm surprised they aren't sold out of everything," Joshua said. "This store doesn't look like it's been pillaged like some of the ones in bigger cities."

"Yet," Jack said.

"Not as crowded as I'd expect either," Joshua added.

"Nobody lives here," Jack said. "We're off the beaten path."

"Precisely why we picked it," Joshua responded.

They split up and filled their shopping carts with everything that seemed like it could be useful: batteries, canned foods, pre-packaged meals, all of the salt, pepper, sugar and coffee on the shelves as well as bandages and other medical supplies.

***

The young woman kept her distance from the tall man in the tan baseball cap and his teenage son. She followed them down two aisles at the store, watching their every move. During one stop the man grabbed what appeared to be a lifetime supply of toothpicks. She snapped their picture on her smartphone before they rounded the corner and disappeared from her line of sight.

She sent the picture to someone with a text: *Aren't these the dudes we tried to rob Saturday night? When the old man rescued them? And trashed ur truck LOL.*

The response came instantaneously: *Think so. Where r u? Not funny abt truck.*

Store. Now I know where they shop. If you were here we could handle this now.

We'll have our chance.

***

The four men loaded their supplies into the Suburban and left the store. Jack's face lit up with a big smile as they pulled into the driveway at an old shack with a sign that simply said "Guns and Ammo."

"My buddy runs this place," Thomas said. "Good place to stock up. He always keeps some set aside for me." They bought a significant amount of ammunition and several knives before the group departed for camp.

"How was the ride?" Rebecca asked as Joshua made his way into the cabin.

"Good. The good news is that we are truly off the beaten path. The bad news is that we have to make a fairly long drive for nearly *anything* we need, which exposes us for longer periods of time than I'd like. But we stocked up on ammo."

"While you were gone I checked on the chickens and cows. They all seemed fine, but still no eggs."

Joshua groaned. "Not good. They're probably still in shock from the trip here. Let's check on them tonight and maybe we can let them out to roam a bit tomorrow."

That night everyone congregated at the shelter, where Jim was grilling portions of the bear meat. Rebecca helped Joshua maneuver his plate and drink to compensate for his still-bandaged right hand.

Joshua pointed at Perry's arm. "What's up with the sling? Did you break a bone?"

"No, but the gash was bad enough that Keri thought it would be wise to keep it immobilized for a few days."

Joshua sighed. "At the rate we're going we're going to look like a camp full of the walking wounded soon."

After a few minutes Jim and Keri joined the group.

"So, how are my patients?" Keri scratched her dirty blonde hair.

"Hanging in there," Joshua said. "Thanks for taking care of us."

"Glad to help. I didn't know I'd be running an urgent care clinic our first few days here!"

Her comment was received with laughter, but the truth

of it worried Joshua. *If things are already this difficult, this fast, how will people respond when the going* really *gets tough?* He bit his lower lip.

"Jim, the food is excellent as always," Joshua said. "We may make you the official camp chef."

Jim nodded, but Caroline offered a less optimistic appraisal. "I'm sure it's good, but you guys are eating *deer* and now *bear*? I'm not used to seeing all of this strange food. I don't eat meat, and so far there is *nothing* here for me to eat. What will I do when the supplies we brought with us run out? Starve?"

"We'll all have to get out of our comfort zone while we're here," Keri said.

"I guess so." Caroline heaved a despondent sigh. "Isn't there a grocery store somewhere nearby?"

"It's a bit of a hike to the closest one," Joshua said. "And a lot of the stores nearby are running out of everything." Caroline groaned.

After a few minutes Joshua looked over the crowd. "Where's Drew?"

"He took off on that new motorcycle," Jim said. "Took a backpack with him, but not much else. Didn't say where he was going and snuck out before I could ask."

"Well, I hope he gets back before too late."

***

The next morning was colder than the previous two. Joshua's breath was clearly visible in the winter air. Reagan joined him on the porch for a few minutes before pawing at the door, apparently having had his fill of the cold. Rebecca opened the door to let him inside.

"Brr. Don't get yourself sick, Josh."

Joshua nodded, took a swig of coffee and opened his Bible.

Twenty minutes later Jim made his way down the hill, a look of obvious concern on his face. "What's wrong?" Joshua asked.

"Drew apparently never showed up last night. I just checked and he's not in his room. It doesn't look like he came in at all."

Joshua shook his head. "Oh, brother. Go see if Jack is awake. We should go look for him."

Jim threw his hands in the air. "I have *no* idea where to look."

Joshua shrugged. "Me either."

Before Jim could make it halfway across the clearing they heard the sound of a whirring motorcycle engine making its way up the path. Drew pulled up to Joshua's cabin. "Good morning, guys. What's up?"

"Where have you been?" Joshua asked.

"I had a few things to take care of."

"We were worried about you," Jim said. "I was getting ready to wake Jack up."

"Why were you going to wake Jack?"

"Because we were going to look for you," Joshua said.

"Sorry. Didn't mean to scare you guys. But you don't need to worry about me or keep track of where I am. I can take care of myself."

"In a normal world I wouldn't doubt that," Joshua said. "But we are *not* in a normal world, and we all need to be extra careful. *Especially* those of us who are on the council. We have to lead by example."

"Well, I'm not going to promise I'll tell you every time I come and go," Drew said. "But I will take extra precautions to ensure that no one follows me back here or knows where we are."

"What if something happens to you and no one knows where you are?" Jim asked.

Drew brushed off the concern. "That's on *my* shoulders. Again, don't worry about me." He put his helmet on and drove to his cabin.

"I worry that he's being a bit reckless," Jim said.

"Slightly. Well, I'm glad you guys are staying with him. Some of us are hoping you can be a mentor to him."

After raising the flag Bob and Kane went to check the trotlines. Joshua's heart sank when they returned and reported no fish.

Sunset brought more bad news. Not only had the chickens still not produced any eggs, a predator had apparently snagged one of the hens.

The next day offered more of the same: no fish and no eggs.

Joshua frowned. "If the chickens aren't going to lay eggs maybe we should just eat them."

"They'll eventually start producing," Rebecca assured him.

"I hope so, but I'm starting to wonder."

"It's not unusual for chickens to stop laying in the winter," Rebecca said.

"True, but they weren't having any problems last week on the farm," Joshua answered. "I think this move freaked them out."

"They'll be okay."

As they walked from the chicken coop to the cabin Thomas' Suburban made its way down the mountain. He rolled down the window. "Hey guys, how are y'all doing?"

"We're okay." Joshua frowned. "But I'm frustrated that our chickens have not laid one single egg since we've been here."

Thomas shook his head, toothpick dangling from his

lips. "Man, that ain't good. Are y'all giving 'em any laying mash?"

"Laying mash? What the heck is that?"

Thomas took off his cap and scratched his head. "A special feed for hens. Helps 'em produce more eggs."

Joshua's brow furrowed. "Interesting. Never heard of it. We're just amateur farmers and really don't know what we're doing."

"Man, I'm headed out to get a few things. I'll see if I can pick some up." After a few minutes of chit-chat Thomas drove down the path toward the road.

***

A few hours later Thomas dropped a 50-pound bag on Joshua's porch. "Laying mash. Maybe this'll help."

Joshua and Rebecca sprinkled the laying mash onto the ground in the coop. The chickens gobbled it up like they had not eaten in weeks. As they walked back toward the cabin a few raindrops started falling.

"As cold as it is, this could be a mess." Joshua caught a couple of raindrops in his hand. With every step they took the frigid rain seemed to intensify. Reagan took off and made it to the dry safety of the porch. Joshua brushed his hand across the subtle ice glaze on the railing. "Not good."

Shortly after dark Joshua made his way onto the porch. Snow was beginning to mix with the freezing rain and the arctic wind felt like a thousand stabbing needles. *The temperature is dropping fast,* he thought. Branches were beginning to sag under the weight of accumulating ice. Somewhere in the darkness he heard a branch snap and collide with several others before crashing to the ground.

Bob arrived at the cabin, clothed from head to toe in dark green winter rain gear. "This looks like a significant storm. We could lose power. What is your plan for an alternate heat source?"

Joshua shrugged. "Hadn't thought about that."

"Martin and I will secure firewood." Bob did an about-face and vanished into the darkness.

Inside, Joshua turned the television to a 24-hour weather network. He felt his shoulders clench as the announcer offered a frigid forecast. *The winter storm making its way into the North Carolina mountains could last for up 36 hours. The temperature is likely to remain below freezing for several days thereafter.*

A couple of hours later Joshua and Rebecca were relaxing on the couch. Reagan was curled up in the corner and John and Ruth were seated in recliners. It was pitch black outside, save for the giant snowflakes falling between the ice-covered trees. Suddenly the cabin went dark.

"There goes the power." Joshua pursed his lips.

"Didn't the weatherman say this storm could last

another day or so?" Ruth asked.

"Yep," Rebecca said. "Just what we need."

They heard a knock on the door. It was Perry. "I guess your power is out too. It's going to get cold in our camper trailer."

"You guys are welcome to hang out here if you'd like," Joshua invited.

"Thanks. Let me go get my better half."

A few minutes later they heard three more loud knocks on the door. Joshua opened the door, expecting to find Perry. Instead it was Bob, accompanied by Kane. They had armloads of firewood, which they unloaded on the porch.

"Martin and I have secured firewood and can retrieve more if needed," Bob said. "McGee and Jones are securing wood for the second cabin."

"By 'second cabin' I assume you mean Drew's place?" Joshua asked.

"Affirmative. The second cabin."

A few minutes later Perry arrived accompanied by a shivering, whimpering Caroline. "This is miserable," she complained.

Everyone crowded around the fire as it slowly flared to life. Reagan secured the spot closest to the warmth of the flames.

Both cabins were packed wall-to-wall that night. Everyone bundled up in an effort to stay warm.

***

The power was still out the next morning and the floor in the living area was covered with sleeping bags and blankets, most of which were still occupied. Bob was tending the fire.

Reagan pawed at the door. When Joshua opened it the anxious puppy bolted through it and charged down the steps. The deep snow completely engulfed the energetic pup. Frightened by this unknown, fluffy white substance that towered over his head, Reagan let out a yelp and ran back to the familiar safety of the porch. Joshua laughed. "Cold, isn't it, boy?" Confused, Reagan walked around on the porch for a moment, and then went to the far end and did his business there. Joshua followed Reagan back into the cabin, where others were beginning to stir.

"I would *love* a cup of coffee." Caroline sat up and stretched her arms.

"Me too," Rebecca agreed.

"But that's probably impossible with the power out." Caroline frowned.

"Any thoughts on how to handle food without power?" Perry asked.

Of course, Bob had the answer. "We will cook leftover

bear meat in the fireplace."

Caroline groaned. "Bear meat? Eeewww! That's just weird. Don't you have any eggs?"

Rebecca answered. "Unfortunately, no. Our chickens have not laid one single egg since we've been here." Caroline groaned out loud.

Not one to mince words or be politically correct, Bob shared his unsolicited insight: "We must adapt if we are to survive. That includes eating things we are not accustomed to. Adapt or perish, city girl."

Caroline let out an exasperated sigh. Sensing her despair, Rebecca suggested they search the cabinet for something she would find more palatable. Joshua retrieved some of the bear meat and Bob put on his raincoat and went outside.

Caroline returned from the kitchen with a can of assorted fruit, which she held up for Perry to see. "Not optimal, but I'd rather have this than that nasty bear meat."

Joshua put a large, cast iron pan filled with bear meat into the fire and Bob positioned an old aluminum coffee pot atop the wood stove. While it took longer than a modern coffee maker, the resulting brew was more than welcome.

The scene repeated when lunchtime rolled around. Caroline again resisted the bear meat and Perry retrieved something she found more palatable from their camper trailer.

Night came and went, and there was still no power in the camp. Eight sleeping bags cluttered the floor in the living area, each strategically positioned as close to the fireplace as possible. The group was well-fed thanks to the bear meat and they only occasionally dipped into the supply of non-perishable food. Caroline still resisted the meat.

Another night passed and there was still no power. Firewood was running low, so Joshua and the other men bundled up and ventured outside. A strong northerly wind knifed through the mountains, reinforcing the frigid temperature. The penetrating sunlight brilliantly sparkled on the thousands of shards of ice dangling in the trees. Joshua cautiously tested the mixture of snow and ice beneath his feet.

"This stuff is starting to melt," he said.

"It's about time," Perry said. "Maybe we'll get power back soon. It's been four days."

"This is good preparation," said Bob.

"Preparation for what?" Perry asked.

"For the high probability that at some point we will lose power permanently."

Perry groaned.

After the firewood had been replenished on the porch Bob and Kane checked the trotlines. Joshua and Perry trekked up the ice-covered hill to check on the people in Drew's cabin.

Jim greeted them on the porch, his eyes bloodshot and underscored by heavy black bags. "I *really* hope the power comes back soon. There are six children stuffed into this house, not to mention the adults. I think people are about to go stir crazy."

Joshua peered in the door, where the floor was completely obscured by sleeping bags and blankets. "You guys are just a bit cramped."

Jim let out a sarcastic chuckle. "That's the understatement of the day. It's a sardine can in there. The kids are complaining about eating the same thing at every meal. We've tried to explain to them that we can't just go to the grocery store or go out to eat like we could at home, but they don't seem to get it. Even beyond being cooped up in this storm, I'm worried about how they're going to adjust long-term. We could be in for a tough time with them."

Perry nodded. "It would also be an understatement to say that Caroline is struggling to adjust. She bottles everything up, especially since Charlie and Allie..." He choked up, unable to complete the sentence.

Jim's brow furrowed and he scratched his chin. "I'm worried about people sinking into depression and basically giving up."

"That would be bad," Joshua said. "And it could be contagious. Please think on how we can combat it."

Upon returning to Joshua's cabin they found Caroline seated on the floor, crying like a newborn baby. Rebecca and Ruth were seated on either side of her. John had retreated into his bedroom to escape the mayhem.

"What's wrong?" Perry asked.

"I can't live like this!" Caroline answered through her tears. "I... I miss Charlie and Allie... I feel like we're prisoners here. We can't go *anywhere* or do *anything*. You guys are eating all of this weird stuff like deer and bear, and we could run completely out of food. I may be forced to eat that crap. Who knows, the power may *never* come back on in here. I want my life back. *I HATE THIS PLACE!*" She again broke down into tears.

Perry tried to console her, but to no avail. Joshua retreated to his office; Rebecca followed and closed the door.

"I am *really* worried about Caroline," she said. "She is on the verge of a complete nervous breakdown, and we've only been here a week."

"And it could become contagious," Joshua observed.

"We need to--"

A shrill scream pierced Joshua's ears. He and Rebecca

rushed into the living area. A cold, deathly chill shot down Joshua's spine as he saw Caroline lying on the floor with blood splattered across her shirt. Perry and Ruth were scrambling frantically. Bob burst through the front door, surveyed the scene, then spun and rocketed off the porch in a full sprint.

"What happened?" Joshua swallowed hard.

Perry frantically ripped off his shirt and wrapped it into a ball, pressing it against Caroline's left wrist. "She cut herself!"

Rebecca knelt beside Caroline and put her hand on friend's cheek.

Perry was frenzied. "We've got to get the bleeding under control!"

Caroline began shaking violently as Joshua and Rebecca applied pressure to her slashed wrist with a wad of paper towels. Perry cupped his wife's head in his hand and pressed his face against hers, bawling. "Why? Why would you do this?"

Bob returned with Jim and Keri in tow. Keri examined the wound. "Thankfully it's not a very deep cut. Keep applying pressure to get the bleeding stopped, then we need to clean this up and get it wrapped."

Joshua collapsed onto the couch, leaned back, closed his eyes and let out a deep sigh. *I am NOT equipped to deal with this. What was I thinking bringing these people here?*

Once Keri had Caroline's bleeding under control, Rebecca went to her husband and buried her face in his chest. "I can't believe this is happening," she whispered.

Joshua put his arms around her and kissed her on the head. "Please don't *ever* do that to me."

Rebecca's head snapped around and she gazed at him through tear-filled eyes. "I think you *know* me better than that."

"I do, but I thought I knew Perry and Caroline better than that too." He hugged her tightly.

***

Later that afternoon Thomas made his way down the mountain to Joshua's porch. "Man, I heard about Caroline. Is she okay?"

"She should be," Joshua said. "Well, okay *physically*. I'm not sure how she's doing emotionally."

"Man, I know it's got to be tough losing your kids. Can't even imagine. How are the rest of y'all holding up?"

"We're hanging in there. I think people are getting cabin fever. Do you think we'll get power back in the near future?"

"Man, I got enough of a signal to call the power company earlier," Thomas answered. "It should be back on in the next day or two."

Joshua groaned. "Next day or two?"

Night came and went, and there was still no power in the camp. Bob pulled Joshua aside as the men were cutting firewood. "We have weak links in this camp. They will hold us back and could compromise us. We must consider how to handle."

"People are struggling. That's obvious. But I am *not* about to kick them out into the cold. I recruited them to come here, and I have a responsibility to help lead them through this."

Bob shook his head. "As you wish. But they are a liability."

"Understood, but I am not going to kick them to the curb."

The power finally came back on around noon.

***

That afternoon Joshua was joined by Rebecca and Jim on Drew's porch. "Jim, I wanted to follow up on our conversation about the fact that some folks are having difficulty adjusting. I agree with you that we could see a major bout of depression if we're not careful, and that could be deadly."

Jim nodded. "The worst thing people can do is bottle it up."

"What would you think about having a couple of small

groups like we had at our old church? It would give people a chance to vent, get things off their chest and hopefully support and encourage each other."

"I think that's a wise plan," Jim said. "Maybe each group can have a couple of families in it?"

"That's what I was thinking. It seemed to work at church."

"I like the small group idea, but that's *not* how we should set them up," Rebecca interjected. Joshua cocked an eyebrow.

"What are you thinking?" Jim asked.

"The women here are processing this whole thing much differently than the men," she said. "We saw that with Caroline. I think the men and women should be in separate groups."

"You're probably right," Jim said. "Joshua, what do you think?"

"I've learned *never* to argue with her." Joshua chuckled.

Rebecca smacked him on the arm.

CHAPTER 8

The sunrise offered a spectacular patchwork of pink, orange and red as it penetrated the darkness, spreading across the mountaintops and glittering through the still-icy trees. The wispy clouds glowed a deep red. A few birds could be seen searching for food and a lone squirrel jumped from tree to tree.

As he enjoyed the morning quiet Joshua reflected on the past couple of days. Warmer weather had melted most of the snow and ice, and camp residents' moods had risen with the temperature. The chickens had finally begun producing eggs and Bob had retrieved a catfish from the trotline. Things were slowly beginning to look up. *Slowly.*

The morning quiet was shattered by the rumbling of a motorcycle. Drew made his way down the path, sporting a blue backpack. He waved as he passed but did not stop. *Where is he going this early?*

Bob and Kane had begun constructing defensive structures around the edges of the camp to minimize the chance of unwanted intrusion at otherwise vulnerable points. Bob was a student of military history, and these barricades would be scaled-down versions of the hedgerows used by the Germans in World War II. Jim and Keri had begun contacting camp residents about the men's and women's small groups, receiving mostly favorable responses.

While things were looking up – at least for the moment – Joshua knew they could not afford to become complacent. His gut still told him that the chaos and conflict raging throughout the nation would eventually find its way here. As the camp's leader, it fell on his shoulders to motivate the others to use this time to prepare for challenges that would inevitably come. He heaved a sigh. *Easier said than done.*

Joshua went inside and turned on the television. The news anchor rehashed the events of the prior few days: *America is still reeling from the recent attacks on our nation. Most of the federal government's functions are effectively nonexistent, and the same can be said of states like North Carolina where the state capital was hit. With the federal government decimated, people who have relied on government benefits for their daily sustenance are doing without.*

The newscast switched to a shot of empty shelves in a grocery store. *Stores are reporting that they are having difficulty getting shipments of food, and an increasing number of international shipping lines are refusing to dock at American ports due to heightened security concerns.*

A crowd of people shouting outside of what appeared to be a city hall flashed across the screen. *State and local governments are being inundated with people angrily demanding that they provide benefits previously offered by the federal government. They do not have the resources to handle the crushing demand. The problem is especially great in urban areas where most residents do not have the knowledge, skills or resources to grow or hunt their own food. People in rural areas and farming communities are faring better, but even those areas are not without hardship.*

The newscast cut away to looters carrying stolen food from a store. *The sudden food shortage is sparking an increasingly violent crime wave. People are breaking into grocery stores, robbing other shoppers and even breaking into homes to steal food. State and local law enforcement agencies are being overwhelmed by the sudden surge in crime.*

Next, the report displayed heavily-armed personnel wearing uniforms with the Department of Homeland Security logo patrolling the streets in a small town. *With state and local law enforcement struggling to keep up, President Armando is dispatching troops and Homeland Security police to quell the violence. We are receiving reports of federal personnel using heavy-handed tactics and, in many cases, harassing people who are not part of the crime wave. Martial law remains in effect in numerous areas, and we are receiving reports of federal officials demanding that law-abiding citizens surrender their firearms.*

"Wow," Rebecca said. "It's getting worse and worse."

Joshua frowned and shook his head. "Indeed. We're watching the disintegration of the America we know and love."

***

Joshua was in the clearing when Thomas' Suburban made its way down the mountain. Tommy jumped out of the passenger side and ran over to meet him. "Mr. Winston, Dad wanted me to give these to you." He handed Joshua a stack of the proposed camp rules. "Me and Dad are headed to see if there's anything left at the store. Y'all need anything?"

"Not that I can think of. Are you taking any of our security guys with you?"

"I don't know."

Thomas and Tommy made their way to the store in Robbinsville, where the shelves were almost barren. Before they made it out of the store Thomas said, "Son, I forgot to get batteries. Go back and get 'em and meet me outside."

Tommy took the crisp $20 bill from his father. He looked for batteries but could not find them anywhere.

"We're running out of a lot of things," the store manager told him. "And we're getting very few shipments of anything that isn't produced locally." Tommy thanked the manager and went outside.

***

"Nine eggs," Rebecca said. "Not a bad day."

Joshua nodded. "Maybe this 'laying mash' stuff Thomas picked up actually works."

They met Bob and Kane in the clearing. "We have completed the first set of defensive structures along the road," Bob informed them. "To the naked eye they appear to be part of the natural terrain, but are difficult for individuals or vehicles to cross. Additionally, we have constructed passageways inside them that can be used to travel around the perimeter undetected. We will resume work tomorrow. It will take some time to fully encircle the camp."

"Sounds good," Joshua said. "I'll take a look at them tomorrow. I've got to finish getting ready for tonight's meetings."

"Both Thomas and Drew took off, didn't they?" Rebecca asked. "Will they be back in time?"

Joshua answered, "I hope--"

Thomas' Suburban rocketed up the path from the road, kicking up dirt and rocks in its wake.

"Why is he in such a hurry?" Rebecca wondered aloud. The vehicle's brakes locked and it skidded to a stop. Tommy jumped out, pale and shaking.

"What's wrong, Tommy?" Joshua asked. "You look like you've seen a ghost."

"Dad..." Tommy stammered and handed Joshua a sheet of paper. "Th.. this was on the truck..."

Joshua examined the paper. He frowned and handed it

to Bob, who read it aloud. *We have your father. You were able to escape when the old man bailed you out on the mountain road. If you want to see your father again, bring the old man who rescued you to us. 4:30 p.m. today, same parking lot where you found this note. No cops, and no one else. If you do not comply, YOUR FATHER IS DEAD.*

"Where did this happen?" Bob asked.

"Um, at, the.. um, grocery store."

"*What* grocery store?"

Joshua jumped in. "Tommy, was it the grocery store over in Robbinsville where your Dad took us last week?"

Tommy nodded.

"How did this happen?" Bob asked.

"We went through the checkout line and then Dad realized he'd forgotten batteries," Tommy said, sounding a little more composed. "He gave me a twenty and sent me back in. When I got back to the truck the keys were hanging in the door and this note was on the seat."

Bob continued his rapid-fire questioning. "Did you immediately drive back here after finding the note?"

"Um, yes."

"Were you followed?"

"Not that I know of."

"Are you certain?"

"Um, no."

"Martin, perform immediate border security check along the road."

"Yes, sir!" Kane answered.

"Joshua, postpone tonight's meetings. Round up people from the other homes. Rebecca, go with Tommy and talk to Mr. Page's family, then bring him back here."

Bob explained the situation after Joshua rounded up Perry, Jack and Chuck.

"McGee, come with us," Bob said. "Mr. Edwards and Mr. Jones, stay here and guard the camp. Let Mr. Davidson and the people in the other cabin know what has happened and that tonight's camp and council meetings are postponed."

"Will do," Perry answered.

After a short time Rebecca and Tommy made the trip back down the hill in Thomas' Suburban.

"How did Kim take it?" Joshua asked.

"She pretty much lost it," Rebecca said. "I assured her that it'll be all right and that we'll get Thomas back."

"Tommy, we need for you to go with us to get your Dad back," Bob said.

Tommy nodded, still shaking.

"Rebecca, please stay with Kim until we come back," Joshua advised. "Bob, what's your plan?"

Bob's eyes narrowed as he checked the magazine on his 1911 and forcefully pumped a round into the chamber. "Well, they said they wanted me. Let's give the morons what they asked for."

Kane returned from the woods and ran toward the cabin, stone-faced. "Bogey vehicle parked up the hill from the gate, sir. Two people in the vehicle. One man, one woman. Another man *thinks* he's hiding in the woods across the road."

"They followed Tommy when he returned here and are planning to ambush us when we leave," Bob said. "The vehicle is a decoy, and the other man is likely the shooter. Martin, was Mr. Page in the vehicle?"

"Unable to discern, sir."

Bob's eyes narrowed as he outlined his plan. "Priority one is to ascertain Mr. Page's location and retrieve him securely. Priority two is to ensure that our location here is not compromised."

Joshua shot Bob a puzzled look. "How do you plan to avoid our location being compromised since they are right outside the gate? Hasn't it *already* been compromised?"

"That is why we must eliminate the three bogeys."

"By 'eliminate' you mean 'kill'?"

"Affirmative. They will likely initiate conflict and force our hand. The larger challenge is ascertaining Mr. Page's location before we eliminate the threat."

"Won't that just draw attention to us?" Joshua asked.

"If they are allowed to escape they will absolutely compromise us. And they have made their intentions clear."

"What about local law enforcement? Shouldn't we call them?"

"Negative! In the wake of all that has happened, and particularly in light of the incident at the farm, we cannot rely on or trust anyone. We must handle this ourselves."

Joshua took a deep breath.

Bob barked out orders. "Martin, position McGee at a secure vantage point near the gate and yourself at the highest possible vantage point with eyes on the bogey in the woods. McGee, keep eyes on the bogeys in the vehicle. I will drive Mr. Page's Suburban to the gate and exit the vehicle when I have eyes on the enemy. Joshua, follow me down the path but stay far enough behind to avoid being spotted. Be prepared to initiate pursuit if the other vehicle flees. McGee, be prepared to join Joshua in his truck."

Kane nodded and motioned for Jack to follow him as he headed into the woods in the direction of the gate.

As Kane and Jack started for the woods Bob said, "Martin, we will wait ten minutes before proceeding to give you time to get into position. You have the green light to engage at the first sign of hostility."

"Yes, sir!"

"What about me?" Tommy asked.

Bob put his hand on Tommy's shoulder. "Son, things have changed now that the enemy has found us. You should stay here. I don't want to put you in harm's way."

"NO! He's my Dad, and I want to go."

Bob looked at Joshua for guidance.

"Tommy, are you sure?" Joshua asked.

"YES!"

"Wait here, son." Bob walked to his utility trailer, returning with two vests and a helmet. He handed a vest and the helmet to Tommy. "Son, put these on and ride in the back. If you hear shots, get down in the vehicle and *stay down*." Tommy put on the vest and helmet and opened the door to the back seat of his father's Suburban and settled in. "Not the back seat, son. *All the way* in the back. As far out of sight as possible." Tommy did as Bob instructed. Bob also donned a vest and covered it with his dark green coat.

After exactly ten minutes Bob began slowly driving down the path toward the gate. Joshua followed him, keeping his distance. His heart was beating a million miles a minute as he kept his hand near his 9mm. *I feel like we're in a war zone, but I'm not even sure who our enemies are. These guys seem like random criminals.*

The short trip down the winding dirt path seemed like an eternity. As Joshua rounded the last curve before reaching the road he spotted the defensive hedgerow that Bob and Kane were constructing.

Bob stopped before reaching the gate. Joshua watched as he concealed his pistol under the back of his coat and walked out into the narrow two-lane road. A shot rang out and Bob went down. *Relax, he's wearing a vest*, Joshua thought. Tommy disappeared down into the SUV. As Bob hit the ground another shot rang out, followed by the sound of tires screeching and another shot.

Bob was back on his feet in a flash. Jack rushed from the interior of the hedgerow and sprinted to the passenger side of Joshua's Silverado.

"Martin, clean up the mess," Bob yelled.

Bob motioned for Joshua to follow as he gunned the Suburban. The tires screeched as he spun out of the driveway onto the road. Joshua floored it and followed him out. *Here we go!* He saw another vehicle off in the distance speeding away. Bob was in hot pursuit and Joshua tried to catch up. Kane crossed the road behind them, presumably going in the direction of the shooter.

"What happened?" Joshua asked Jack.

"Kane took out the shooter. I took a shot at the vehicle, but it began a quick U-turn as soon as I squeezed the trigger and I missed the driver." Jack frowned as he replaced the spent rounds in his rifle. "I think I took out a female passenger."

Joshua's heart pounded as he followed Bob and the bandit. He gripped the steering wheel tightly with both hands as the mountainside streaked past in a dizzying blur. The old Silverado shook and rattled as it hugged the narrow, winding mountain road. *They didn't cover this in drivers' ed,* he thought.

"I just hope Thomas is okay and that we find him," Joshua said.

"We will," Jack assured him.

Joshua felt beads of cold sweat on his forehead as the chase continued for several miles. As they rounded a curve he spotted the getaway vehicle streaking down a narrow dirt path on the right. Bob did not follow them, instead passing the entrance to the path and continuing down the road.

"Should we turn?" Joshua asked.

"No, follow Bob," Jack answered. "I think I know what his plan is."

When they rounded the next curve they found Bob pulled off onto the shoulder. A thick cluster of trees obscured the view of the valley and the path down which the getaway vehicle had fled. Joshua's old Silverado skidded to a stop.

"What's the plan, Bob?" Joshua asked.

"They think they lost us. Joshua, go back past the dirt path and drop McGee off. McGee, you go into the woods and come down the right side of the dirt path. I will enter the woods here and come down the left side. Joshua, you maintain position in your vehicle, out of sight, from a vantage point where you can see any vehicles coming up the path. Keep your eyes open, and if you see the other vehicle trying to escape use your truck to block its exit."

"What about me?" Tommy asked.

Bob's tone transformed from that of a commanding officer to a concerned father. "Son, you stay here in your Dad's vehicle. We'll get him back for you." Tommy nodded.

Bob disappeared down the mountainside and Joshua drove back up the road past the dirt path down which the getaway vehicle had turned.

"Let me out here," Jack said.

Joshua obliged and Jack began his trek down the embankment.

***

Bob nimbly made his way down the side of the mountain into the small valley where Thomas' kidnappers had fled. Halfway down the incline he spotted the getaway vehicle parked between a small brown house and a rickety old wooden barn in the clearing below. *Is this where they're holding Thomas?* he wondered. A dark red El Camino was parked near the getaway vehicle and a run-down trailer sat near the property's edge. The yard was cluttered with rusty barrels, five-gallon buckets, boards and three lawn chairs.

The embankment was steep, but Bob was unhindered as he stealthily descended toward the house and barn. As he neared the base of the slope a man exited the back door and rushed to the barn. Bob watched him through a telescope. During the brief instant the barn door was open he spotted Thomas, blindfolded, gagged and tied up against a pole. A shot of adrenaline pulsed through his veins. *We're in the right place.*

After reaching the edge of the yard Bob surveyed the steep hill on the other side of the house. Jack was still far up the mountain, slowly descending.

Bob clenched his teeth. "Hurry up, McGee," he mumbled under his breath. "I don't have all freakin' day."

Bob froze as a mangy brown mutt stepped around the corner of the barn and stopped. He could feel the dog's glare laser-focused on him. He put his hand on his holstered 1911. Bob swallowed hard. *If he starts barking I'm blown.* The dog silently fixated on his position for what seemed like hours, then abruptly turned and slowly meandered away from the barn. He exhaled as the dog disappeared into the woods off to his right. After the dog was safely out of sight Bob began a slow belly crawl forward.

Yelling and cursing rang out from the barn. Bob had crawled about halfway to the structure when the door opened. He froze and watched as the man he had seen earlier left the barn and returned to the house. Bob heaved a sigh of relief when the house door slammed shut without the man noticing him on the ground less than fifty feet away. *That could have imperiled the mission.*

Bob un-holstered his 1911 and continued his silent belly crawl to the barn. Once there, a quick glance between the loosely fitted boards confirmed that Thomas was still tied to the post. He again studied the adjacent hill, where Jack was only about halfway down the mountain. *I don't have time to wait on you, McGee.*

Bob stealthily slipped around to the back of the barn, putting it between himself and the house. He quietly slipped through the door and made his way toward Thomas.

"Thomas, it's Bob Kendall," he whispered. "We're here to--"

He felt a blow to his back and fell forward onto his knees. His pistol flew from his hands and skidded across the dirt floor, out of reach. Bob vaulted up and spun toward his unknown attacker. WHACK! His face was met by the broad side of a shovel. He tumbled backward, dazed. The last thing he saw was the shovel descending toward his face.

***

Joshua was growing impatient. He studied the valley below through a pair of binoculars, unable to get a clear view of what was happening. *What's going on down there?* Off to the right he spotted Jack, still making his way down the mountainside. *It's not that far. I could make it down the path in no time. I might even be able to beat Jack there...*

***

Groggy, Bob struggled to regain his senses. His swollen right eye resisted his efforts to open it. He was inside a dimly lit structure that was permeated by a dank, musky odor. After a moment he realized it was the barn where Thomas had been held. He tried to stand up, but the tightly bound ropes would not allow it. As the blurriness receded Bob realized Thomas was still tied up a few feet away. His blindfold had been removed. A tall, skinny man in worn jeans and a frayed green flannel shirt stood ten feet away holding a shotgun.

"Old man, you destroyed my truck the other day. Today you killed my little brother and my girlfriend. Now it's *your* turn!" He punched Bob repeatedly, then kicked him in the ribs and spit in his face for good measure. "I'm gonna enjoy this! You'll watch your friend here die. Then you're next!"

Where is McGee? Bob thought. *Slow bastard.*

The man squatted near Bob, the heavy stench of his foul breath saturating the air like a toxic cloud. "Who do you think you are? Rambo? Jack Bauer? You're just an old man who will be forgotten in a week!" He pumped a shell into the chamber of the shotgun as he walked away.

"I'm the one you want," Bob pleaded. "Let him go and kill me. He's done nothing to you."

"It's too late for that! He's seen our faces," the man snarled, pointing at Thomas. "And the last thing *you* see before you die will be proof that you *failed* to save him!"

Bob's heart sank under the weight of his inability to accomplish his mission. "Thomas, I'm sorry I failed you." Thomas looked at him helplessly.

The kidnapper let out a sadistic laugh and took aim at Thomas. Bob closed his eyes, unable to watch. He heard one shot, then a pumping shotgun, then a second blast. Then a body hitting the floor. *Thomas was on the ground. That person was standing up.* Bob opened his eyes and saw the kidnapper lying on the ground, blood oozing from beneath his lifeless corpse. Tommy stood in the doorway closest to the house, a smoking 12-gauge in his hands.

"Dad..." Tommy ran to his father.

"Son!" Tears streamed down Thomas' face. "You saved my life! But you shouldn't have risked yourself!"

Tommy stood up straight with an air of defiance. "I couldn't sit up there and do nothing!" He laid the shotgun on the ground and began untying his father.

"Your father is right, you shouldn't have come down here." The stranger's voice was followed by the sound of a pumping shotgun. "Hands up. NOW."

Another man stood in the doorway. Bob's heart sank as he realized *this* was the man he had seen go from the house to the barn and back earlier. *How could I not have suspected there were two of them? Where the hell is McGee? He should be here by now.*

"Do what he says, son," Thomas said. Tommy raised his hands.

"It won't help." The man checked the fallen kidnapper's body for a pulse. "Boy, you killed my cousin!"

"He was going to kill my Dad!"

The gunman snarled in response. "Well, now I'm going to kill *all* of you!"

Thomas pleaded for his son's life. "No! He's just a boy!"

"He should've thought about that earlier!"

The man raised his shotgun and pointed it at Tommy. Tommy dove and landed behind an old red crop sprayer as the kidnapper fired off a shot. The shotgun blast echoed within the barn, followed by the sound of metal clanging against metal. Bob cringed as ricocheting pellets pelted his legs, arms and torso.

"Boy, you can't hide." He pumped another shell into the chamber. "I *will* get you."

Thomas struggled against the bindings, trying to get up. The man hit him in the chest with the shotgun butt, sending him back to the ground. Still bound, Bob watched helplessly. Tommy leapt from behind the crop sprayer and landed behind the wheels of an old blue tractor further from the back door. The man fired off another shot.

"You've got yourself cornered now, boy," the man snarled. "That's the last stupid decision you'll ever make."

Thomas again desperately pleaded for his only son's life. "Don't kill my son!"

The plea seemed only to fuel the attacker's desire for revenge. "Shut up!" He again hit Thomas with the butt of his shotgun. Bob's skin burned as he strained against the ropes, unable to free himself. *If I could just get free...*

As the kidnapper turned back toward Tommy another figure silently shot through the front door behind him. In one sweeping motion Jack did a quick forward roll, spun and kicked the man's legs out from under him. The shotgun flew from the man's hand and slid toward the back of the barn.

Jack and the kidnapper both rocketed back to their feet. Jack pulled out a large serrated knife with a black handle. The attacker grabbed a machete from the barn wall and the two faced off.

"It's about time you got here, McGee," Bob said.

"You shouldn't have come here," the man snarled at Jack. "Now you can die with your friends."

Jack remained silent and kept his steely stare focused on the man. The kidnapper wildly lunged at him with the machete. Jack deftly avoided the blade, but did not seek to strike a blow of his own. He silently squared up, waiting for the enraged kidnapper to make a second move.

Jack avoided the attack as the man again lunged at him wildly. He smoothly pivoted and slashed the kidnapper's back. The man let out a yell, cursed and charged. The kidnapper again missed his mark, this time coming away with a gash on his left bicep.

Tommy picked up the shotgun. Unable to get a clear shot at the kidnapper, he rushed to his Dad's side.

The attacker continued lunging wildly at Jack, while Jack calmly staved off every advance. One fighter completely out of control, another fully under control. Nearly every time the kidnapper swung his machete, Jack's blade was the one that found its target.

The kidnapper backed up, paused for a second and raised his machete over his head. Jack took one step back, baiting him. The attacker let out a scream like a crazed animal and charged head-on, swinging the machete wildly. Jack charged to meet the attack, slid to the ground and knocked the attacker's feet out from under him. As the kidnapper's back hit the ground Jack spun and forcefully drove the knife into his jugular vein. The man gasped for breath and reached for his throat, then faded into oblivion.

Jack quickly retrieved his knife from the fallen kidnapper's neck and wiped it off on the man's shirt. Tommy finished untying his father and then released Bob while Jack checked the area for additional kidnappers.

Bob rubbed his swollen eye. "What took you so long, McGee?"

"You're welcome, sir," Jack answered.

"Why didn't you just shoot the guy?"

"Where's the sport in that?"

"McGee, this isn't a joke."

"I couldn't get a good angle without putting you guys in the line of fire," Jack said. "We need to clear this scene and get out of here." He found a set of keys on one of the bodies and threw it to Tommy. "Can you pull their vehicle around behind the barn?"

Jack found two gas cans in the corner of the barn and emptied one of them onto the dead bodies. "Bob, let's check out the house." Bob frowned and followed him.

Bob carefully opened the back door. With weapons raised they cleared the door and stealthily entered the living area, which was unoccupied. Jack led the way as they conducted a room-to-room search with military precision. In one bedroom they found the lifeless body of a young woman with a gunshot wound to the head.

"This is who I hit when I shot at their vehicle," Jack whispered. "Sad. Pretty young lady. Hate that she got mixed up with these dirtbags."

Bob shrugged. "She made her choices."

As Jack opened the final interior door they were met by a strong ammonia-like odor. Bob spotted two glowing eyes in the back of the room. A large, angry Rottweiler let out a deep, echoing bark, charged and jumped. Jack deftly avoided the canine missile and in one lightning-fast motion holstered his pistol, unsheathed his knife and sank it into the airborne canine's upper ribcage, followed by a second quick blow to the dog's chest. The enraged dog struggled to continue its attack, but quickly lost its will.

"And why didn't you shoot *him*?" Bob frowned.

"Too much noise," Jack said. "You guys already woke up the whole mountain. Plus I have a hunch that setting off a gun in this room could be bad news."

"What do you mean?"

"Smell that? Smells like a meth lab."

Bob sniffed the air. "Good call, McGee."

They cautiously entered the room, where they found two large tables covered with an assortment of jars and other containers, rubber tubes, gas cookers, a funnel, rubber gloves and other items. Shower curtains covered the windows.

"Yep, looks like a meth lab," Jack said. Bob nodded.

"This is good," Jack said. "Go tell Tommy and Thomas to get in the truck and be ready to leave. Then get that second gas can and pour a trail of gas from the bodies to the house, and bring a little gas in here. We can use the meth lab as the source of an explosion."

"Good idea. Will do," Bob said.

Jack poured liquids into the cookers, but did not turn them on. Next, he went into the kitchen and put all of the silverware he could find into the microwave, along with several bullets and an entire roll of paper towels. He set the timer on sixty minutes but did not press 'start'. He pulled the gas stove away from the wall and turned on the gas logs in the fireplace.

When Bob returned they moved the dead woman's body into the living area near the fireplace and covered it with the remaining gasoline. Jack knocked the hose off of the gas line to the stove so that gas flowed freely into the house. Bob turned the meth cookers on high and Jack hit the 'start' button on the microwave. They rushed out and Jack quickly drove up the mountain.

***

Joshua paced back and forth in front of his truck. *I should've gone down there. What's taking them so long?*

The kidnappers' SUV raced up the mountain trail. *What in the world?* Joshua jumped into the cab of the truck and gripped his 9mm. His heart pounded like a bass drum as he moved to block the exit. *Where are Bob and Jack?* Joshua positioned the truck across the end of the path, got out and used the vehicle to shield himself, keeping his pistol out of view. He exhaled a deep sigh of relief when he saw Jack behind the wheel. He ducked when an explosion rang out from the valley below, followed by a second, much louder blast.

"What happened?" Joshua asked.

"I'll explain it when we get back, but we need to get out of here," Jack said. "You take Thomas and Tommy with you. Bob and I will dispose of their vehicle and meet you at the camp. If we're not back in two hours send Kane to look for us."

Joshua nodded as his brow furrowed. *Looks like Jack has taken the lead. Interesting that Bob would let that happen.* He pointed at Bob. "Looks like you got banged up a bit."

"It's just a scrape." Bob lit up a cigar. "Besides, chicks dig scars."

Thomas and Tommy retrieved two shotguns from the kidnappers' vehicle and headed back to camp.

"What happened?" Joshua again asked.

Thomas shook his head. "Man, I don't know where to start." He put his arm around Tommy. "I'm just happy we're alive."

Joshua pressed the issue. "Let's start with how these guys kidnapped you in the first place."

Thomas explained everything that had happened. "Bob came in to rescue me and one of the guys surprised him and knocked him out."

Joshua cocked an eyebrow. "Caught *Bob* off guard? Wow. That's hard to do. That explains his swollen eye."

"I know, man. He tied Bob up and beat on him a bit. Said he was going to kill me and then him. Tommy came out of nowhere and shot him." Thomas looked at Tommy and choked up. "Son, you saved my life, but I wish you hadn't risked yours to do it."

"Dad, I wasn't just going to sit up here and let them kill you without doing something."

Thomas continued his account, emphasizing that Jack had saved the day. "Man, that guy is tough. He's something else. I think he's as tough as Bob, but not as wild. He really took charge of the situation."

Joshua nodded. "We're lucky to have them both. Kane, too."

As the gate came into view Kane appeared out of nowhere and opened it. He closed it behind them and vanished into the woods.

When Kim saw Thomas and Tommy alive she broke down into tears and ran to hug them, followed by Tommy's sister, Laura. Laura's black hair matched that of her mother, while Tommy's hair was light brown like Thomas'.

Rebecca hugged Joshua and Reagan pawed at his ankles. Joshua explained what had transpired.

"Wow," Rebecca said. "I guess it's getting more and more dangerous out there. No sense of law and order."

"Apparently not." Joshua shook his head.

Thomas sheepishly walked over to Joshua and Rebecca. "Man, I can't thank you guys enough. That goes for Jack and Bob too. I'm glad we have 'em here. Man, you were right when you said it would be a lot easier to make do if we had the right group of people with us here. We wouldn't have made it two weeks without y'all."

"I hate to say 'I told you so', but I did," Joshua admonished Thomas. "You *really* need to be more careful when you're out and about."

"I know, man."

***

"Any sign of Drew?" Joshua asked Rebecca.

"Nope."

Joshua shook his head, irritated by Drew's repeated

disappearing acts. "I just hope we don't have to go on another missing person hunt. I've had enough excitement for one day."

As the sun set over the tree line an hour later Joshua heard a motorcycle engine whirring up the mountain. A few minutes later there was a knock at the door.

"What time are the meetings tonight?" Drew asked.

"They're postponed 'till tomorrow."

"Why?"

Joshua explained everything that had happened and added, "Where in the world have you been? It's dangerous leaving without security."

Drew loudly blew his nose, then rubbed it with his handkerchief. "It was safe where I went. Don't worry about me."

Joshua shook his head as Drew drove away.

***

A cold breeze whipped through the shelter the next morning, giving Rebecca goosebumps. She warmed her hands over the fire as Keri opened the discussion. "Ladies, this is just a chance for us to get together and talk about whatever we're dealing with. Bottling it up won't help any of us. We're obviously in a whole new world compared to what we're used to. We don't, and probably won't, have access to the luxuries we've become accustomed to. We've had a tough couple of weeks, and I know it has to be weighing on each of us."

"That's the understatement of the century," Kim interjected. Everyone nodded in agreement.

"This time is informal," Keri continued. "The main rules we have are that we will open and close in prayer. So let's do that now." Everyone closed their eyes and bowed their heads as Keri prayed. When she finished she heaved a deep sigh. "All right, who wants to go first?"

Kim spoke up immediately. "Well, my husband has almost been killed twice. We're used to living in the country, but not having to watch our backs all the time. This is ridiculous. We've always been pretty laid back. I guess those days are over."

"That's a good point, Kim," Keri affirmed. "What do the rest of you think?"

Rebecca offered her input. "We all have to be on our toes from here on out. I'm not used to it either. As Keri said, we have to come to grips with the fact that the world we're used to doesn't exist anymore."

Caroline stroked the tightly wrapped bandages on her left wrist. "I feel like I'm a prisoner here. I know you guys say it's the safest place we could be, but it sure doesn't feel like it. If it's so safe, why did Thomas almost get killed yesterday? I still just can't believe all of this. I'm used to living in a nice house in a nice neighborhood, and now I'm sleeping in a stupid camper trailer. I'm used to being able to go where I want to go, do what I want to do, buy the things I want to buy. I'm used to wearing nice clothes and eating nice meals at nice restaurants, and here it seems like I'm destined to eat these strange animals even though I'm a vegetarian. I'm used to being independent, and not having to rely on anyone else. If I wanted something, I could go get it. Here, I am completely dependent..." Her words trailed off as she broke down into tears.

Rebecca choked up.

"Feeling totally dependent on someone else can be a terrible feeling," Keri said. "But, if we really look at it, we were all more dependent on others than we would like to admit, even before all of this happened."

"How so?" Andrea asked.

"Well, think about it. If you needed money, you relied on the bank to have it in the ATM. If you wanted to go somewhere, you relied on the gas station to have gas. If you wanted food, you relied on the grocery store or restaurant to have it. If your car was broken down, you probably relied on a mechanic to fix it."

"That's different!" Caroline retorted sharply.

Keri continued her line of thought. "It *is* different, until you consider the fact that people outside of this camp don't have access to a lot of those very same things right now. People out there who relied on grocery stores to have food are wondering where their next meal is going to come from. A lot of people out there who relied on the gas station to have gas are walking everywhere they need to go. People out there who relied on the police to keep them safe are now fearful for their lives. People out there who relied on government benefits don't know how they are going to make it."

"I hadn't thought of it that way." Caroline pursed her lips.

Keri continued, "We've all relied on many things, and we likely took them for granted. And a lot of people all across the country are now painfully aware of how dependent they are. *Very* painfully. But we have food, we are alive and well, we have people to protect us. Even though things are different for us, we need to take a step back and count our blessings. We're going to have to help each other cope. If we try to do it alone, we won't make it. And we have to rely on God."

"How could God even let this happen?" Caroline interrupted. "I've been a Christian since I was little, but right now I wonder if God is even up there."

Rebecca bit her lower lip. She noticed several women in the group squirming in their seats.

"That's a perfectly understandable feeling in a situation like this," Keri calmly answered. "And while I don't understand what God's plan is in all of this, I know He has one."

"Some plan this is," Caroline sneered.

Keri was unfazed. "Caroline, I can understand your skepticism. And I'm not going to try to talk you out of it. These are natural questions, and I appreciate you being open and honest. I'm willing to bet some others here feel the same way." Sheri and Ruth admitted that similar thoughts had crossed their minds. Keri continued, "None of us will benefit from keeping this inside, and that's why we wanted to start meeting like this."

After a lengthy discussion Keri moved on to the next topic. "Okay, how are your kids handling things? Our two are hanging in there."

"Ours are pretty much used to being up here in the mountains," Kim said. "Although I'm worried about Tommy given what he's been through."

"Our three are struggling," Sheri volunteered. "They're used to living in a nice house, having their smartphones, and being able to keep up with their friends on Facebook. Now the five of us are stuffed into a cramped RV and they're cut off from the world. They're just not old enough to understand."

"Billy is hanging in there," Andrea said. "He was a bit rattled by what happened at the gas station on the way here, but he's a tough--"

Caroline began wailing loudly. "I just wish Charlie and Allie were here! I still can't believe they're gone."

Keri put her arm around Caroline. Rebecca noticed Ruth's face overcome with pain, tears streaming down her cheeks. "Ruth, what is it?"

"John and I haven't talked about it publicly, but our only daughter had just started a job in Washington on February 16," Ruth said between sobs. "She was working for a congressman. He had gotten her a ticket to watch the State of the Union from the gallery. She was so excited..."

A wave of gasps rolled across the group. To everyone's astonishment Caroline rose and went to embrace Ruth, stroking her shoulder-length blonde hair as they shared a common grief.

For a moment no one spoke. Keri broke the silence with a soft prayer from Psalms: "Praise the Lord. How good it is to sing praises to our God, how pleasant and fitting to praise him! The Lord builds up Jerusalem; He gathers the exiles of Israel. He heals the brokenhearted and binds up their wounds. He determines the number of the stars and calls them each by name. Great is our Lord and mighty in power; His understanding has no limit. Amen."

***

That afternoon, a loud rumble shook the forest as Joshua and Perry made their way up the path from the lake.

"What in the world?" Joshua asked. He could feel the trail vibrating under his feet.

"No clue," Perry said. "Strange..."

Joshua gripped his 9mm as they approached the clearing. His jaw dropped and he stared in bewilderment at a semi-trailer tanker truck passing in front of them. Thomas was at the wheel and Drew followed in Thomas' Suburban. Drew grinned and waved as he passed. Speechless, Joshua and Perry watched as the truck wormed its way up the path past Drew's cabin before pulling into the woods and backing into a cleared area on the opposite side of the trail. Several of Thomas' contractors jumped out of the Suburban and began working to conceal the truck with a makeshift shelter. Drew disappeared into his cabin.

Joshua pointed at the truck as Thomas climbed down out of the cab. "What in the world?"

"Hey man," Thomas said. "Let's just say we won't have to worry about where to get gas when the stations run out."

Joshua cocked an eyebrow. "This had to cost a fortune. How did you manage this?"

"Drew took care of it."

Joshua shook his head in bewilderment.

***

After dinner that night Joshua turned the television to a

national news station. *The chaos we have seen throughout the nation appears to have made its way to western North Carolina. A house and barn near Robbinsville exploded and burned to the ground yesterday. Two bodies were found in the barn and a third in the house. Authorities first attributed the explosion to an accident related to a meth lab in the house. However, a fourth badly burned body was found on the edge of Lake Fontana, several miles east of the dam. Authorities have identified this body as the brother of one of the two men whose bodies were found in the barn. While his body was badly burned, the cause of death was determined to be a gunshot wound. Authorities now believe the two events are related. There are no suspects at this time.*

"Not good," Joshua said. "I'd better go tell Bob."

***

The next night, Joshua called the camp meeting to order and opened with a prayer and the Pledge of Allegiance. The meeting was a short one as there was little discussion of the camp rules, which were adopted without opposition. After the camp-wide meeting Joshua called the council meeting to order using the same gavel he had wielded as mayor. Rebecca, Jack, Jim, Ruth and Chuck stuck around to observe.

Joshua outlined a standard agenda he planned to follow for council meetings, which included a review of outside news, discussions about security, the importance of developing a sustainable food supply, other needed supplies, health, Andrea's plans to help the children continue their education, overall camp morale and any other issues that needed to be addressed from week to week.

"I feel compelled to point out that most of the items on this list *never* showed up on our agendas when I was on the town council or in the legislature," Joshua said. "It never seemed relevant to talk about security of this nature or our food supply. The mere fact that these items are even on our agenda is indicative of the unique situation in which we find ourselves. We cannot afford to get complacent or let our guard down. Yesterday's events bear that out. Let's start with security. Bob, can you give us an update?"

Bob discussed the hedgerows that he and Kane were constructing around the camp border. He reiterated the need to avoid drawing attention to the camp and the importance of traveling in groups, with security, when leaving the camp.

"That means you, boy." Bob pointed at Drew. "Your unaccompanied trips outside of the camp put us all at risk."

"Don't worry about me." Drew pushed his glasses against his face. "I take great pains to stay low-key and ensure that I am not followed."

"Drew, I share Bob's concern on this," Joshua said.

"Something could happen to you and no one would know."

"Again, don't worry about me. If I don't come back, give my house to Jim and his family."

"Boy, I don't think you get it," Bob said. "You're putting *ALL OF US* at risk."

Drew turned beet red and waved his finger at Bob. "You need to consult your oracle and make sure you've got your facts straight before making accusations. How many times have you had to rescue me or come to my defense since this whole thing started? *NONE!* You've had to rescue or defend almost every man in this camp *except* me, and yet I'm the one you keep singling out. Something is wrong with you!"

Joshua's stomach twisted as Bob shot up from his seat, his fists clenched and his nostrils flaring like an angry bull, and took a step toward Drew. Drew turned his back toward Bob. Thomas stepped between them.

"Man, let's all take a deep breath and relax," Thomas said. "Drew, I have to agree with these fellas. I was a bit too laid back about this whole security thing, and it almost got me killed yesterday."

"If I don't come back, don't come looking for me," Drew reiterated.

"Let's move on." Joshua's brow furrowed. "Drew, I'll talk with you one-on-one about this later."

The council discussed the camp's progress toward

developing a sustainable food supply. The trotlines were slowly beginning to yield fish and several of the men had begun fishing farther out on the lake using the canoes Drew had acquired. Kane's hunting continued to yield a steady supply of meat and Joshua's chickens were now producing eggs daily. The dairy cows Thomas had acquired were producing milk. While vegetables were in short supply inside the camp it would soon be time to begin planting a garden. In the meantime, Thomas had identified several places they could acquire fruit and vegetables from local farmers. Others in the camp were beginning to hunt and fish and many still had most of their non-perishable food supply.

"So far, we're hanging in there in regard to developing our food supply," Joshua said. "However, this is something we have to focus on *every single day*. And we also have to realize that, if people outside of this camp who are struggling for food find out we are here, they could become a threat."

The council covered its remaining agenda items and adjourned.

***

Drew caught up with Jack as everyone began to head their separate ways. "Jack, you seem like a decent guy. I was hoping to ask you for a favor?"

"Sure, what is it?"

Drew looked around to make sure no one else was in earshot. He swallowed hard. "Well, I'm almost embarrassed to ask this, but I was hoping you could teach me how to properly shoot a pistol. I bought one today while I was out. I've fired a shotgun, but didn't grow up around handguns and have no idea how to use it. I don't want to ask that Bob guy... I know how that will go."

Jack chuckled. "Yep, he'd give you a little grief. I'll be glad to help. Where did you find a pistol?"

"A guy Thomas introduced me to. Let me know if you want his name."

***

After breakfast the next morning the men in the camp got together for their version of a small group. Jim offered a prayer and opened the meeting. "Guys, thanks for being here. I want to start by saying that this is not some sort of support group. Proverbs 27:17 says, 'As iron sharpens iron, so one man sharpens another.' That's why we're here, to sharpen each other as men and as leaders. Any questions before we start?"

Joshua spoke up. "I don't have a question, but do have a couple of comments. First, thank you to Jim for his willingness to lead this. This is important. Second, thank you to all of *you* for coming. Please take this seriously."

"I'll take it seriously as long as it doesn't turn into some kind of namby pamby girl talk session," Bob said, blowing a puff of cigar smoke.

Jim chuckled. "I don't think there's much risk of that with this group. However, I do think we can help each other. And for those who are willing, we should pray for each other."

"Guys, I'll start," Perry volunteered. "Please pray for me to be strong for Caroline. She seems to be on a bit more solid ground, but I'm still worried she may have another breakdown." He choked up. "I've hidden all of the knives in our camper."

Several of the other men shared things their families were struggling with. Bob, Kane and Drew were silent.

"It occurs to me that virtually all of these requests have one thing in common," Jim observed. "They all relate to our *families*, and to how we can be strong for them. Anyone else?"

"I have a couple of prayer requests," Joshua spoke up. "First, pray for me in the leadership role you guys have entrusted me with. Second, pray for both Rebecca and me as we adjust. Third, let's all pray for the safety of everyone here. Finally, we need to pray for our nation, or what's left of it, as a whole. I fear we're seeing America's last days."

***

The violence has mushroomed into full-scale riots across America. In many areas federal Homeland Security police and military personnel are using extreme force to quell the violence – a move that continues to meet with resistance from some governors and local officials. President Armando continues to reject their criticisms as unwarranted.

The newscast cut away to the Governor of Texas. *The State of Texas does not recognize the right of so-called Homeland Security police to patrol our streets. We will not stand idly by and allow these unconstitutional federal agents to oppress our citizens, and our National Guard and local law enforcement stand ready to defend the people of the Lone Star State. Furthermore, I will pardon any Texas citizen who is accused of a crime for defending his or her freedom – or that of his or her neighbors – against this federal intrusion, which is nothing more than a blatant step toward tyranny.*

The anchor came back on screen. *Several other governors have publicly said that they stand with Texas, including the governors of South Carolina, Tennessee, Georgia, Montana and Ohio. This list is sure to grow.*

President Armando appeared on screen. *These statements by the Governor of Texas and other governors are uncalled for, irresponsible, and downright un-American. This is a blatant act of rebellion against the United States. I call on these governors to renounce their statements and resign their offices immediately. Any shots fired against our Homeland Security police by the National Guard or local law enforcement personnel in these states will be considered an act of treason against the United States and we will respond accordingly. I will not stand idly by and allow this republic to be split by rebellion any more than Abraham Lincoln before me.*

The anchor again came on screen. *The Governor of Texas offered some strong words in response to President Armando's attempt to compare himself to Abraham Lincoln.* The newscast again cut away to the Texas Governor. *That is a completely ludicrous statement by an un-American, dictatorship-minded politician who is barely a shadow of the man to whom he is comparing himself. If he's Abraham Lincoln, then I'm Bugs Bunny.*

"The country is falling apart at light speed." Joshua shook his head and switched to a local newscast.

We have more information about a story we first reported yesterday. Authorities have matched a bullet taken from the body found at Lake Fontana yesterday to one taken from the body of a federal agent killed in Chatham County two days after the attack on Raleigh. Both bullets were fired from the same .308 rifle. So far authorities have not been able to track down the owner of the rifle. The case has been turned over to Homeland Security police.

Joshua looked at Rebecca, stunned. He found Bob and described what he'd heard on the newscast.

Bob shook his head and frowned. "It sounds like those were the bullets fired from Martin's rifle. The good news is that the weapon was acquired from a non-traceable source. The bad news is that these Homeland Security police will be nosing around this part of the state now. We need to get rid of the rifle before they stumble onto this camp."

As they were talking Thomas' Suburban pulled up to Joshua's cabin. Jack was in the vehicle with him.

"Hey guys, we're headed to pick up some things and ditch this vehicle," Thomas said. "What are y'all up to?"

After Joshua explained the situation and the need to get rid of Kane's rifle Thomas said, "Man, I think I can help with that. I have a buddy who runs a gun store but also sells 'em off the grid, if you know what I mean. He can get it out of this area. Where's the gun?"

Bob found Kane and they hid the rifle in Thomas' Suburban. As they were doing so Drew came down the mountain and hopped into the back seat. He had a blue backpack over his right shoulder. Bob silently glared at Drew.

As the vehicle headed down the mountain Bob said, "That Thompson boy still worries me."

"He worries me sometimes too," Joshua agreed. "But he has a point that we haven't had to defend or rescue him yet."

Bob sent a puff of cigar smoke in Joshua's direction. "Yet!"

PART III

CHAPTER 9

The full moon pierced the cloudless pre-dawn sky, illuminating the ripples atop the water like a million tiny stars. The mountains rose around the lake like walls on a stone fortress and the waves gently lapped against the canoe. Joshua's breath was visible in the cold, pre-dawn air. The darkness was not defiled by man-made lights, penetrated only by the moon and stars.

Joshua took a deep breath of the cold winter air. He scratched Reagan behind the ears and the now full-grown dog raised his head in response. *I can't believe how much you've grown*, Joshua thought. *For that matter, I can't believe we've been here a year.* Reagan was a best friend to everyone in the camp but was at the same time territorial, fearless, protective and always on the alert for anything that might pose a threat.

Joshua's mind wandered to the events of the past twelve months. So much had happened since they had made the trek to their new home in the mountains. On the one hand, it was hard to believe they had been in the camp a full year. On the other hand, it seemed like they had been here forever. Their farm, his time in the legislature – it all seemed like a distant memory.

The terrorist attacks had left the United States a mere pale reflection of what was once a shining city on a hill. In their aftermath hunger had reached epidemic proportions.

Grocery stores were cut off from their supply chains and few Americans had the knowledge or skills to grow or hunt their own food. This, combined with the abrupt halt in government benefits and the collapse of the nation's financial network, left millions desperate for food and put the nation on the pathway to widespread violence that overwhelmed state and local governments and law enforcement. The death toll from the hunger and violence was nearly as incomprehensible as the number killed in the terrorist attacks.

In Texas, Arizona and New Mexico, Mexican drug cartels had taken advantage of the chaos to seize control of the southern border. In many cases the remnants of local law enforcement and National Guard personnel were split between defending the border and sparring with Homeland Security police.

Street gangs had claimed control of large chunks of territory in urban areas. In Texas and Arizona gangs were battling drug cartels for control of many cities' streets. In the remnants of New York and Chicago the gangs' primary opposition was newly emboldened organized crime.

AIS had made good on its threats to launch ground attacks on American soil. The first came in Philadelphia, where they had seized control of a large chunk of the city, destroyed the Liberty Bell in a mainly symbolic victory and raised an Islamic flag over the city hall. The terrorist group was eventually defeated – not by local law enforcement or the American military, but by a well-organized, well-armed street gang that wanted the city for itself.

AIS had launched attacks in other areas, primarily along the east coast. In Virginia, they surrounded and burned a Methodist church full of worshipers. A Catholic church in Maryland met the same fate. The terrorist organization launched an all-out offensive in New England, where they seized and still maintained control of significant portions of Massachusetts, New Hampshire and Vermont.

Throughout the country AIS-affiliated suicide bombers had blown themselves up in crowded areas. AIS militants and lone-wolf copycat terrorists launched small-arms attacks targeting civilians. No one felt safe anywhere, and the peace and comfort so many Americans had long taken for granted was no more. Local law enforcement was ineffective or nonexistent in many areas. The American people had no one to defend them; they had to defend themselves.

Closer to home, AIS had seized control of the port in Morehead City. The terrorist group had begun an inland move from the port before being met by forces from Camp Lejeune led by U.S. Marine Corps Major General Samuel Cloos. The conflict had not yet reached the mountains, but Joshua's gut still told him it would in due time.

While the teetering nation was reeling from the brutal attacks and lawless chaos on its streets, those living in the camp had gone relatively unscathed in the months following Thomas' kidnapping. Most had learned the lessons of the incident and now willingly followed Bob's security protocols.

Drew was the only person who consistently left the camp without a security escort, and he was remarkably bull-headed on this issue. Though he had not yet caused any known security breaches, his secretive ways and obstinate refusal to follow basic security protocols frustrated Joshua and raised suspicions among other council members.

Most camp residents had become adept hunters, fishermen, farmers or gardeners. Thomas had secured and planted several full-grown apple and peach trees, and they had already produced fruit. Camp residents had grown a variety of vegetables, including squash, tomatoes, lettuce, cabbage, potatoes, collards and corn.

The camp had done such a good job of generating its own food supply that several families still had portions of the non-perishable food they brought with them a year earlier. Drew never hunted or fished, yet curiously never seemed to need food from others.

All in all, morale was high. Caroline still had bouts with depression and some of the kids in the camp still struggled to adapt, but most residents seemed to have adjusted well and developed strong community bonds. Notable exceptions were Drew, always the loner, and Bob and Kane, who kept to themselves when not performing official duties.

Andrea had put her background as an educator to use teaching the children. Despite the wide age range among the children her efforts seemed to be working, and the teenagers were helping the younger kids along. Since there were no textbooks Andrea made do with what she had: Bibles, copies of the U.S. Constitution, *The Boy Scout Handbook*, biographies Joshua had brought along and an assortment of books Thomas had in his cabin.

Jack taught the teenagers how to safely use firearms and other weapons. Thomas educated them on construction and farming, Bob instructed them on military strategy, personal security and physical fitness and Joshua taught them about the U.S. Constitution and the American government. Joshua reflected that the lessons on the American government now seemed like a *history* class, not a civics class. Joshua and Perry gave fishing lessons and Keri taught basic first aid.

Jim was still leading a weekly worship service, which nearly everyone attended. Drew attended but usually seemed disinterested. Bob and Kane were typically present but appeared to be there only out of a sense of duty.

John and Ruth were no longer in Joshua's cabin. They had made a deal with Thomas, who built a small, two-room cabin for them across the clearing from Joshua's. They were sociable at times but tended to keep to themselves.

Jim and his family were still living in Drew's cabin.

Joshua again scratched Reagan on the head. "We've come a long way in a year, haven't we, boy?" Reagan's tail thumped against the canoe in response. Things were going well. Almost *too* well. Joshua's instincts told him more storms were coming.

Joshua closed his eyes and took a deep breath of the cold winter air. The sound of the mountain breeze was relaxing. He had always been drawn to the water; that was one of the reasons he had taken up fishing as a hobby. Now, fishing was more than a hobby – it was a necessity for survival. Still, he enjoyed the peace and quiet of the lake, particularly at this time of morning. While it paled in comparison to the ocean, which he missed, the lake was a quiet place to think, reflect, and connect with God's creation. Reagan seemed to look forward to this time of day alone with Joshua.

Others, particularly Caroline, had stated that they felt like they were prisoners in the camp, but in many ways Joshua felt freer than ever before. He didn't have to go to someone's office and punch a time clock. There were no income taxes, no homeowners' association rules, no zoning laws, no rat race – none of the sources of stress that seemed to burden so many people before the attacks. The more modern and "advanced" society had become, the more stressed people had become. Life here was *simple*.

The organizational structure they had developed in the camp emphasized personal freedom combined with personal responsibility, and it had not been contaminated by the same encroachments on freedom that had clouded government in America in recent decades. *Not bad*, he thought. *So far.*

Two hours, two largemouth bass and three large catfish later Joshua paddled the canoe back to shore. Deep red streaks were beginning to pierce the darkness, but the orange ball had not yet risen from behind the mountain. Reagan stood on the nose of the canoe, silently scanning the shore for potential threats. His ears and tail were perked up and he was as motionless as a hood ornament.

When they reached the shore Joshua quickly cleaned the fish and hid the canoe and fishing equipment. The uphill climb back to camp was now an easy stroll – quite a change from a year ago, when the mountainous inclines took a toll on his cardiovascular system.

As Joshua and Reagan approached the clearing Drew's motorcycle whizzed by, headed toward the road. He was wearing the same blue backpack he wore every time he left the camp. Joshua shook his head. No one knew where Drew went, and he refused to tell anyone where he was going or what he was doing. Joshua had considered having Bob or Kane follow him one day, but decided that might cause more problems than it solved.

Joshua kicked off his boots and left them on the porch. When he entered the cabin he was greeted by the welcome aroma of brewing coffee. Reagan followed him in and curled up in the corner.

"Any luck?" Rebecca asked as she came down the hall.

"Decent." Joshua took the fish out of the bucket and put them on a plate on the counter. "Two bass and three catfish."

"Not bad. Ready for tonight's meeting?"

Tonight the residents would elect their new council. Deep down Joshua wished someone else would step up and assume the chairmanship, but he wasn't holding his breath. "Not yet, but I'll work on that in a bit."

They ate breakfast and Joshua took his Bible and coffee and sank into one of the rocking chairs on the front porch, perching his cup on the rail. Reagan sat on the edge of the steps and kept watch.

A short time later Reagan growled, stood up, and walked down to the bottom of the steps, his tail pointing straight up into the air. When Bob and Kane entered the clearing he relaxed, wagged his tail and returned to the top of the steps. "Good boy," Joshua said. Reagan's tail wagged a bit harder.

Bob and Kane raised the American flag as they had done nearly every day since arriving in the camp. Kane disappeared into the woods and Bob made his way to the porch. "Joshua, do you have a moment?"

"Sure, Bob, what's up?"

"I wanted to give you a heads-up about tonight's meeting. As you are aware, I believe we would be well served to have someone other than Drew on our council. I have spoken with Ruth and she has agreed to accept my nomination. I believe we have enough votes to elect her. Everyone is obviously planning on voting to re-elect you, Thomas, Perry and myself."

Joshua felt his stomach twist. "I've had some concerns about him myself, but I'm not sure this is the way to address them. Drew has a pretty strong relationship with Thomas, and Thomas has been very gracious in letting us use his land."

"I understand your concern, but I feel strongly about this." Bob removed his camouflage cap and scratched his short, gray hair. "I trust you will not tip Drew off."

"I doubt if we'll see him before tonight." Joshua avoided directly answering the question. "I saw him heading out this morning when I was walking back from the lake."

After Bob left Joshua went inside. "I think we may have a problem."

"What kind of problem?" Rebecca asked.

"You know Bob has had it in for Drew from day one. He

just told me that he's talked Ruth into running against him tonight."

"Well, it's an open election. He has the right to nominate her."

"True, but it worries me. Drew seems pretty close with Thomas, and Thomas has been awfully gracious to us. And most of this land *does* still belong to him."

***

As the sun was setting camp residents gathered in the shelter next to Drew's cabin, now referred to as the community center. The community center had detachable walls that protected those inside from the cold wind but which could be removed during warmer weather. People huddled near the fire pit as they waited for the meeting to start.

Seven o'clock rolled around and Joshua called the meeting to order. Jim offered an invocation. The sound of Drew's motorcycle grew louder as the prayer commenced, and he arrived at the community center just as Jim said "amen." He was now often the last to arrive – a marked change from his behavior before the attacks, when he was always one of the first to arrive at any event. Drew used the mirror on his motorcycle to comb his hair before dismounting. As Jack led the Pledge of Allegiance Joshua wondered whether the nation whose flag they were saluting really still existed.

"Folks, we all know why we're here." Joshua ascended onto the massive stump that Thomas had converted into a makeshift dais. "Our main business tonight is the election of our council for the next year. Every adult over the age of 18 who resides in the camp has one vote. Tommy, that means you get to vote this year!" Everyone gave Tommy a round of applause.

"If there are more than five candidates voting will be by secret ballot," Joshua continued. "The top five vote getters will be elected. Unless there are questions, the floor is now open for nominations."

Perry raised his hand and said, "I nominate Joshua Winston."

"I had a feeling that was coming," Joshua chuckled.

Thomas nominated Drew, Rebecca nominated Perry, Drew nominated Thomas and Chuck nominated Bob.

"We have nominations for Bob Kendall, Thomas Page, Drew Thompson, Perry Edwards and me," Joshua said.

Bob raised his hand. "Mr. Chairman, I nominate Ruth Moore."

Drew's head snapped around in Bob's direction. Bob glared back at him with a condescending grin.

"Are there any further nominations?" Joshua asked.

After a few moments of awkward silence Jack moved to close nominations. The motion carried.

"We have six nominees for five council spots," Joshua said. "That means we will have an election by secret ballot and the top five vote-getters will be elected." Rebecca was furiously tearing sheets of paper into small strips. "Rebecca is in the process of making ballots. I will appoint Jim, Chuck and Andrea to serve as tellers. Everyone must sign in to get their ballot. After all of the ballots have been cast the tellers will count the votes."

The tellers made their way to a table and everyone lined up to cast their votes. Drew was fidgeting nervously and Bob had a confident smirk on his face.

As the first people received their ballots Thomas stood up. "Joshua, can I say something?"

"Sure, Thomas, what is it?"

Thomas removed the toothpick from his mouth and twisted it between his fingers. "Man, I've never been one for serving on boards and committees and stuff like that. I agreed to be on the council last year because y'all seemed to really want me there. You folks seem like you've got it pretty well under control, and I don't need to be on the council. I'd like to withdraw my name."

Bob's confident grin immediately turned into a scowl. "Son of a..." he muttered out loud before catching himself.

Joshua was also caught off guard. "I, um... Thomas is withdrawing from the race. That leaves us with five candidates for five seats."

"Man, I'd like to make a motion that we elect those five candidates to the council for next year," Thomas said. Kim seconded the motion.

"We have a motion and a second," Joshua said. "Is there any discussion?"

There was no discussion so Joshua called for a vote. There was a loud chorus of "ayes." When he asked if there were any opposed a lone voice rang out: Bob's.

"Ruth, welcome to the council," Joshua said. "You've got a lot to offer and I look forward to working with you. Thomas, thank you for your service during the past year. That concludes our business at this meeting. Our governing rules state that the council is to elect a chair immediately following this meeting, so I will now call the council meeting to order. Those of you who are not on the council are welcome to stay, but I certainly understand if you have other things to do."

Joshua began the council meeting. "It has been a tremendous honor and a great responsibility to serve as your chair for the past year. We've come a long way, and I greatly appreciate the trust you've placed in me. With that said, if someone else is interested in serving as chair, I would gladly step aside." He noticed Rebecca cock an eyebrow.

Perry immediately interjected, "Joshua, I think you need to be our chair for at least another year."

"I realize I sprung this on you guys," Joshua said. "If you want to sleep on it, I will accept a motion to table the chair vote for one week."

"I stand by my statement that you need to be our chair again, but if you want us to think it over I'll make the motion to table this for a week," Perry said. Ruth seconded the motion, which passed unanimously.

Bob stormed over to Joshua immediately following the meeting, red-faced. "You tipped Drew and Thomas off, didn't you?"

"No, I did not." Joshua shook his head. "I was as surprised by his withdrawal as anyone."

"I'm not sure I buy it," Bob said.

Drew walked up as Bob was speaking. "Bob, predicting that you would nominate someone to get rid of me was so easy it was pathetic. You may know military tactics, but I know *political* strategy, and I saw your move coming a mile away. I didn't know it would be Ruth, but I knew you would talk *someone* into it. *No one* had to tip me off."

Bob glared at Drew but did not speak.

"Drew, are you saying you *asked* Thomas to step aside?" Joshua inquired.

"No," Drew said. "I did talk with him about the fact that I felt like Bob would try to get rid of me, and he *volunteered* to step aside. He said that serving on the council just wasn't his thing and that he trusted us to take care of things." Drew smiled like a victorious warrior. "Oh, by the way, Bob, that was *six weeks ago*." He pointed at Bob's chest. "Your move was all too easy to predict." He rubbed his nose with his handkerchief, then turned and strutted away.

"Joshua, I apologize for implying that you tipped them off," Bob said. "I was just surprised and upset by what happened."

"Don't worry about it," Joshua said. "I've been on the losing side of some elections and have reacted the same way myself. Consider it water under the bridge."

As soon as Bob left Drew made his way back to Joshua. "I gather from Bob's statement that you had advance knowledge that he was trying to get rid of me?"

"He told me about it this morning." Joshua pursed his lips. "That's when I found out, and I didn't see you until the meeting started tonight."

"Hmm. That's fine." Drew said. "On a different note, if you're serious about wanting someone else to step in as chairman, what would you think about me in that role?"

Joshua froze. "Umm... Let me sleep on it. This has been a somewhat tumultuous meeting and I want to process everything. If you'd like I can also talk with the other council members and see what they think."

"Sure thing," Drew said. "Be sure to bounce it off of Bob and let me know what he says."

After a few minutes Joshua and Rebecca began walking back down the hill toward their cabin. "I think we've got another problem."

"What is it this time?" she asked.

"Well, Bob accused me of tipping off Drew and Thomas about his plan to knock Drew off of the council, which I did not. And then Drew seemed upset that I knew about Bob's plan ahead of time and didn't tell him, even though I didn't know until this morning."

"Well, you can't please everybody all of the time," she assured him. "That's something you've said for as long as I've known you."

"True. But now Drew wants to be the chair if I decide not to do it again. I just don't think that will fly."

"Probably not," she said. "On that note, I wish you'd told me you were thinking about stepping back as chair before you announced it to everyone else."

"Sorry about that." Joshua pursed his lips. "But I know you've always wanted me to step back from politics and leadership roles."

Rebecca grabbed his arm and stopped him in his tracks. She looked into his eyes with a deep, penetrating gaze. "Yes, I have wanted that. I never liked everything that goes along with politics, all of the public appearances and glad-handing. But this isn't about politics. It's about whether or not we *survive*."

Joshua looked down for a moment, then into her brown eyes. "I'm sorry I didn't mention it to you. I thought it's what you'd want."

"You should know better than to think you can read my mind by now. If you'd asked me, I would've told you not to make that announcement. I'm not sure there's anyone else here I trust in that job."

"Well, the cat's out of the bag now," Joshua said.

"So what are you going to do?"

"I don't know yet. I need to talk to others on the council."

When they opened the door Reagan almost knocked them over. "I think he needed to go out," Joshua observed.

Joshua sat down, leaned back and closed his eyes. Rebecca poured two glasses of water and sat beside him on the couch. He sat motionless for what seemed like an eternity.

After a while she broke the silence. "What's on your mind?"

Joshua opened his eyes. "Just thinking about everything that happened today. This morning I would've bragged how well everyone had adapted and how smoothly everything seemed to be going in the camp. Tonight it seems like things are suddenly going to hell in a hand basket. There is a lot of tension, and we are too small to be divided like this. And I have to admit that it doesn't sit well with me that people who should *know* better would think I wouldn't shoot straight with them."

Rebecca put her hand on his knee. "You've always said leadership is a tough business that requires a thick skin. You can't get hung up on what others think. Their reactions say more about *them* than anyone else."

"I guess so," Joshua said. "I just didn't expect all of this today."

***

"You said you had something you wanted to discuss." Perry's breath was visible against the backdrop of the cold, pre-dawn winter air, and the breeze gently rippled across the lake. "What's on your mind?"

"The council." Joshua re-baited his hook and dropped it back into the water. "That's why I wanted to talk to you out here, where we can have some privacy. You know I'd like to step back as chair, and I know you want me to stay in the position. One of my goals when I decided not to run for the legislature was to spend more time with Rebecca. Now here I am, stuck in another political role."

"That's true from a certain point of view, but these are not ordinary times," Perry said. "You couldn't have predicted all of this."

"After last night's meeting another council member approached me and said they would be interested in the chairmanship if I stepped back."

"Who was it?"

"Drew."

"Oh, *hell no!*"

"Well now, how do you *really* feel?" Joshua chuckled. *Perry NEVER uses profanity!* "I have a feeling others will have the same reaction."

"I would vote for ANY of the other council members over him," Perry said. "Even Bob... sometimes he scares me, but I'd take him over Drew."

"I have a feeling Bob will say the same thing," Joshua said. "And given that he was able to talk Ruth into running against Drew, I think she might go along with him."

"Joshua, it *has* to be you. I'm not cut out for the job, and neither is anyone else on this council. *You* brought us here. You are a natural leader. The people here trust you. *They are here because of you.*"

Joshua's brow furrowed. "I see where you're coming from, but I'm not so sure about that trust thing."

"Seriously?" Perry blurted out. "What in the world are you talking about? Of course they trust you!"

"Well, Bob accused me of tipping off Drew and Thomas about his plan, which I didn't, and then Drew was upset that I knew about Bob's plan and *didn't* tip him off."

"Well, the fact that both Bob and Drew were upset probably proves that you did the right thing. That's why it *must* be you."

"We'll see. I'm not going to make an immediate decision."

"It's amazing that we're even here talking about this," Perry reflected. "A year ago we were at your farmhouse getting ready to watch the State of the Union, with so much hope for a new direction under President Wagner. So much has changed so quickly."

The conversation was interrupted by a strong tug on Perry's fishing pole. He hauled in a big trout. "This will make a nice meal!"

A couple of hours later they made their way back to shore as the sun overcame the darkness and pierced the dense fog that hovered over the lake. Reagan lay flat in the bottom of the canoe, shielding himself from the cold wind.

Joshua felt his shoulders clench up when Rebecca opened the door. Her eyes were red and tears were running down her cheeks. "What's wrong?" he asked.

"Something *terrible* has happened," she answered morbidly.

Caroline emerged from behind the door, tears streaming

down her cheeks.

"What's wrong?" Perry pressed.

"I don't even know where to begin," Rebecca stammered.

"Rebecca, *what's WRONG?*" Joshua stepped toward her.

"Nothing, we're just cutting some very potent onions," she said with a laugh. "But we had you going for a minute."

Joshua looked at her and then Perry, rolling his eyes. "That you did," he said with a forced chuckle. "You scared me to death. I owe you one."

Joshua spread the morning's catch out on a tray beside the sink. Three trout, one very large catfish and several bass.

***

Joshua approached Bob, who was cleaning some squirrels in the woods near the lake.

"Bob, I wanted to talk with you about the council," Joshua said. "As I've told you before, my main goal in life for the past couple of years has been to spend more time with my wife. Even though something like being the chairman of our council is nowhere near as time consuming as serving in the legislature, it's still a burden. That's why I said last night that I would be willing to step back from the chair position."

"What are your plans?" Bob puffed on his cigar.

"I'm not sure yet. I did have someone express interest in serving as chair if I step back, and I know *exactly* how you'll react when I tell you who it is."

"Then it must be that Thompson boy," Bob interjected.

"Yep."

"Over my dead body," Bob said. "I will seek the chairmanship myself before I will allow that weasel to have it."

"I had a feeling you'd say something along those lines."

They stood in silence as Bob continued cleaning the squirrels. After a few minutes Bob broke the silence. "I hope you will serve again, Joshua."

"Does that mean you'd support me if I decide to do so?"

"Affirmative."

***

Later that morning Joshua went out to make his rounds. It had been his practice to visit every residence in the camp nearly every day since they had moved here, if only for a moment or two. As the leader he felt it was important to stay connected with everyone, yet it felt burdensome on occasion. Today he felt it was particularly important given the newfound tensions within the camp.

His first stop was John and Ruth's new cabin, the only one that had been built since they arrived. Their cabin was smaller than Joshua's. It had one bedroom, a second room

---

that John used as a study, a kitchen, one bathroom and a small living area. The exterior was dark brown wood, similar to Joshua's cabin.

Joshua shared his thoughts with them as he had done with Perry and Bob. Ruth's reaction was similar: she would not vote for Drew, but encouraged Joshua to serve another year. Eventually he made his way up the mountain to Thomas' cabin. Thomas was outside repairing the fencing on his chicken coop.

"Hey man, what's up?" Thomas twisted the toothpick between his lips as he greeted Joshua.

"Just making the rounds," Joshua said. "Pretty good morning fishing. Three trout, one big catfish, and several bass."

"That's cool, man. Let me know when you're having the fish fry," Thomas said. "Sure was an interesting meeting last night."

"That it was. I don't like the tension and infighting we saw."

"Man, that's why I love having my cabin up here, away from everybody. Don't need the drama. That Bob fella sure does have it in for Drew."

"That's putting it mildly," Joshua said. "This kind of stuff is why I wouldn't mind stepping away as chairman. That drama does get to be a headache."

271

"Do it, man," Thomas said. "Just live your life. Heck, I'm not even sure we need all this structure anyway."

"I do think we need *some* structure. None of us were prepared to have to live like this. But I agree with you that we don't need too much."

"Man, I think they would find a way to make it work if you stepped back. People will find a way to get by. Take some time and try to enjoy your life."

"Drew said he'd be interested in taking over as chair if I step down."

"I think he'd do great, man," Thomas said. "I'd vote for him if I was still on council."

"I've talked with the other council members and he just doesn't have the votes," Joshua explained. "They *all* say they will vote for someone other than him, and Bob said he would run before he would let Drew have it."

"Man, that's a shame. Drew's a good guy. I like him a lot. And that Bob guy scares me. I don't want him in charge of any more of my property than he already is."

"I had a feeling you'd say that. And most of it *is* still your property."

"Why don't people like Drew?"

"Well, I personally like him, but I have to admit there are moments I don't trust him," Joshua said. "He is so secretive, and the fact that he disappears, won't tell anyone where he's going and refuses to follow any of our security protocols worries me. Bob just doesn't like him, and I think that with some of the others it's a trust issue. He just hasn't connected with people."

"Man, that's a shame," Thomas said, shaking his head. "They should try to get to know him. He's a good fellow."

***

Jim was Joshua's fishing partner the next morning. He had been a mentor to Joshua even before they made the trip to the mountain camp, and Joshua needed his insight now more than ever. Reagan wagged his tail and pawed at Jim's knee, paying more attention to him than Joshua.

"It is beautiful out here," Jim observed. "Great place to get away."

"I love this time of day," Joshua agreed. "It's quiet and peaceful, and you are right, it's a beautiful corner of God's creation."

"So what's on your mind? You said you wanted to talk."

"I'd like your take on how things are going in the camp and what I should do."

Joshua described his concern about the recent infighting in the camp and the reactions he had received from others. "In a nutshell, Bob said he'd run for chair before he'd let Drew have it. I think he'd have the votes to win. But Thomas was pretty emphatic that he doesn't want

273

Bob to have any more control over his land than he already has. I just don't like where this is headed."

"What are your reasons for not wanting to serve as chair again?" Jim prodded.

Joshua outlined the same reasoning he had shared with Perry.

"I can understand that, and I had a feeling that's what you'd say," Jim said. "But this is a different time. We live in a different world than the one in which you made plans to step back from leadership roles. Don't forget that *you* are the person who organized this group and led us all here. I believe God put you here, and we're better off for it."

Joshua shook his head and looked down. "I'm just *tired.*"

"Then you need to make more time for yourself," Jim admonished. "Don't push yourself so hard. Don't stress yourself out over everything, especially things you can't control." Jim paused and leaned forward, scratching Reagan's ears. "But you need to take more time for yourself *within the context of being our leader.*"

"Easier said than done. A big part of me feels like the only way I'll be able to do that is to step away from the chairmanship. I wanted to bring everyone here to give us a chance to survive, but I didn't sign up for all of this drama or to babysit people. It's just frustrating."

"I understand that sentiment," Jim said. "But you have to remember that almost everyone in the camp came here with the assumption that *you* would be the leader. That's one of the reasons they came. Heck, it's one of the reasons *I* came. And, to be honest, if you step back as chair now you'll probably have to step back in later to clean up the mess."

Joshua sighed and nodded. "That's probably true."

"Only you can decide what you have to do," Jim said. "Talk it over with Rebecca, pray about it and you'll know what the right move is. Speaking of Rebecca, what does she think?"

Joshua chuckled sarcastically. "Well, she was a bit perturbed that I announced that I was thinking about stepping back before I mentioned it to her."

Jim smirked and shook his head. "Didn't you learn *anything* in our pre-marital counseling sessions?"

"Apparently not."

"Well, if you do stay on, spend some time developing other leaders to help carry the load. And set some personal boundaries to make sure you take care of yourself."

"I'm worried that we'll keep having internal bickering no matter what I decide," Joshua lamented. "Bob and Drew are both council members, and they just flat despise each other."

"You can't control them," Jim said. "But what you just said should factor into your thinking about whether *you* should be the chair instead of either one of them."

"Good points, as always," Joshua said. "I appreciate your advice and insight. I'll talk with Rebecca and we'll pray about it."

***

Benjamin Leibowitz sat alone in one of the soft leather chairs at the oak conference table. A Presidential seal adorned the wall behind the high-back chair at the head of the table and an American flag stood at its right. Several pictures of President Armando dominated the wall space.

Benjamin pondered the past year's turn of events. Things had played out quite differently than he envisioned when joining President Wagner's administration a year earlier. One of his first assignments had been to accompany the designated survivor, then Secretary of Homeland Security Nelson Armando, on the night of President Wagner's first State of the Union address. *That's the only reason I'm alive today,* he thought. *If I had been given a different assignment, I would've been killed in the attack on Washington.* With Armando's ascension to the presidency, Benjamin's entry-level job had transformed into a de facto cabinet position in the new president's administration.

"Good morning, Benjamin." Anthony Russo, who spoke with a thick New York accent, was the second to arrive.

Anthony, a top Homeland Security staffer, was a holdover from the previous administration. He was followed by Richard Webb, an aide to President Wagner who had been named the White House Liaison to the Department of Homeland Security. Others filed in until all but three of the twenty seats were full.

Everyone rose as President Armando entered the room, flanked by four Secret Service agents and his two top lieutenants, Abdar Al-Haziz and Adilah Hassan. Benjamin felt a spark of anger flow through him at the mere sight of Abdar and Adilah. He gripped his pen tightly, hoping to conceal his disdain for them. Armando seated himself at the head of the table. Abdar and Adilah took seats on either side of him and the Secret Service Agents stood behind him.

"Take your seats," Armando said in his heavy New York accent. "We have a lot to cover. What's first on the list?"

Abdar spoke with a strong middle-eastern accent. "We are monitoring communications and identifying people supportive of the governors who have challenged our security efforts."

"What about the rogue general in North Carolina?" Armando asked.

"Major General Cloos." Abdar nodded. "Our top commanders have told him to stand down." Benjamin clenched his teeth as Abdar spoke.

"Mr. President," Richard interjected. "Forgive me, but

what has Major General Cloos done that deserves a reprimand?"

"He disobeyed a direct order to stand down," Abdar retorted.

"You mean he was ordered to leave American citizens defenseless and let the terrorists in Morehead City have their way?" Richard asked.

"The bottom line is that he disobeyed a direct order," Abdar said. "We cannot and will not tolerate this type of insubordination." Benjamin tightly clenched his fist below the conference table.

"Mr. President, I am greatly concerned," Richard said. "Some in this administration seem to place a greater priority on controlling American citizens than protecting them from terrorists."

"I resent the implication!" Abdar slammed his fist on the table. Benjamin briefly made eye contact with Anthony, who was watching the back-and-forth with his eyebrow cocked.

"Then prove me wrong!" Richard raised his voice. "AIS controls large chunks of land in the northeast and this government has made *no* visible move to confront them. On top of that we are actually discussing reprimanding an officer who took action against the terrorist invaders. Unbelievable!"

Abdar shot up out of his seat and waved his fist. "Major

General Cloos disobeyed a direct order!"

"An order that should never have been--"

"That's enough for today," Armando interrupted. "This meeting is adjourned. We will reconvene tomorrow."

Armando left the room. Abdar stormed out behind him, glaring at Richard as he exited, followed by Adilah. Richard slammed his binder into his briefcase and stomped out. *I guess I'm not the only one who sees Abdar for what he is,* Benjamin thought as he walked out with Anthony.

"That was interesting," Anthony whispered. "Richard raises some good points."

Benjamin was non-committal. "His comments were certainly thought-provoking."

"I hope he can get the President's ear," Anthony added.

"We shall see." Benjamin nodded, looked at his watch and quickly walked away.

***

AIS has launched an attack in western North Carolina.

Joshua and Rebecca immediately stopped what they were doing, fixated on the television.

AIS militants have surfaced in the North Carolina mountain town of Asheville. The terrorists have claimed control of much of the city's downtown area where they seized a church, beheaded the pastor and hung his head on a fencepost in front of the church. The AIS flag now flies over the church and the city hall. White-hot rage coursed through Joshua's veins like bubbling magma. The anchor continued: *These terrorists are relentless and seem determined to show that they can attack anywhere. Numerous vehicles filled with AIS militants were seen leaving Asheville today.*

"That's too close to home." Joshua shook his head.

"Asheville is still close to 100 miles away," Rebecca reassured him.

"*Still* way too close to home," Joshua frowned.

The anchor continued: *Meanwhile, President Armando seems more focused on exerting control over states that are bucking federal authority than defending America against the AIS militants. The president has made no effort to reconstitute Congress, which was decimated by last year's attack on the State of the Union. President Armando's tactics, combined with his ongoing use of Homeland Security police and military personnel in American streets, continue to draw strong rebukes from a number of governors.*

The screen broke away to a shot of several governors standing together at an undisclosed location. The Governor of Texas was speaking, flanked by governors from South Carolina, Tennessee, Georgia, Montana, Ohio, Louisiana, Alabama, Mississippi, Arkansas and Oklahoma.

As we have said individually on multiple occasions, we

do not recognize the right of so-called Homeland Security police to patrol and control streets in our states, the Texas Governor said. *Now, we stand TOGETHER, united, to make that same statement in an unmistakable way. We do not recognize Nelson Armando's rogue regime. Armando is blatantly ignoring our Constitution and appears bent on manipulating this crisis to turn America into his own dictatorship. Nelson Armando – I will not call him 'President' -- has made no effort to reconstitute Congress, and he seems more focused on fighting fellow Americans than fighting the terrorists who did this to us. Make no mistake. We will not stand idly by and allow these agents to oppress our citizens. Our National Guard and local law enforcement stand ready to defend the people of our states. Every governor here has committed to pardon any citizen in our states who is accused of a crime for defending his or her freedom – or that of his neighbors – against this federal intrusion, which is nothing more than a step toward tyranny.*

The anchor came back on screen. *Several other governors have publicly said that they stand will stand with Texas, including the governors of Nebraska, Arizona, Iowa, Wyoming, Indiana, North Dakota and South Dakota. However, President Armando appears to be unyielding.*

Joshua turned off the television. "I thought Armando was bad news from day one, and he's worse than I ever imagined." He shook his head and changed the subject. "By the way, I've talked to everyone on the council. After lunch

I'm going to take Reagan and go up on the trail and just spend some quiet time thinking."

"It's going to be cold up there." She peeked out the window at the light snow falling.

"I'll be fine," Joshua assured her. "I'll put on plenty of warm clothes."

***

Joshua donned his camouflage winter weather hunting suit, green ski mask and insulated hunting cap with earmuffs and zipped the suit up to his chin.

"That should keep you warm, but camouflage won't do much good against the white backdrop of the snow." Rebecca chuckled. "You'll stick out like a sore thumb."

"Then it's a good thing bears hibernate in winter." Joshua gave her a quick kiss and went out into the cold. Reagan followed without hesitation and seemed energized by the brisk winter air. The intensifying snowfall and cold wind stabbed at Joshua's face as they made their way up the trail.

"Maybe this wasn't such a good idea, boy." Reagan's tail wagged when Joshua spoke, but he remained unfazed by the cold.

The swirling snow pelted Joshua as they climbed the trail. They eventually reached their destination: an area in a brief downhill climb shielded from the wind by rocks on all sides and where the snowfall was impeded by overhead trees. This was the perfect place – quiet and secluded.

Joshua situated himself on a rock and removed his Bible, journal and pen from his backpack. Reagan explored the immediate area but never wandered out of sight. Joshua's mind drifted into deep thought and he lost track of time, staring off into space. He reflected on the past year. He and Rebecca had abandoned their farm and he had led a group of people to this remote mountain camp. They had willingly followed him. They had *trusted* him. Somehow, everyone made it here in one piece. A year later the camp remained intact, and everyone was alive and healthy. *Not bad.* Things weren't so good outside of the camp. The nation he loved was a pathetic shadow of its former self. Joshua sighed. He had so looked forward to spending time with Rebecca on their farm, just the two of them, away from all of the pressures associated with leadership and politics. But the events of the past year had dictated otherwise. Here he was, again thrust into a leadership role, this time against his will. He took a deep breath and closed his eyes for what felt like an eternity.

Suddenly a light bulb went off in his head and he began scribbling furiously in the journal. Half an hour later he closed the journal and Bible. "Come on, boy." Joshua put the journal and Bible into his backpack. "Let's head down."

Reagan led the way as they pushed through the blowing snow. They wound down several curves to an area where the trail passed through a wide clearing. Joshua felt his stomach turn as Reagan suddenly stopped and began growling. The dog's ears perked up and his tail pointed straight up into the air. Joshua drew his pistol and got down on one knee behind a small, barren tree. "What is it, boy?" he whispered. *This tree doesn't offer much cover,* he thought.

Reagan took several steps forward, tail straight as an arrow, still growling. Joshua's heart pounded as he quietly removed his backpack, took out a small telescope and scanned the open space in front of them and the mountainside behind it. He saw nothing.

After a few minutes Reagan abruptly turned and came to Joshua. He looked back at the horizon several times, his growl fading into a low moan. Joshua's heart raced as he scratched Reagan's head. "What was it, boy?" Reagan turned and again pointed, emitting a faint growl.

"Let's stay here for a bit."

Reagan sat beside him. Joshua waited for a few minutes before moving across the clearing, staying low as he progressed.

"Rebecca was right that this camouflage doesn't help against a white backdrop," Joshua mumbled to himself, his heart racing. "I need a white winter suit."

Joshua kept his 9mm drawn the whole time. After what seemed like an eternity they reached the other side of the

long clearing and entered a thickly wooded part of the trail.
After rounding a curve Joshua went about fifteen feet up
the side of the mountain and hid behind a rock. "Let's wait
here and see if anyone or anything follows us." His heart
pounded as his right hand still gripped his Beretta. He
pressed his left hand against Reagan's neck, hoping the
touch would keep the curious canine from compromising
their position.

Joshua waited. The time moved like cold molasses, but
his gut told him he should wait and see if anything out of
the ordinary happened. Nothing did. After some time he
again began making his way down the trail. Reagan kept an
eye out ahead of them and Joshua kept checking the trail
behind them. Again, nothing. Joshua's heart was still
pounding, but Reagan appeared completely relaxed. *How
can you go from being on high alert to completely calm so
quickly?*

When they reached the edge of the camp Joshua entered
the inside of the hedgerow. He looked back one final time
before moving down the dark passageway. *Someone or
something was watching us back there.*

The inside of the pitch-black passageway was dank and
musky. Joshua reached out into the darkness. *So this is
what it feels like to be blind.* The ground squished beneath
his feet as leaves and branches brushed across his face and
torso. He stumbled forward, nearly falling. *What did I just
trip over?* He reached out into the darkness with his left

hand, trying to feel anything that might guide his steps. He heard something moving up ahead. *I sure hope that's Reagan.* SMACK! Joshua felt twigs and branches jab into his face and arms. *I guess there's a sharp turn here.*

A voice penetrated the darkness. "Who goes there?"

"Who is that?" Joshua answered with a question of his own.

"Joshua? It's Bob. What are you doing in here?"

Joshua described what had happened on the trail. "I just had an uneasy feeling about it. I felt like we were being watched, but I didn't see anyone or anything."

"Martin and I will keep an eye out."

Bob led them to an exit near Drew's cabin. Joshua met Jim as he entered the clearing.

"You look like an Eskimo," Jim said. "Where have you been?"

"I went up the trail to clear my head and collect my thoughts about what I should do in regard to the chairmanship. After our conversation I thought getting away from the camp to think would be helpful."

Jim smiled. "Did you come to a resolution?"

"I think so, but I still want to sleep on it," Joshua answered. "Either way, I need to spend more time away from the camp where I can think with a clear head."

"That would be good for you." Jim nodded.

Joshua decided not to tell him about the incident on the trail, feeling it was better not to alarm anyone else – especially since he was not sure what exactly had happened up there. They parted and Joshua made his way back to the cabin, where Rebecca greeted him with a hot cup of coffee.

"I thought you could use this after being out in the cold for so long."

Joshua removed several of his outer layers of clothing. Reagan had beaten him to the fireplace and was curled up, already sound asleep.

"How did it go?" she asked.

"Went well. I think I know what I'm going to do."

"And?"

"I don't see any other choice but to serve again." He shook his head, grabbed Rebecca's hands and looked into her eyes. "I am SO sorry that our plans for a quiet life together fell apart. I *really* did want to spend this time with just you and me."

She smacked him on the leg. "We already covered this, Josh. We really don't have a choice."

***

Abdar spoke as he took his seat beside President Armando at the boardroom table. "I have some sad news.

We have learned that Richard Webb was killed last night. It appears he was assassinated by AIS terrorists."

Benjamin felt a wave of tension surge throughout his body, struggling to conceal his reaction. *AIS didn't do this,* he thought. *This was an inside job.* He noticed the look of utter horror on Anthony's face. *Russo agrees. This happened because Richard dared to challenge Abdar in the last meeting.*

President Armando lowered his head. "This is terrible news. Please join me in a moment of silence for our fallen comrade, Richard Webb."

Benjamin surveyed the room through squinted eyes. Anthony's face still conveyed utter shock. President Armando seemed genuinely saddened. Abdar and Adilah were stone-faced.

"Thank you." Armando opened his eyes. "Abdar, prepare a press statement about Richard's death."

Anthony raised his hand. "Mr. President, I believe any statement we make should include a pledge to bring Richard's killers to justice. We cannot let this go unanswered."

"Leave the press statement to me," Abdar interjected.

"With all due respect, Abdar, I wasn't talking to you. I was speaking to the President."

"And I speak *for* the President."

"Not until *he* tells me you do." Anthony said. "Mr. President, if AIS can kill a member of your inner circle without fear of retaliation, why should they fear coming after *you*?"

"You let me worry about that!" Abdar slammed his fist on the table.

This is getting out of hand, Benjamin thought. *Anthony is going to find himself in the same cemetery as Richard.* He raised his hand. "Mr. President, May I speak?"

"Go ahead, Leibowitz," Armando said.

"While I respect the chain of command and the fact that you have delegated press work to Abdar, I do share Anthony's concern that AIS will take a direct shot at you," Benjamin calmly stated. "I don't think any of us – Abdar, Adilah, Anthony or me – want that to happen. We've also read the reports of AIS gaining a foothold in the North Carolina mountains, and they still control the port at Morehead City. At some point citizens are going to wonder why we're not moving to stop AIS. If the people are going to have confidence in this administration then we have to show them we are doing *something*." Benjamin noticed Adilah whispering something to Abdar while he was speaking.

"You make good points, Leibowitz," Armando said.

"Mr. President, what do you want to do?" Anthony asked.

"I have a man on the ground in western North Carolina who is working to get things under control," Abdar interjected. "And I have a plan to gain control of the Morehead City situation."

"Mr. President, what do *YOU* want to do?" Anthony again asked.

Armando sat silent for a moment, staring off into space. "I don't know."

***

The following Tuesday Joshua called the camp meeting to order. "Folks, I've done a lot of soul-searching since last week's meeting. I've met with many of you this week and heard your insights. In particular, Jim pointed out that many of you – him included – came here with the assumption and understanding that I would be in a leadership role. He didn't say it, but the implied message is that I would be letting you down if I just stepped away from the chairmanship at this point. That is the *last* thing I intend to do. With that said, I will remain as chair for this year if that is what the council desires."

Applause rang out from the crowd.

"Before we move into the council meeting and elect a chairman, there are a few things that I think need to be said," he continued. "We're a small group, and we have done remarkably well over the past year. Things have gone downhill at a dramatic pace all over the country, but we have been relatively unscathed. We're virtually self-sufficient. Unfortunately, I worry that we have become complacent. We've done well when we have been united, when we have put our differences aside and worked toward a common goal: *survival*. This week, I've seen some dangerous cracks in our unity. We have seen infighting, and that infighting worries me. It's okay to disagree -- in fact, it's healthy *if done properly* -- but at the end of the day we must stick together if we are going to survive. We must not let honest disagreements become personal. We are too small and too vulnerable to be divided among ourselves. We must be united, and that unity has to start with those of us who are on the council. If you elect me as your chair again, this is something I will push every day."

Another round of applause rose from the crowd.

"With that said, let's move into the council meeting," Joshua said. Perry immediately nominated Joshua for chair and Bob seconded. Drew moved to close nominations and elect Joshua. The motion carried unanimously.

"Thank you for your trust," Joshua said. "We have a good thing going here. We just have to keep it going, and that will require all of us working together."

***

Attired in a green and khaki service uniform, Major General Cloos leaned back in his high-back leather chair and kicked his feet up on the expansive cherry desk, which was flanked by an American flag and a U.S. Marine Corps flag. The desktop was clear apart from a bankers' lamp, notepad and silver pen. "Where do we stand, Major?"

"Sir, all of the terrorists have retreated to the port and we have them contained there," Major Michael Chinn said. "We have established a blockade to prevent them from escaping by boat."

Cloos brushed his fingers along his chiseled chin, which was adorned by a dark five o'clock shadow. "Well done, Major. What is our timeline for retaking the port and eliminating the terrorists?"

"We--"

A young woman in uniform stuck her head in the doorway. "Major General, I'm sorry to interrupt, but you have a video conference call coming in from Abdar Al-Haziz."

Cloos pursed his lips. "Who the hell is that?"

"President Armando's acting chief of staff."

Cloos let out an audible grunt. "Put him through."

The video screen on the back wall of Cloos' office flared to life. Abdar appeared on screen along with President Armando, a young woman and two men.

"Major General Cloos," Abdar began the conversation.

"You've got him," Cloos responded gruffly.

"I am joined by President Armando, Adilah Hassan, Anthony Russo and Benjamin Leibowitz. The President and our entire team are gravely concerned by your refusal to follow our direct order to stand down."

"Can you tell me why in the hell you would want to let these foreign invaders push inland on American soil without fighting back?" Cloos cocked his eyebrow.

"It is not your place to question our strategy!" Abdar raised his voice.

"What strategy?"

"You are out of line, Major General!"

"Abdar, or whatever the hell your name is, I don't report to you and don't give a rip what you think," Cloos growled. "Mr. President, who is calling the shots? I see no evidence of a strategy and no indication that your administration has any plan whatsoever to purge these terrorists from American soil."

President Armando remained silent. Abdar stood up and waved his fist at the camera. "Who do you think you are?"

"I am a Major General in the United States Marine Corps, and I took an oath to support and defend the Constitution of the United States against all enemies, foreign or domestic. I just never thought the 'domestic' part of that oath would seem so relevant. Mr. President, it's apparent you have nothing to say. Call me when you do."

Major General Cloos motioned for his team to kill the video connection. As the screen went blank he leaned back in his chair and rubbed his fingers across his face, his brow furrowed. "Colonel Brookhart, put all defenses on high alert. Be on the lookout for a drone attack. Also tell our IT staff to increase our security against intrusions from anyone outside of this base, including those who are affiliated with the U.S. Government. Tell them to block any intrusions or cyber-attacks and trace the source."

"Will do, sir," Colonel Kenneth Brookhart responded. "But do you *really* think President Armando would authorize an attack against his own military?"

Cloos clenched his teeth. "Better safe than sorry. And I'm not sure Armando has control of his own government."

***

Benjamin unlocked the door to his small apartment in Virginia Beach, the city which had served as the Armando administration's base of operations since the attack on Washington a year earlier. As he did every night, Benjamin drew his pistol and went room-to-room searching for intruders or other signs that something might be awry. Terrorists might want him dead because of his job with the Armando administration. Or because of his Jewish heritage. Or someone might simply break in looking for food, which was nowhere to be found in the now-empty stores in and around the Hampton Roads area. So far, he had not encountered problems. *So far.*

Benjamin opened his refrigerator and surveyed the full supply of milk, food and other conveniences. They were conveniences to him, but they were necessities that many on the outside would kill for. Benjamin felt a pang of guilt. He only had a full refrigerator because he worked for the President of the United States.

***

Joshua sipped his coffee as the TV flared to life. The newscaster offered a sobering report. *AIS appears to have once again struck at the heart of the U.S. Government. Richard Webb, a top Homeland Security staffer and member of President Armando's inner circle, was reportedly captured and beheaded in Virginia Beach this week. We have not seen a video of the purported beheading, which supposedly happened overlooking the Chesapeake Bay.* Joshua shook his head and planted his face in his palm.

President Armando condemned the killing. Joshua again focused on the television as Armando came on screen. *Our prayers go out to the family of our fallen colleague, Richard Webb. This attack against the U.S. government will not go unpunished. We will find his killers and bring them to justice.*

CHAPTER 10

A week later Joshua, Perry and Jack made the trip past the dam to the local exchange. This was an outdoor area where farmers and others set up shop and traded goods. Given that the dollar was effectively defunct, nearly everything was traded on the barter system. If you wanted to obtain something of value, you had to have something of value to offer.

After arriving at the market Joshua, Perry and Jack unloaded the valuables with which they would trade: eggs, venison from one of Bob's kills and several jugs of gasoline. In return they secured coffee, vegetables, ammunition and sugar. Joshua thought about asking the trader how he was able to obtain coffee, but decided not to look a gift horse in the mouth.

The three men loaded their acquisitions into Perry's truck and began the trip back to camp. They perked up as they rounded a curve.

"Look!" Joshua pointed at the plume of thick, black smoke billowing through the otherwise clear blue sky.

"I see it." Jack drew his Glock .40.

Perry gripped the steering wheel tightly with both hands as they rounded a curve and came upon a pickup truck engulfed in flames. He stopped about a hundred feet from the inferno. "Let's check it out."

The three men cautiously approached the burning vehicle. There was no trace of another human being, dead or alive.

"No sign of people, but this fire is still fresh," Jack observed. "That's strange."

WHOOSH! The three men turned in unison as a fire-propelled streak shot from the mountainside. A thunderous boom consumed Joshua's ears. He felt himself flying backward through the air, then crashing to the ground on his back with a painful thud that took his breath away. When he opened his eyes a shadowy, masked figure in a black robe stood over him. Groggy and struggling to regain his senses, he saw the butt of a rifle descending toward his face.

***

Rebecca nervously twisted her hair as she paced impatiently in front of the warm, cozy fire. *It's been three hours. They should be back by now.* She jumped, startled by a knock on the door. She opened it to find an equally worried Caroline.

"Any word from Joshua and Perry?" Caroline asked.

"None!" Rebecca felt a lump forming in her throat. "I'm worried. We should send someone to check on them."

Caroline nodded. They rushed up the path to Drew's cabin, where they found Jim. Rebecca explained the situation and Jim headed off into the woods, returning thirty minutes later with Bob and Kane.

Bob twisted his cigar between his fingers. "Don't worry, Mrs. Winston, we'll find them." Stone-faced, Kane nodded. The two soldiers retrieved a stockpile of weapons and sped off toward the gate in Bob's Yukon.

***

Joshua slowly regained consciousness, not sure where he was or how he got there. As he struggled to open his swollen right eye he realized he was on the floor inside a small church. The church's white walls were adorned by dark, stained crossbeams and ornate stained-glass windows. A large cross hung behind the dais and a smaller cross emblazoned the front of the pulpit. The stained wooden pews looked as though they could be hand-me-downs from centuries past.

The rope felt prickly against Joshua's wrists as he tried to move, and the piece of cloth used to gag him tasted like stale bread. Perry and Jack were tied up beside him, along with two other prisoners whose identities were unknown to him.

A tall man in a black robe and mask was seated in a chair across the room. Joshua's heart sank. *AIS. We're in a fix.* The man sharpened a foot-long knife using slow, ominous strokes, glaring at Joshua and the other prisoners.

***

"Martin, be alert," Bob snapped.

"Yes, sir." Kane pumped a round into the chamber of his Kimber .45 and re-holstered it.

Bob stopped his Yukon about a quarter-mile from the charred remains of two vehicles: one of which had burned, another which had been blown to bits. He studied the scene and surrounding area through binoculars while Kane stood ready with an AR-15. Once convinced that whomever or whatever had caused the damage to the two vehicles was no longer an imminent threat Bob moved his Yukon closer. The acrid smell of smoke permeated the area as Kane walked into the still-smoldering debris and silently held up the remnants of an object.

"RPG," Bob said. "Not good." He picked up a piece of dark blue shrapnel from one of the vehicles. "This does appear to be from Mr. Edwards' truck."

After surveying the area Bob and Kane returned to camp.

***

Joshua, Perry and Jack watched helplessly as five masked terrorists scurried around within the church. They tore down the cross that stood behind the dais and covered the pulpit with a sheet. The militants hung a flag featuring bold blue, green and white horizontal stripes and red Arabic

300

lettering underscored by a black sword in front of the pulpit, then set up a video camera and tested the sound. They communicated in Arabic.

Joshua clenched his teeth and balled up his fists as two of the militants rushed over and grabbed one of the other prisoners. The man kicked and tried to scream as they dragged him across the floor, his helpless cry muffled by the gag. They forced him into a chair facing the camera with the flag behind him. Joshua's heart sank as the terrorist who had been sharpening the knife positioned himself behind the imperiled hostage and removed his gag.

Another militant turned on the camera and began recording. The terrorist with the knife spoke in near-perfect English with a neutral Midwestern accent. "Are you a Christian?"

The hostage gulped. "Yes."

Joshua closed his eyes and swallowed hard as the militant grabbed the hostage by his hair, violently yanked his head back and savagely cut his throat. The man's blood-curdling scream quickly faded into a low gurgling sound. The terrorist severed the man's head and held it up for the camera as the slaughtered hostage's torso collapsed onto the floor.

"These infidels will meet the same fate if they do not renounce their Christian faith and their loyalty to the American government." The terrorist pointed toward

Joshua, Perry, Jack and the other hostage.

***

When Bob and Kane returned to camp a crowd had gathered around Joshua's cabin. Rebecca rushed to meet them, followed by Caroline. "Did you find anything?" Her voice quaked anxiously.

"We located the remains of Mr. Edwards' vehicle," Bob said. "It appears to have been destroyed by a rocket-propelled grenade. There was another burned vehicle nearby. We did not see any sign of Mr. Winston, Mr. Edwards or McGee. There were no bodies in the vehicles, so we have to assume they are alive. We will search the area and find them."

As Bob finished speaking Keri emerged from Joshua's cabin, appearing troubled. "You guys need to get in here and see this."

Rebecca's heart raced wildly as she rushed inside, where the television was tuned to a national news channel.

Disturbing images from western North Carolina today. A group of AIS militants have seized what appears to be a small church and taken several people hostage. They have just uploaded a video in which they beheaded one man for simply saying he was a Christian and are threatening to kill the other hostages if they do not renounce their Christian faith.

The screen showed a clip of the lead militant speaking. A cold chill overcame Rebecca when she spotted Joshua tied up in the background. "Oh my God!" She clasped her hands over her mouth and collapsed to her knees on the floor in front of the television, trembling violently. Caroline let out an ear-piercing shriek.

"I've been to this church," Thomas said. "It's right up the road a few miles."

"How do we get there?" Bob asked. "We don't have much time."

While Thomas explained how to find the church Rebecca rose to her feet and disappeared down the hall. She returned with a .22 rifle in her hands and her Beretta .380 on her hip.

"Mrs. Winston, what do you think you're doing?" Bob asked.

"Going with you." Her eyes narrowed.

"Ma'am, I don't think that's such a good idea. These people are crazy, and they *will* kill every one of us if they have the chance. They won't spare you or show mercy because you're a woman. I shudder to think what they would do to you."

"They also won't show mercy to Josh." Rebecca felt her blood boil. "If he goes, then I go with him and I take as many of them out as I can. *I'm going*, and you'd best not try to stop me."

"Yes ma'am, but I still think it's a bad idea." Bob puffed on his cigar. "So it's Martin, Mrs. Winston and me."

"And me," Tommy interjected.

"Son, you can't go with them," Thomas said.

"Dad, I'm an adult now, and I think I showed I can handle myself last year," Tommy insisted. "Besides, Mr. McGee saved my life last year, and I'm not going to sit here and let these people kill him."

"Son--" Kim cut him off, leaned over and whispered something in his ear.

"Mr. Page, McGee says that your son is a fine fighter and that he has lots of potential." Bob walked over and put his hand on Tommy's shoulder. "Son, I understand that you want to go with us, but someone has to stay here and guard the camp with Jones. I think that needs to be you. If you're willing, *I'm counting on you* to stay here and keep these folks safe."

Tommy paused for a moment. "Yes, sir. You can count on me."

Bob nodded at Thomas, then did an about-face and headed for his Yukon. Kane and Rebecca joined him.

"I still don't think you coming is a good idea," Bob said.

"It's *not* your call." Rebecca pursed her lips.

"Well, I learned a long time ago never to argue with a woman," Bob said with a chuckle. "Let's go."

***

The stench of blood hung over the church sanctuary as Joshua waited, helpless to escape. After what seemed like an eternity the terrorists re-entered the church. Without explanation they moved the prisoners, flag and video equipment outside.

The small, white church was perched near the edge of Lake Fontana, which along with the mountains provided a picturesque backdrop. The steeple was topped by a cross that stretched toward the heavens. The property was encircled by a picket fence and a small family cemetery sat behind the building. As the militants set up the camera equipment it became apparent that they wanted to use this scenic backdrop as the setting for their next gruesome production. Joshua shuddered as one of the militants began recording. Another removed the American flag and church flag, threw them on the ground and raised the AIS flag in their place. *They want to show that they can strike deep into the heart of America and that no one is safe anywhere. God help us.*

Joshua's heart pounded as the terrorists huddled in a group, then abruptly dispersed. His blood boiled as three of the militants walked over to the other unknown prisoner, picked him up and dragged him toward the camera. The man had a look of horror on his face and tears streamed down his cheeks, but he did not resist. The terrorists positioned him in front of the camera and removed the gag.

The terrorist leader positioned himself behind the poor soul. "Are you a Christian?"

"Yes," the man said sheepishly.

"Renounce your Christian religion or die, infidel."

The hostage hesitated before answering. "I... I can't do that."

A potent combination of rage and terror pulsed through Joshua's veins as two militants kicked the hostage in his ribs. The man bowled over in pain, screaming in agony. The terrorists forced him back into an upright position.

"Again, renounce your Christian religion or die." The man again refused, and they kicked him again. The third try was the charm: the man renounced his faith. And then the militant leader beheaded him anyway.

As the man's lifeless body fell to the ground the terrorist leader held up his head for the camera like a trophy. "Now these infidels will meet the same fate." He tossed the man's head onto his lifeless body.

Joshua's stomach twisted into knots as the same three militants who had dragged the most recent prisoner to the place of his death walked toward them. He looked down and closed his eyes. *God, if you're up there, please help us.*

***

All Perry could think about was the fact that these so-called "people" had launched the attacks that killed Charlie and Allie. His precious children. Every ounce of his being hated these pieces of sub-human scum. He thirsted for revenge. If there was any justice in this world, this seemingly hopeless situation would somehow turn in a way that allowed him that revenge today. Rage boiled within him and hate pulsed through his veins. He could not help but make eye contact with these men, if they could be characterized as such, whom he so desperately wanted to kill.

The moment Perry made eye contact the militants grabbed him and dragged him toward the camera. He briefly made eye contact with Joshua, who struggled in a futile effort to break free from his restraints. Perry kicked one of the terrorists in the shin and twisted his body in an effort to escape, but his resistance was short-lived. He cringed in pain as the inhuman beasts punched him repeatedly in the head and abdomen, but refused to be broken. *If they kill me, I will go out like a man. I will not cower before these animals.*

Perry stiffened his body as the men forced him to his knees facing the camera, removed his gag and spaced themselves out behind him. *I MUST find a way to break free and kill these bastards.* The terrorist leader positioned himself behind Perry and began speaking to the camera, once again in perfect English.

"We told you we would bring the fight to America, to your homeland. Now, we are here, in a most remote part of your country. Let this prove that we can strike you anywhere. And know that we will strike you *everywhere*."

The man turned to Perry. "Are you a Christian?"

I will not give in to you, Perry thought. *Never!* He glared at the inhuman eyes that stared back at him through the black mask, but did not answer. The man kicked Perry in the ribcage. "Answer me, infidel!"

Perry grimaced as the pain pierced his torso and radiated throughout his body. He defiantly forced himself back to an upright position and glared at the terrorist, rage pulsating through his veins like molten lava. All he could think about was revenge.

"Do you have any last words?" the terrorist asked.

"To hell with you!" Perry's nostrils flared like an angry Brahma bull. "You may kill me, but you will die in this place today, you piece of terrorist scum, and I hope you burn in hell!"

***

The terrorist leader paused for a moment, appearing caught off guard by Perry's boldness. He grabbed Perry from behind and began moving the blade toward his throat. Joshua closed his eyes, unable to watch the certain, bloody death of his best friend, knowing that he himself would soon meet the same fate. *Is this somehow my fault for bringing everyone here?*

A shot rang out. Startled, Joshua jumped. As he opened his eyes the terrorist leader's lifeless body fell to the ground. Four more rapid-fire shots rang out, each finding its target. One by one, the other terrorists fell.

Joshua heaved a deep sigh of relief as Bob raced out of the woods, his 1911 still raised. *Bob saves us once again,* Joshua thought. Bob rushed to Perry. "Are you okay?" Perry nodded, and Bob moved on to Joshua and Jack.

"Looks like we got here just in the nick of time." Bob removed Joshua's gag and then began unbinding his wrists.

Horror shot through Joshua like a bolt of lightning as he saw the shadowy figure approach Bob from behind. "Bob, look out!" The warning came too late. The terrorist appeared out of nowhere, grabbed Bob and cut his throat in one quick, ruthless motion. A deathly chill overcame Joshua as Bob dropped to his knees, grasping for his neck as blood poured down the front of his torso. Joshua clenched his fists as the terrorist shoved Bob's dying body to the side and took a menacing step toward him. Bob managed one final, raspy breath as he hit the ground. Two more militants emerged from behind the church. *Where did they come from?*

Suddenly a loud scream rang out from the mountainside near the church: "Noooooooo!" Kane had arrived a moment too late to save his mentor. Enraged, he raised his AR-15 and fired a shot, which removed the head of Bob's killer. He killed the other two militants in rapid-fire fashion. Two more terrorists emerged from the front of the church, walking into a hail of bullets from Kane's rifle. Kane kept his weapon trained on the door, waiting for more targets.

Joshua's heart sank when another terrorist rounded the back corner of the church and fired a rocket-propelled grenade in Kane's direction. The rocket did not score a direct hit but impacted the mountainside just below Kane's position. The force of the explosion brutally slammed him against the rock wall.

A tsunami of hopelessness swept over Joshua as he watched Kane's seemingly lifeless body roll down the mountain and disappear into the brush below. He swallowed hard. *There is no way we get out of this alive.*

***

Rebecca watched helplessly from her hiding place as the rocket exploded against the mountain, sending Kane careening out of sight. *Oh my God,* she thought. *Bob and now Kane?* Her heart was pounding a million miles a minute.

She cautiously peeped around the boulder and watched as seven more armed militants emerged from the church.

Eight. No way I can get them all. The terrorists dragged
Perry back to the area where the other prisoners were being
held. Rebecca cringed as the militants hit and kicked
Joshua and the other hostages, seemingly to communicate
that they were still in control. They also secured Perry's
wrist restraints and gagged him once more.

Rebecca slid down behind the rock and pressed the
barrel of her Beretta against her chin, her hand shaking
like a major earthquake. She closed her eyes, slid her finger
across the trigger and took a heavy, deep breath. After a few
uncertain moments she opened her eyes and re-holstered
the pistol. *What do I do? There are too many of them. I have
to--*

Her train of thought was interrupted by the sound of a
commotion. Rebecca peeped from behind the rock.
Adrenalin surged through her veins as the terrorists
dragged Joshua toward the camera.

***

The newly self-appointed terrorist leader picked up the
knife used by the militant who carried out the earlier
beheadings. He positioned himself behind Joshua and
spoke to the camera in a thick, middle-eastern accent.
"Your infidel came here and killed my brothers. He killed
fellow warriors." He pointed the knife at Bob's lifeless body.
"He is dead." Next, he pointed the knife at Joshua. "Now
this man will pay for his friend's sins."

Joshua closed his eyes, bracing himself for the gruesome fate he knew was imminent. His life flashed before his eyes. *What will Rebecca do? Will she ever even know what happened to me? I hope and pray she never sees a video of this. Perry and Jack... I know they're next. How will the people in the camp survive with Bob, Kane and Jack gone? Will AIS find the camp? Is this the end of the free world as we know it? How could God allow this to happen? Why?*

Joshua tensed as he felt the terrorist's hand grab his head and pull it backwards. He anticipated the imminent sensation of a blade slashing through his neck. Instead, he heard a voice screaming "Nooo!" followed by a shot. This was a familiar voice. A *female* voice. *Rebecca's voice! What is she doing here? They'll kill her!*

As Joshua opened his eyes the terrorist fell to the ground, lifeless. *She's always been a good shot.* Another shot rang out and another militant fell to the ground. He spotted Rebecca positioned behind a large rock near the base of the mountain and watched as she calmly fired off another shot from her rifle, taking out a third terrorist. *That's my girl. Three down, five to go.*

The remaining militants spotted Rebecca almost as soon as Joshua did. He clenched his fists as they turned in unison and began firing wildly in her direction. She fired off another shot and killed another terrorist, then screamed and shielded herself behind the boulder. One of the terrorists began blasting at the rock with a fully automatic rifle. Joshua shuddered, horrified and helpless, certain of what an unspeakable fate she would meet if they reached her.

Two of the terrorists ran toward the area where Rebecca was hiding, while two stayed put and guarded the remaining prisoners. *Are these the only four left? Are there more hiding in the church?* Joshua watched in horror as the militants easily overpowered Rebecca and dragged her to the area where he was being held. She was bound and gagged within seconds.

Rage coursed through Joshua as one of the terrorists stooped near Rebecca, stroked her face and groped her. He groaned and struggled against his restraints, but was helpless to defend her. The terrorist walked over to the other three militants, pointed at Joshua and then Rebecca, said something in Arabic and laughed. The lump in Joshua's throat was the size of Jupiter. He looked at Rebecca in horror. *I cannot imagine what these animals plan to do to her. Lord, please find a way out of this. If that is not your will, please end it quickly.* Rebecca returned the gaze, but her expression was different. Amazingly, in spite of the seemingly hopeless situation in which they found themselves, the look in her eyes was one that was happy to see him. *How can she be so calm when we are about to die?*

Joshua perked up as the four terrorists picked up their weapons and pivoted toward the road, where a jeep turned into the driveway and began making its way toward the church. The jeep's four occupants were dressed in AIS garb. Joshua looked at Perry and then Jack. Jack shook his head. *Their reinforcements are here,* Joshua thought. *No way out.*

The four new arrivals exited the jeep and silently walked toward the terrorists. Without warning they raised their weapons and shot the terrorists. Caught off guard, the militants' fates were sealed before they knew what hit them. *What the heck?*

Two of the new arrivals silently stood guard near Joshua and the others while the other two entered the church, weapons raised. *Who are these people? Are they really on our side?* After some time he heard a shot ring out from inside the church. Then silence. Then another shot. Then silence.

After what seemed like an eternity the two men emerged from the church. The first gave a thumbs-up sign, after which all four of the men removed their masks. The men all appeared to be in their 40s or 50s and their faces were worn by hours spent outdoors in the sun. The leader, a man with graying hair and a moustache, spoke in a strong Western North Carolina accent. "I assume one of you is Joshua Winston. We got to y'all just in time."

Joshua's brow furrowed as he nodded.

He pointed at Bob's bloody, lifeless body. "Too late for

your friend here. I hate that."

They removed the gags from Joshua, Rebecca, Jack and Perry and untied them. Joshua immediately jumped up and embraced Rebecca tightly. "What in the world were you thinking coming here? They would have raped you a thousand times and then killed you!"

"I just couldn't let you die here without doing something," she said, tears streaming down her face.

"You are crazy!" He cupped her head in his hand. "I love you, but you are *crazy! Please* don't ever put yourself at risk like that again."

Joshua turned to Perry and Jack. "You guys okay?" They both nodded.

"Thank you." Joshua turned to the four newcomers. "But I'm confused. Who are you, how do you know my name, and how did you know we were here?"

"My name's Ray," the leader said as he donned a camouflage baseball cap. "That's plenty for now."

"But how do you know my name, and how did you know we were here?"

As Joshua finished his question three more pickup trucks entered the driveway. Each vehicle contained at least two men, all of whom were armed.

"Relax, they're with us," Ray said. "Just know that we were sent here to make sure you got out of here alive. We've got instructions to drop you off at Fontana Dam and wait there until you have been out of sight for thirty minutes. But now we need to focus on getting out of here."

"Kane!" Jack jumped to his feet. "One of our men was up on that hill, where you see the blast mark." He pointed at the mountainside. "They didn't hit him directly. Come on, let's see if we can find him."

Jack, Perry, Joshua and several others scaled the mountain toward Kane's last known location. The incline was steep and climbing was an arduous process. Joshua, Perry and Jack were slowed by the beating they had taken at the hands of the militants, but the others ascended like agile mountain goats. Kane was alive but unconscious. They carefully moved his injured body down the slope.

A tall, slender man in a brown flannel shirt stood guard with a double-barrel shotgun while Rebecca and Joshua tended to Kane, who slowly regained consciousness. Jack and Perry helped the other men clean up the mess.

"One of these terrorists is still alive," a short, stocky man in a denim jacket and burgundy cap called out.

"Which one?" Perry asked.

The man pointed at a barely conscious militant who was gasping for breath. Perry picked up the large knife that the terrorist leader had used to execute the two hostages.

"This is for my son, you bastard." Perry gripped the knife

with both hands, raised it over his head and plunged it deep into the militant's abdomen. He pulled the knife out and plunged it in again, twisting it for good measure. "And this is for my daughter."

Then he lost control, screaming and stabbing the dead body over and over. A morbid chill came over Joshua as he and Rebecca stood up, stunned by this unprecedented outburst of rage from their usually calm friend. Jack rushed over and grabbed Perry's wrist from behind.

"Come on, buddy," Jack said. "He's dead. You did what you wanted to do."

Perry let go of the knife without resisting, collapsed onto the ground and began sobbing uncontrollably. After a few minutes he regained his composure. "I've waited for this moment ever since they killed my children. I've thought of little else besides making these bastards pay for what they did to my Charlie and Allie. I somehow thought it would bring more closure than this." He wiped the tears from his eyes. "Guess I'll have to kill a few more."

"I can understand that feeling," Jack assured him. "Just try and calm yourself. It's over."

"For today," Perry said.

Joshua and Rebecca again turned their attention to Kane, who was now somewhat coherent. He tried to sit up, but groaned and laid down once more.

Frank L. Williams

"You're banged up pretty bad," Joshua said. "Looks like you've got a broken arm, but we'll get that fixed up. Just try and rest."

"Command Sergeant Major Kendall..." Kane did not finish the thought.

Joshua and Rebecca looked at each other and Joshua put his hand on Kane's shoulder. "I am so sorry." He swallowed hard. "I know how much he meant to you."

Kane broke down into tears, bawling like a baby. This was the first show of real emotion Joshua had ever seen from him, and it came like an avalanche.

Shallow graves were dug for the slaughtered hostages and crosses made from wood found near the church were placed at the head of each grave. The terrorists' bodies were piled up in the yard. Joshua and Rebecca constructed a crude splint for Kane's arm using a small board and some towels from the church.

"What should we do with your friend's body?" Ray asked.

"I'd like to take him with us," Joshua answered. "We'll give him a proper burial where we live."

They wrapped Bob's body in sheets found inside the church, then again in plastic, and put it in the back of one of the trucks. Joshua retrieved Bob's Springfield 1911. *This should go to Kane,* he thought.

Jack and Ray retrieved every weapon the terrorists had brought to the church. There were automatic weapons, high-powered rifles, several rocket launchers, hand grenades, quite a few large knives and lots of ammunition.

"Half of this is yours," Ray said.

"We'll take it," Jack quickly responded. "But I agree with Joshua that I'd really like to know how you knew we were here."

"Let's talk about that at our next stop. We need to get out of here."

Jack nodded. The men divided the weapons and ammunition equally and put it into the back of two trucks. Everyone piled into their vehicles. One of the men poured gasoline onto the dead terrorists' bodies and ignited it.

Rebecca grabbed Joshua's hand and squeezed it tightly as they rode up the hill. When they reached the road Joshua was surprised to see several more trucks and groups of men standing guard near the driveway. Bob's Yukon was parked on the roadside about a quarter of a mile away.

Jack took Bob's Yukon and the convoy made its way along the winding mountain road, eventually reaching Fontana Dam. The lead vehicle stopped near a red crew-cab Ram pickup parked on the road.

"Which one of y'all is Perry Edwards?" Ray asked.

"That's me." Perry cocked an eyebrow.

Ray pointed at the truck and tossed a set of keys to Perry. "Then this is yours."

"That can't be." Perry snatched the keys out of the air. "My truck was destroyed in the attack this morning."

"That's why this is yours," Ray answered.

Perry looked at Joshua and Jack, dumbfounded. Joshua shrugged. The men loaded Bob's body into the back of his Yukon and placed half of the weapons and ammunition in Perry's new truck.

"We'll wait here until you've been out of sight for 30 minutes," Ray said. "Good luck. Maybe we'll meet again sometime."

Joshua extended his hand. "Thank you. I *am* still curious about how you know our names and knew we needed help."

"Well, it's a long--"

The tall man in the brown flannel shirt got out of his truck and rushed to Ray. "Just got a report on the radio. Another AIS group nearby with hostages. Got their location."

Ray turned to Joshua. "Change of plans. We're out of here. Got some more terrorists to kill." Joshua nodded. Ray called out to his group as he fired up his truck. "Lock and load, boys. I'll relay instructions over the CB. Let's hit it."

The convoy sped off, clearly on a mission. Perry got into the drivers' seat of his new crew-cab truck and Kane claimed the passenger seat. In the back seat Rebecca buried her head in Joshua's chest and he squeezed her tightly as they rode back to the camp in a heavy, somber silence.

***

The sun was beginning to dip below the mountains when Reagan suddenly started growling and walked to the bottom of the steps, tail sticking straight up. Caroline tensed, fearing the worst. *I'm sure they're bringing terrible news. How will I make it without Perry?* She looked down at her scarred left wrist. *Maybe I should finish what I started.* She swallowed hard. *Caroline, don't even START with those thoughts.*

Chuck and Tommy raised their weapons, then let their guard down as Drew's motorcycle made its way up the path from the road to the cabin.

"I didn't even realize he had left the camp," Chuck said.

"Me either," Jim agreed. "I guess we were all preoccupied."

Drew parked his motorcycle beside Joshua's cabin, removed his helmet, combed his hair and dismounted.

"Where in the world have you been?" Chuck asked.

"I had to take care of some things," Drew replied

nonchalantly.

Drew's ambivalent attitude sent a spark of rage through Caroline. "You were out running *errands* on a day like today, when Perry and Joshua have probably been killed by these terrorists?" She put her left hand on her hip and waved her finger at him. "Have you no respect? What is WRONG with you?"

Drew did not respond. Caroline glared, seething with anger as he made his way onto the porch and claimed one of the rocking chairs. *Snot-nosed brat.*

A short time later Reagan again started growling. Chuck and Tommy went on high alert as a strange red truck made its way toward the clearing. *NOW the terrible news is coming*, Caroline thought. *I don't think I can live without Perry.* Her eyes narrowed as she again stared at her scarred wrist.

"Do you recognize that vehicle?" Chuck asked.

"No, sir," Tommy replied, raising his shotgun.

"It's just dark enough that I can't see who's inside," Chuck said. "Get into position."

Tommy found a vantage point behind a tree near the path. As the vehicle made its way into the clearing Chuck stepped in front of it and raised his Ruger .44 Magnum Revolver.

"Relax, it's us," a familiar voice called out from the

truck.

Caroline sprang up from her seat on the porch and raced toward the truck. "Perry! I thought for sure you were dead!"

Perry stepped out of the truck and rushed to meet her. Caroline gripped him tightly. "I thought I was never going to see you again," she said, then broke down into tears.

"I'm here," he said, holding her close.

***

Reagan rocketed off of the porch at the sight of Joshua and Rebecca, running so hard that he knocked Joshua onto his rear and then licked him across the face. "I'm okay, boy. I'm okay." Joshua laughed as he scratched Reagan's head. Bob's Yukon came up the path as he climbed back to his feet.

"Thank GOD you guys are safe," Jim said as he made his way down the porch. He pointed at Joshua's swollen right eye. "Looks like you got beat up pretty good." He cocked an eye as Jack climbed out of the Yukon. "Where's Bob?"

Joshua shook his head and Kane again broke down into tears.

"Oh, no." Jim shook his head and looked down at the ground. A solemn mood descended over the crowd.

"I know." Joshua heaved a deep sigh. "Kane has a

broken arm. Keri, can you help take care of that?" Keri nodded.

"What in the world happened?" Jim asked. People crowded around to hear the answer.

Joshua described everything that had transpired. "I thought we were done for. And then these local guys disguised as terrorists showed up. They wound up killing the militants and freeing us. Their leader knew my name and said they had been sent there to help us today."

"That's strange," Jim said. "Any idea who they were?"

Joshua shook his head. "Just--

"Let me guess, Ray dropped you off at the dam," said Drew.

Joshua's jaw dropped. He was speechless.

Drew followed up with a question. "Perry, how do you like your new truck?"

Everyone stared at Drew in silence, shell-shocked at the revelation.

"You are all obviously perplexed, so I'll explain it for you." Drew leaned the rocking chair back and kicked his feet up on the rail. "You know those trips I've been taking by myself? The ones you asked me to stop taking, the ones you said were jeopardizing our security?" He pounded his chest with his fist. "I've been building relationships with people in nearby communities. Don't worry, they don't know where I live, and I've never given them details about the camp. However, unlike some others I've long believed that completely isolating ourselves was a recipe for disaster."

"How do you know these particular men?" Jack asked.

"A few years ago I worked as a field rep for a campaign in this part of the state. One of my jobs was organizing coalitions, including a sportsmen's coalition. I kept lists of my contacts, and that network proved useful today. When I heard what had happened I found Ray and told him you needed help. I haven't met most of the other guys, but I'm pretty sure they're from his hunting club."

"What did you tell him about me?" Joshua inquired.

"I didn't go into great detail. I simply told him that you were someone who was of like mind, a natural leader, and that you were in trouble and needed help. He said he'd take it from there."

Joshua shook his head. "I don't know what to say."

"The truck," Perry interjected. "How did you do that?"

Drew smiled. "I'll explain that some other time."

Joshua somehow overcame his bewilderment. "Drew, thank you. We all owe you a debt of gratitude."

"I have to agree," Perry concurred. "And I have to admit that I always thought you were one who might go off the reservation, especially after the last couple of council

325

meetings. I know you were interested in serving as chair if Joshua decided not to run again, and I wasn't sure how you'd react to the way things went."

"I never really wanted to be chair anyway," Drew said.

Joshua cocked an eyebrow. "Then why did you express interest?"

Drew chuckled. "Let me guess how things played out. After I expressed interest you talked to the other council members. They said they would not support me, and someone probably even said they would run to make sure I didn't get the job. You didn't want to see the camp divided, and you were uneasy about the other person who expressed interest serving as chair, so you felt like the best way to keep the camp united was to agree to serve again. Correct?"

"Umm... yes."

Drew smirked. "My expressing interest in serving was the best way to ensure that *you* would agree to serve again." He winked. "Not bad for someone who is nothing but a political hack, huh?"

***

Major Chinn unrolled a map of the port at Morehead City. "Sir, we have troops stationed in Beaufort, Fort Macon and Morehead City to prevent the terrorists from escaping via land. We are maintaining a constant lookout from the Atlantic Beach bridge. Just before nightfall we will begin amassing ground forces near the entrance to the port property. After sunset those forces will begin maneuvers which will serve as a distraction and while we launch an amphibious attack from the channel. I believe we can catch them off guard and reclaim the port with little difficulty."

"Good plan," Cloos said. "Keep me posted, Major."

Colonel Brookhart threw open the conference room door. "Major General, it appears your hunch was correct. We have detected a drone headed our way."

Cloos pursed his lips. "Shoot it down. And make sure we get this on video. After we shoot it down we need to recover the wreckage."

"Then what?"

"Then we will call the President."

***

Joshua and Rebecca slept until late morning, exhausted and sore from the previous day's challenges. After they ate a brunch comprised of four large eggs and very potent coffee Joshua planted himself on the couch and turned on the television. "I'm almost afraid to watch."

The news anchor was talking about the previous day's events. *A bizarre ending to a tragic story. As we told you yesterday, a group of AIS militants seized a church near Fontana Dam, executed at least two hostages and threatened to kill others. Now, we are receiving reports that locals found a pile of burned bodies that appear to be those of the militants. There are two freshly-dug shallow graves nearby, and the local who tipped us off said there were more spent shell casings than he could count. No one seems to know what happened to the other hostages or who is responsible for what appears to have been either a daring rescue or a retaliatory attack. Meanwhile, President Armando said this kind of 'vigilante justice' is uncalled for and would not be tolerated.*

Joshua clenched his teeth. "Sometimes it seems like this so-called 'president' is not even on our side. He should be *thanking* Ray for picking up his slack."

The anchor continued. *We are receiving reports of federal Homeland Security police sparring with local law enforcement and National Guard personnel in a number of states, including North Carolina, South Carolina, Tennessee, Georgia and Alabama.*

"Josh, I'm not sure the America we knew and loved exists anymore," Rebecca said.

Joshua shook his head. "Sadly, I think we are living in the days after the republic."

***

Benjamin rushed into the already-full conference room where President Armando convened his inner circle. The president was already seated, along with Abdar, Adilah, Anthony and ten others. "I apologize for being late, Mr.

President."

"No need to apologize, Leibowitz," Armando said. "This was a hastily called meeting."

Major General Cloos appeared on the videoconference screen, flanked by two other men in uniform.

"Major General, you called this meeting," Abdar said. "What do you want to discuss?"

"Two things," Cloos said. "First, we have recaptured the Port of Morehead City and the terrorists there have been eliminated. That's the good news." Cloos puffed on a cigar and blew smoke in the direction of the camera. "Now the bad news. Our base was attacked yesterday."

"You invited this attack by engaging the terrorists without our consent," Abdar said. "You should have known they would respond."

"I said we were attacked," Cloos said. "I did *not* say we were attacked by AIS."

"Then what are you saying?" Anthony asked.

Cloos leaned toward the camera and took another puff on his cigar. "We were attacked by a United States military drone, which we shot down. Mr. President, I have to ask, was this attack sanctioned by your administration?"

Benjamin clenched his teeth but did not speak. Armando sat speechless, looking like a deer in the headlights.

"Mr. President?" Cloos persisted.

"This is an outlandish accusation!" Abdar stood up and shook his fist at the camera. "How dare you?"

Cloos turned to a tall officer with light brown hair and wire-rim glasses. "Colonel Brookhart, roll the footage."

Benjamin cocked an eyebrow as the monitor showed a zoomed-in clip of a drone bearing an American flag. The video zoomed out as a surface-to-air missile destroyed the drone, then zoomed in on a recovered fragment that included a portion of the flag.

"This was clearly an *American* drone," Cloos said. "So the question remains, did your administration sanction this attack, or is someone else controlling our drone fleet? Mr. President?"

President Armando finally spoke up. "No such attack was authorized by me."

"What about by anyone else in your inner circle?" Cloos pressed the issue.

Abdar again stood up and shook his fist at the camera. "This line of questioning is insulting to the President! How dare--"

"Son, I didn't attain the rank of Major General by being an idiot. Either someone in this administration sanctioned this attack, or you have lost control of our drone fleet. I want to know which."

"Who do you think you are?" Abdar yelled.

"Son, be careful what you ask for or I might come up there and *show* you who I am." Cloos motioned for his team to kill the videoconference. The screen went blank.

***

The top of Bob's grave was covered in neatly arranged stones and a wooden cross had been placed at the head.

Jim delivered a eulogy and several camp residents spoke. Kane was the last to speak. He approached the grave and fell down on both knees, his broken left arm in a sturdy splint. He brushed his right hand across the grave.

"You were the only true friend I have ever had," he said in a choked voice. "And you were the closest thing to a father I ever had. I don't know how I will make it without you."

Kane broke down into tears and Jack put his hand on his shoulder. Joshua surveyed the crowd; there was only one dry set of eyes present: Drew's. He stood stone-faced, staring at Bob's grave.

***

Welcome news from eastern North Carolina today.

Joshua and Rebecca perked up as the anchor spoke.

American military forces have defeated a group of AIS terrorists and reclaimed control of the Port of Morehead City.

President Armando appeared on screen. *We are thankful to the brave members of our Armed Forces who executed our plan to win this great victory. This is a critical step toward restoring order in our great nation.*

"Maybe Armando is finally starting to wake up and do something right," Joshua said.

"Maybe," Rebecca said. "But don't forget a piece of advice I've often heard you give others."

"What is that?"

"Don't believe everything you see on the news."

***

Major General Cloos felt his face flush red with anger as he watched the newscast. He slammed his fist on his desk. "Those bastards claimed credit for a battle *our* soldiers fought."

Colonel Brookhart nodded. "A battle they ordered us *not* to fight."

Cloos spat loudly into a Styrofoam cup. "Well, I guess it's clear what kind of people we're dealing with."

***

A stern warning for residents in Western North Carolina today. Joshua fixated on the television.

The newscast cut away to a pre-recorded video of an AIS terrorist standing in front of a flowing mountain stream. *To the American who killed our brethren at your infidel house of worship. We will find you. We will kill you. You cannot escape. And we will kill everyone who matters to you. Revenge will be ours.*

***

The following Tuesday camp residents gathered for the weekly council meeting and a special camp meeting.

Joshua began the camp meeting by rehashing the events of the previous week. "We all owe a debt of gratitude to Drew. The relationships he developed saved my life, Jack's life, Perry's life, Rebecca's life and Kane's life. Drew, thank you." A round of applause rang up from the crowd.

"It goes without saying that we will miss Bob," Joshua solemnly continued. "Over the past year he saved many of our lives, and we also owe him a debt of gratitude. May he rest in peace. Please join me in a moment of silence in Bob's honor."

Everyone closed their eyes. After the moment of silence Joshua continued. "As you all know, Bob was a member of our council and functioned as head of security. His death creates a huge void, one that we must now decide how to best fill. While *no one* can replace Bob, we have to determine how we can best move forward without him. That begins by deciding who will fill his seat on the council and act as head of security. With that said, nominations are now open for one seat on our council."

Kane raised his hand. "Sir, I would like to be considered. I served and studied under Command Sergeant Major Kendall, and he taught me virtually everything he knew. I believe this is what he would want."

Joshua nodded. "Kane Martin has nominated himself. Do we have further nominations?"

Thomas raised his hand. "Man, I'd like to nominate Jack McGee. I saw him in action when he rescued me from those kidnappers last year, and he can do this job. He seems like a natural born leader."

"We have nominations for Kane Martin and Jack McGee. Are there further nominations?"

Drew made a motion to close nominations. The motion passed. Rebecca passed out ballots and Joshua appointed Jim, Ruth and Chuck to serve as tellers. After a few minutes Ruth handed Joshua a sheet of paper.

"Folks, the votes have been counted," Joshua announced. "Congratulations to our new council member, Jack McGee. Jack will also serve as our head of security. Kane, thank you for your willingness to serve. You have made valuable contributions to this camp, and I wish we had room for both of you on the council."

Kane stood at attention and saluted in Jack's direction. "Congratulations, sir!" Jack extended his hand.

Joshua spoke up again. "Before we adjourn, there is one

more thing I would like for you to consider. I have long feared that this conflict would make its way to us here. Unfortunately, that happened this week. Now, my fear is that we have not seen the last of it. We must remain vigilant, and we must face the stark reality that we have multiple enemies. The first is obvious. AIS. Based upon the news reports I've seen, the second enemy appears to be the remnant of our own U.S. government, particularly in the form of these Homeland Security police. Beyond those, we also have to consider the fact that the world outside of this camp is increasingly dominated by lawlessness, which means *anyone* could be our enemy. We must stay alert and stick together."

***

Caroline squeezed Perry's hand as they walked up the trail, where Jack was seated under an awning in front of his camper trailer. She smelled the aroma of gun oil – a once-foreign odor that she viewed with increasing acceptance. Jack's AR-15 was partially disassembled on a small fold-out table under the awning along with a gun cleaning kit. His 30:06 leaned against the camper beside a 50 caliber sniper rifle, crossbow and compound bow.

"That's quite a collection of weapons, Jack. Do you have a minute?" Perry ducked to avoid hitting his head as he made his way under the awning.

"One for every occasion. Sure, what's up?"

Perry squeezed Caroline's hand. "Coming face-to-face with AIS made me realize how unprepared I am for a fight. I'm not bad with a rifle or pistol, but have no real training in hand-to-hand combat." He cleared his throat. "Can you help us?"

"I'll do my best." Jack leaned his reassembled AR-15 against the trailer and began disassembling his 30:06. "Is there anything specific you want to learn?"

"Everything you can teach us." Caroline stroked the scars on her left wrist. Her eyes narrowed. "They killed my babies. I want to be ready if I ever have my chance."

"I can help with that," Jack said. "I do feel like I should let Joshua know what we're up to."

"That's fine," Caroline said. "He's welcome to join us."

***

Several days later Joshua, Rebecca and Reagan were returning from a hike up the trail. The weather was unseasonably warm and there was not a cloud in the clear blue sky. This was a much-needed opportunity for Joshua to spend quality time alone with those he valued the most – time he desperately craved after the gut-wrenching events of the past few weeks. As always Reagan led the way, trotting about ten feet ahead. Joshua and Rebecca walked hand-in-hand, winding down several curves to an area where the trail passed through a fairly large open clearing – the same clearing where Reagan had become agitated several weeks earlier.

History repeated itself. As they entered the open space Reagan began growling, his tail pointing straight up. He fixated on some mysterious point on the mountainside.

"Again?" Joshua drew his pistol.

Rebecca looked at him quizzically. "What do you mean 'again'?" she whispered. "Has this happened before?"

"He did the same thing when I came up here to think and clear my head before deciding to serve as chair again. In this very same spot."

"And you didn't tell me?"

"We don't have time to debate this now, Becca."

"Josh, I don't like being kept in the dark. Why didn't you tell me?"

"I didn't want to frighten you. *Let's talk about this later.*"

Rebecca huffed. Reagan continued growling and scanning the horizon for several minutes, then abruptly turned and came to Joshua. Joshua studied the mountainside through his telescope, and then handed it to Rebecca. Neither of them saw anything.

After a few minutes Joshua motioned for Rebecca to follow him. They silently moved forward, keeping low to avoid detection by whatever had spooked Reagan. Reagan stayed with them, still agitated but no longer on high alert. Once they made it through the clearing to a more thickly wooded area Joshua found a vantage point from which they could watch the trail.

"I don't know what Reagan sees up there, but both times this has happened I had the strange feeling that I was being watched," he whispered to Rebecca. "Something isn't right."

They stayed put for some time, but again did not see anyone or anything out of the ordinary. After sufficient time had passed they resumed their trip back to the camp.

As they completed their hike Joshua pondered the events of the past few weeks and wondered what the future might hold. The great republic known as the United States of America was all but gone. The conflict that had brought the once-great nation to its knees had reached this remote part of the North Carolina mountains, and a key member of the camp had been lost in the process. These events had tested the camp's unity and Joshua was unsure how the residents would hold together moving forward. Now he had the uneasy feeling that someone or something was watching him on the trail, possibly watching the entire camp. Things were peaceful for the moment, but Joshua's gut told him that the peace would be short-lived. He feared that life after the republic would bring a series of unfamiliar and unpredictable challenges and that the conflict that had engulfed America would soon hit close to home once again...

STAY TUNED FOR BOOK II

The story of Joshua, Rebecca and those fighting to survive after the fall of the Republic is far from complete.

The saga will continue in the second book in the *After the Republic* series. To receive updates about future books in the series, please sign up for our email list at www.AftertheRepublicBooks.com.

Please also connect with us on social media.

 /AftertheRepublic

 @AfterRepublic

ABOUT THE AUTHOR

Frank L. Williams grew up in Northwest, a rural farming community in Brunswick County, twenty minutes from the historic Port City of Wilmington in southeastern North Carolina. A prolific reader at an early age, he read many of the books in *The Hardy Boys* mystery series before completing third grade. Frank's family has a love of America and a history of civic leadership that spans generations. He has followed in that tradition, having been actively involved in the political process for more than two decades. After graduating from North Brunswick High School in 1988, Frank earned a degree from North Carolina State University's Department of Communication in 1993. In August of 2001 he formed Pioneer Strategies, a public relations agency he still owns and operates. In his free time he enjoys writing, reading, action movies, politics, fishing, the beach and rooting for the N.C. State Wolfpack. For more information, please visit www.FrankWilliams.biz.

 /FrankLWilliams10

 @FLWilliamsBiz

Made in the USA
Charleston, SC
13 February 2016